MW01103189

The Convertible

by

Jerry Land

Copyright © 2007 Jerry Land

ISBN-13 978-1-60145-147-7
ISBN-10 1-60145-147-4

All rights reserved. No part of this publication may be reproduced, stored in a retrieval system, or transmitted in any form or by any means, electronic, mechanical, recording or otherwise, without the prior written permission of the author.

Printed in the United States of America.

The characters and events in this book are fictitious. Any similarity to real persons, living or dead, is coincidental and not intended by the author.

Booklocker.com, Inc.
2007

This book is the result of a joint effort with my wife, Sharon, without whom I never would have completed it.

Finding a classic mid-fifty's Chevy convertible that had been locked in a garage for forty three years is a dream for any car collector. For David Jordan, it was a life changing event.

CHAPTER 1

It was eleven o'clock Sunday morning when David decided to retrieve the items out of the Chevy' trunk. He drove the two miles to Jim's Storage Yard where the car had been towed after the auction. As he turned into the driveway, leading up to the front gate, he saw two sheriff's cars blocking his path. "What the hell is going on?" he said to himself. An ambulance and an unmarked squad car were parked in front of Jim's mobile home. Yellow tape stretched across all entrances to the storage yard. He glanced over the fence to where he had last seen his convertible. The space between the two late model cars where Jim had parked it was vacant. The Chevy was gone!

David parked and hurried over to the first sheriff's car. A young deputy stepped out and asked what business David had here. "I bought an old Chevy convertible at auction yesterday and Jim towed it out here last night. He parked it right there next to that Lincoln. Now it's gone! What happened here?"

The tall lanky deputy looked David up and down, "There's been a murder. Jim Ballantyne was shot and killed sometime during the night. He's right over there under the blanket by the step." David looked in disbelief at a form under the plaid blanket. "When was the last time you saw Jim?" the deputy pulled a small notebook out of his pocket. "Better yet, let me get the Sheriff Woodford out here, I know he would like to talk to you."

He spoke into the microphone attached to the shoulder of his uniform. The entire time keeping his eyes focused on David. "We've got a possible witness here. He was here last night. He may have been the last person to see Jim alive."

A heavyset man in a sheriff's uniform, with a very determined look on his face, came out of the mobile home and walked over to where David and the deputy were standing. "I am Sheriff Woodford. We're conducting a murder investigation here. If you know anything about the events that happened here in the last 24 hours, I need to know about it. But first, we need to see your identification." David hesitated for a moment thinking to him self, "Am I going to be a suspect?" He knew better than to argue with someone with a gun and a badge so he pulled out his billfold and handed his drivers' license to the sheriff.

The sheriff glanced at David's California driver license, "Deputy Passmore, call the station and have them check out Mr. Jordan, this is a California license." Handing the license to Passmore, Wolford turned to David, "Mr. Jordan, I'm going to record our conversation, I am sure you won't mind." The sheriff was acting very professional and doing a hell of a good job of it. He pulled out a small hand-held recording device from his shirt pocket and clicked it on.

David suspected he did not have any choice in the matter. He could hardly believe Jim was dead. He had seen him last night. In addition, his Chevy was gone! What the hell was going on here? Did one thing have something to do with the other? He could not believe the old Chevy was worth being killed over, so it must be some other reason.

"How and when did you meet Jim Ballantyne?" the sheriff wanted to know. David told his story including how he came to own the Chevy. Fortunately, the sheriff knew about the auction and had heard about the 43-year-old car hidden in Mrs. O'Ryan's garage.

After David repeated his story twice, Woodford finally said, "We don't know what all was taken besides your car and Jim's service truck. Mrs. Ballantyne called our office about six this morning and said someone had shot her husband. She was hysterical. Oh, by the way, I need the names, telephone numbers, and addresses of the people you were with last night."

David wished he could give the sheriff a telephone number. The best he could do was to give Kathryn's name and the Holiday Inn telephone number where they were staying. He did describe the waiter at Irv's Chicken Shack and the waitress in the cocktail bar where he and Kathryn had drinks together.

Sheriff Woodford hesitated long enough to listen to his deputy say, "Mr. Jordan checked out okay. No record, no wants, or priors."

"Good," he said and continued. "The first deputies on the scene found Jim laying on the steps right in front of the door to the mobile home. His wife was kneeling beside him sobbing. Their young boy was asleep in the back bedroom. Jim had been shot once in the forehead with a small caliber gun. Jim's wife has not been much help. The paramedics gave her something to calm her down. They're with her now in the mobile home. As soon as she gets her self together, we'll get a statement."

"Do you think she had anything to do with Jim's murder?" David asked.

"No. Of course, we can't rule anything out. Jim and his wife had some good fights. We've been out here a number of times, Jim was a little rough on her, but I really don't know if she would have the guts to pull the trigger. However, strange things do happen. We'll know more after the crime lab is done. I'm waiting for them now. They have all the fancy equipment for examining a crime scene like this. Those guys are really good, I expect we'll get some answers by the time they finish."

David had other concern's "Sheriff, do you think you could have some of your men take a look around and see if by some chance Jim moved my Chevy to some other location?"

"Yeah, I think that would be all right." He motioned to Passmore, "Take Mister Jordan here and look around in back and see if you can find his car." He pointed his finger at David. "Stay with Passmore and don't touch a goddamn thing." They spent 30 minutes snooping around the junkyard. There was no trace of David's old Chevy. There were two other '56 Chevrolets, both sedans, parked next to the back fence one on top of the other. There were over 500 junk cars in the back lot.

One thing, in particular, stood out in David's mind about Jim's junkyard. It did not look prosperous. There was not a barn or any kind of shop where dismantling could take place. No bins full of old generators, starters, and transmissions: just parked junk cars. The storage yard contained a few late model cars, several RVs, half a dozen boats, and two trailers with snowmobiles on them. Jim must have been making a living doing something besides the junk business. David wondered if the towing service paid enough to support a wife and child.

By the time they finished walking the endless rows of junk cars there was six more vehicles parked alongside the driveway leading up to the front gate, including a truck sprouting a huge dish antenna and the coroners van. Three people wearing white lab coats and blue rubber gloves were bent over the body at the mobile home's doorstep. David could see Jim lying on his back, blood covered his face. He thought he could see a small black dot in the middle of the dead man's forehead.

The impact of the whole situation was just now beginning to catch up with him. Last night's emotional high and this morning's incredulous murder were just about more than David could handle. His brain was going in six different directions and he felt like this was some kind of weird dream. He wished he could wake up and start over again. His daughter was not going to believe him when he got back to Chicago.

"I want to get back to my daughter's home as soon as possible. How long do you think it will be before I can leave town?"

"Didn't you say you were staying at the Holiday Inn?" David shook his head. "Stay there and we will find you. It won't take long as soon as the homicide detectives get here. The sheriff will want you to provide a written statement. Just don't try to leave town."

On the way back to his car, a man in a dress shirt and tie confronted David. Holding a microphone, he asked him, "Did you know the deceased? We understand you may have been the last persons to see the victim alive." It was a TV reporter from Rockford. David could see a second man with a heavy camera on his shoulder and cartridge-type battery belt behind the man who was sticking a microphone in his face. David was at a loss for words, he had never been on television and had no idea what to say or even if he should say anything. Quickly he spurted out, "I, I, just met Jim yesterday, and we did some business together. I have no idea what happened last night."

The cameraman was only a few feet away and the reporter was pressing for more information. "What kind of business did you have with the deceased? Did you know Mr. Ballantyne had just been released from prison several months ago?"

David was intimidated and confused. He could not reply, he wheeled around, took three long steps, got into his car, and started the engine. Pulling out around the reporter and the cameraman he nearly clipped the TV van. "Slow down you fool!" he said to himself as he braked and slowed the car down to match the speed limit.

He was not involved in the murder. He knew absolutely nothing about Jim's prison record. Now Jim's tattoos made sense, prison tattoos. If he had known, he would have called some other towing service. The disappearance of the old Chevy did not make sense. There was no reason for anyone to kill another person over this old car. Why was it missing? Was there something in it that someone else wanted badly enough to kill for? If that were the case why didn't they just break open the trunk and leave the car?

This situation was the most bizarre thing that had ever happened to him, excluding two tours of duty in Vietnam, of course. This kind of thing only happened on the six o'clock news and in the papers. Now he found himself right smack in the middle of a murder.

Since he was one of the last persons to see Jim alive, David was sure the sheriff was looking at him as a suspect.

CHAPTER 2

As David drove into the small faming community of Dumont, he could see the town square was nearly empty with just a few cars parked along the curb. He stopped and parked the rental car as far from the other visitors as he could. He found a wooden bench facing a statue of a WWI solder, with fixed bayonet, forever fighting the Hun. He sat down and took a deep breath. A huge Elm tree provided a shady environment on a well cared for green lawn that allowed David to reflect on the events of the past twenty-four hours.

Vivid memories of last night's episode with Jim at the storage yard were foremost in his mind. It all began when he asked to use the phone in the main house at the auction site after he had won and bought the old Chevy. His request for a tow truck was answered in less than fifteen minutes. David was on an emotional high, he was realizing an old dream of owning a car he remembered from childhood. And he had met the most wonderful woman he could imagine.

Jim's Towing and Storage Service turned out to be nothing more than a large junkyard, two miles outside of town. David followed Jim's flatbed service truck, loaded with the convertible, through the main gate held open by a very pregnant young woman. She yelled something to Jim as he roared by and Jim gave her the finger in response. They drove past an old single wide mobile home that served as an office and residence. A small child and his toys, including a wading pool, were scattered inside a fenced yard, all being guarded by a large mixed breed dog.

After Jim unceremoniously unloaded the car he invited David into his office. David asked if he could barrow Jim's master keys so he could unlock the trunk and see if anything was there. Jim was reluctant at first, "Master keys, hell I don't have any master keys, got a slim jim, but that won't work on the trunk.

After David flashed a twenty-dollar bill, Jim remembered the set of GMC master keys in the lower drawer of his crowded, grease-covered desk. It was a large steel ring containing hundreds of GMC automotive keys. David tried half of the several hundred keys before he found one that felt like it would open the trunk. He was afraid to put too much muscle into it for fear of breaking off the key. Jim's dog was barking furiously just six feet away from his legs. A chain link fence separated them, but the barking made him extremely nervous.

David twisted the key back and forth and each time the tumblers seemed to move just a little more. Finally, the lock clicked open. Not knowing what to expect, David's imagination started to gallop with all kinds of images, dead bodies, valuables, important papers, slowly he raised the trunk lid and peered inside. Light from the sun, low in the western sky, filtered through the overhanging trees reflecting off the Lincoln next to the convertible. He could make out two suitcases a Samsonite and an older, leather, well-traveled bag.

He could not help but notice the remains of a bouquet of flowers lying between the suitcases and the spare tire. The flowers had dried and turned brown with age, crumbing to dust when touched. The flower stems were wrapped in what once was green floral paper. "What's this?" David reached in and picked up a small envelope buried among the dried flowers. Jim's dog was getting more excited by the minute and trying to bite through the fence. David hastily put the small envelope in his shirt pocket. The dog kept on barking and in a flash of temper, he shouted, "I'll be out of here in just a few minutes you son-of–a-bitch, now shut up!" The dog ignored him.

He opened the older suitcase first. Half a dozen small rolls of 8mm home movie film lay on top of neatly folded men's clothing. The much larger Samsonite case contained women's clothes, including a mink stole. He held it at arms length and was amazed at its good condition. The softness of the fur felt luxurious.

David stood motionless for a moment, thinking about what might have happened to the recipient of the flowers? Why were these items left in the car and locked in a garage for four decades?

Closing the trunk lid, David decided to come back in the morning when he would have more time to examine his prize and take inventory of its contents. Right now, he had to get going so he could meet Kathryn for dinner. He walked toward the mobile home and saw Jim watching him from the doorway. Jim called his dog in, "General, come here. Come here boy." The dog lowered his tail, responded obediently. Jim grabbed the General by the collar and held him.

From the relative safety of opposite side of the cyclone fence surrounding the mobile home, David said, "I'll call you when I make arrangements to have the car transported to California."

Jim reached over the fence for his keys. "No hurry. It will be safe right where it's at. We don't have much theft around here. Besides, I turn the General loose at night and nobody gets in without him waking the dead. And I've got protection if I need it," he added, turning his head toward a cabinet on the far wall of the mobile implying a gun inside.

David felt uneasy about Jim. Had he seen him hold the fur piece up to the light? Jim had the keys to the trunk and could open it any time he liked. What if there was something more valuable in the suitcase? Jewelry for example, or money. David was increasingly hesitant about leaving the Chevy vulnerable to the likes of Jim and Jim's friends, whoever they might be. The General might keep strangers out, but Jim was the problem as far as David was concerned.

It was getting late and David hurried so as not to be late for his date with Kathryn. He had decided to come back in the morning and clear out the trunk. He told Jim he would call after he had contacted a car carrier.

"Wait a minute." Jim pulled out a fat wallet and searched through dozens of business cards and receipts finally selected one and handed it to David.

It was a business card for a trucking outfit, "Central Illinois Trucking." There was a name and telephone number, but no address. Jim explained, "We use them to move cars around. The price is right and they're reliable."

"Thanks, I'll give them a call." David remembered putting the card in his wallet, but thinking, could he trust them? As he left the storage lot, he tried to act as though he had not a care in the world. But he definitely did. That was the last time David saw Jim alive.

As he started to drive back to town he suddenly remembered the small envelope in his shirt pocket. Taking the note out of the envelope he held it up to his face trying to read it and drive at the same time. The message, written in poor penmanship, had been scribbled with a ballpoint pen. The name on the outside of the envelope was, "*Cindy.*" The note read:

"Cindy, tonight is the beginning of our life. I have everything ready. Meet me at the old Cooper place at midnight.

I love you."

The note was signed with the letter "*B*".

CHAPTER 3

David's replaying of last nights events in his head were interrupted by several small children running across the grass chasing a soccer ball. David reached out picked it up and tossed it back. They retreated to the far end of the square leaving him alone with his thoughts of Kathryn.

Meeting her had been just as memorable as meeting Jim, but on a much different level. He first saw her after arriving in Dumont yesterday in the early afternoon. The estate of Mrs. Margaret O'Ryan's was not hard to find. Colorful signs were posted on telephone poles announcing "Estate Sale Today". This small town, with its central square resembled hundreds of other Midwestern towns.

The auction had drawn a large crowd gathered under ancient Elm trees surrounding the property. The auctioneer was near incoherent with his babble about perfect examples of 1920's brass table lamps and Philco radios. The newspaper article David had spotted earlier in the day, had mentioned a 1956 Chevy convertible, not running, and that is what David came to see.

Chicago Sun
Times, June 12,
1999

Former Lt. Gov. O'Ryan's Estate Goes on Auction

DUMONT, IL ---Mrs. Timothy O'Ryan passed away in her sleep at her home in Dumont June 1st. She was discovered by her live in housekeeper early in the morning. Private funeral services were held at the local Methodist church last week. She was three days short of her 99th birthday. Her husband, Timothy C. O'Ryan, served as Lt. Governor from 1956 to 1960. He was killed in a mysterious auto accident in 1963. Mrs. O'Ryan is believed to be survived by a daughter Cynthia, whose whereabouts is unknown.

According to neighbors, she lived a quiet life in the northern Illinois farming town of Dumont. She was active in local civic organizations until a few years ago when she suffered a broken hip. According to the executor, Mrs. Millard, an estate sale is scheduled for Saturday, June 12th. Many antiques will be auctioned off including a 1956 Chevrolet convertible, not running. The car has been locked in the garage for the past forty-three years.

David was on vacation from his home in San Pedro, California. Staying with his daughter Kelly and her twin boys in Chicago was great for a few days, but after a while he needed a break and this auction offered an escape. And besides, he always wanted a '56 Chevy convertible. Maybe this would be the time to start a new restoration project.

But where was it. He had to park several blocks away and as he got nearer the Chevy was not in sight. He looked all over the well-manicured lawns and garden but could not locate the car on the property. He reasoned it must still be in the garage next to the alley. Judging by the size of the folding doors, what had been a carriage house in the beginning of this century had been turned into a three car garage about the time Model A's were popular. Trying to peak inside was useless. The window glass was clean but the interior of the garage was dark as coal. The side entrance and folding doors were painted shut and padlocked.

Much to his delight an attractive woman came out from the crowd gathered around the auctioneer's table. "Hello, are you looking for the old car?"

"Yes, I am," David's eyes, shielded by aviator sunglasses, took in every bit of her. She was about forty years old, give or take a few years. Her body looked firm and trim, not thin, but just a little on the plus side to make her a very desirable handful. David had not had sex for a very long time and all of a sudden, he felt a certain tingle in his groin telling him there was definitely life there.

She spoke in a soft voice with a bit of an accent, "The auctioneer said we could show the car to anyone who's interested. When he is finished with all the other items, he will put it on the auction block and sell it as-is. Whoever buys it will have to tow it out of the garage and off the property. We could not find the key to the garage door so I've sent for a locksmith, but he hasn't arrived yet."

David turned so that his back was to the sun and this woman was bathed in bright sunlight, "So, tell me about the car, why has it been locked up all these years?"

"I really don't know too much about it, except it belonged to my great-aunt's daughter Cynthia, and for some reason she never drove it. Forgive me, I'm Kathryn Phillips" holding out her hand.

"I'm David Jordan." Her handshake was firm and cool.

"My aunt owned this property. She passed away two weeks ago and my mother is the executor of the estate. I volunteered to help with the sale. Actually my mother is not in the best of health so I really wanted to be near to watch over her and help out as much as possible."

David made a mental note, she was not wearing a wedding ring. There was a large diamond solitaire on the middle finger of her right hand and a matching bracelet with what he guessed was real emeralds and diamonds. Her clothes were tailored and fit perfectly. Her auburn hair was slightly windblown and she kept brushing it out of her face. She spoke the Kings English with just a hint of a European accent that David could not recognize. She carried herself with grace and self-confidence. David's instinct told him this woman had class.

He wanted to think she was checking him out at the same time he was checking her out. Wishful thinking, he concluded.

Just then, a white utility van pulled in from the alleyway and parked next to the garage. A man in khaki work pants and shirt, with Keystone Key and Lock emblazoned on his shirt pocket, jumped down and asked if this was the address that had called for a locksmith.

"It is, and these are the locks we want opened," Kathryn said pointing to the rusted padlocks on the garage doors. It only took a few moments for the locksmith to open both padlocks. He was gone as quickly as he had arrived.

Kathryn looked at David, gestured toward the side door, and said, "Shall we? I have never been in here, so I really don't know what to expect."

"How do you know anything is in there?"

"Aunt Margaret left a very detailed list of all her belongings. She wrote down instructions about every item, and whom it was to go to when she died, and what to do with the house and furnishings. She specifically wrote in her will that the old car in the garage could be sold for junk for all she cared. 'Sell it as is and have it towed out of here,' were her words."

David tried opening the side door, but it would not budge. He put his shoulder to it, but it was stuck tight. Kathryn suggested maybe the folding doors would open easier. Using all his strength, David moved the folding doors inward and began to fold them to one side. Together, they pushed the doors open exposing a very dusty, dirty, sad-looking 1956 Chevy convertible. The first thing David noticed was the year on the Illinois license plate, 1956.

His heart rate had increased significantly being close to Kathryn and smelling her softness and warmth. Now his heart took another leap with the realization of uncovering a rare automotive find. Actually David knew that nineteen fifty-six Chevy's were not rare. He had read somewhere that there were approximately a million Chevrolets produced that year, including about forty thousand convertibles, but finding one that had not been driven for over forty years was indeed rare.

Although the old car was covered with dirt and pigeon droppings, he could not see any serious rust. The top was in rags and strips of canvas were hanging down. The seats were cracked and rotted. The mice had had a field day.

"When do you think the car will go on the auction block?"

"The auctioneer indicated it would be late in the day. Would you like to see what else we have to offer at auction?"

"Yes, I would," David responded enthusiastically. Spending time with this woman was the best thing that had happened to him in a long time. He felt really good about the prospects of buying the old Chevy. There didn't to be anyone else interested. And he felt equally good about his prospects with the woman he had just met. As they strolled towards the old house a handful of spectators started to gather around the open garage doors.

Kathryn took David on a tour of the property pointing out many features of the 100-year-old Victorian mansion and grounds. David found it very difficult to keep his eyes off the main attraction, Kathryn.   At four-thirty the auctioneer announced he was going to auction off the car that had been hidden from view for the past forty plus years.

The bidding started at five hundred dollars in increments of one hundred. There were a handful of bidders in the beginning. After the price reached two thousand dollars, there were only two, David and an older man with a neatly trimmed goatee. Kathryn was standing by the older man's side looking straight ahead. The man kept bidding until he forced David to bid two thousand four hundred dollars.

"Do I hear two thousand five?" David could barely keep up with the auctioneer's chatter, his knees were beginning to shake and he could see his dream car slipping away.

The other bidder did not hesitate to accept each increase the auctioneer asked for by nodding slightly.

"Do I hear two thousand six?" drawled the auctioneer.

"Yes," signaled David.

"Do I hear two thousand seven?" said the auctioneer, looking directly at Kathryn and the man with her. A nod from the bidder and the auctioneer immediately looked at David and raised the asking bid to two thousand eight hundred dollars.

As David was preparing to go to the next level, he made eye contact with Kathryn, she leaned toward the well-dressed man and said something. David signaled the auctioneer and accepted the two thousand eight hundred-dollar asking price. There was no response from the other bidder despite the pleading from the auctioneer.

"Do I hear two thousand nine? Two thousand nine going once, going twice, sold for two thousand eight hundred dollars to the man right over there!" The bidding was over. David had bought the car of his dreams with a little help from a new friend.

The crowd started to disperse and David handed his Visa card to the cashier. He was elated. But he was also anxious to speak to Kathryn. Why had the man she was with stop bidding? Was the older man her father? I've got to find her and thank her. His brain was on overdrive trying to do business and figure out how to get next to this lovely vision that had taken over his conscious being.

As if prearranged, Kathryn walked up to David as he was signing the necessary paperwork. She smiled and asked, "Are you happy with your new car?" She emphasized the word "new" with a little smile and a look that seemed to say, "You owe me a favor" she said cocking her head slightly, and then added," for helping you buy this car."

She obviously was teasing, but he took her seriously. "Yes, I am. I want to thank you for your assistance. I assume the man with the goatee is your father."

"Yes, one of my chores today was to keep my father from bidding on anything. Well, I knew when he saw the old car, he was going to bid. I didn't want you to be forced to pay more than was necessary. I simply reminded him, that his garage in Ireland is bursting at the seams, and there is absolutely no room for any more automobiles. He agreed. Besides, his interest in classic cars is mostly centered on English and German models, with two or three American early thirties vintage cars."

David wondered how big this garage was and how many cars were in it. Kathryn seemed to sense his silent question and volunteered, "My father has always been interested in cars and has made them his vocation. He buys and sells them on a fairly regular basis. His garage, in Dublin, had twelve or thirteen cars in it the last time I was there. You could barely get in the door or walk between them."

David was much more interested in Kathryn than her father, so he took a deep breath and asked the question. "I would very much like to take you to dinner tonight. I am sure there must be a decent restaurant around here somewhere. I owe you a great deal. It sounded like your father would have paid much more for the Chevy than I could have." David's voice cracked with dryness.

She looked at him for a moment with those wonderful dark eyes and hesitated a bit before she answered with her low breathless voice, "Thank you. I would love to have dinner with you. I have to help my mother finish here and take her and my father back to the motel. We could not stay here in Aunt Margaret's house because of the sale so we're staying at the Holiday Inn south of town. Why don't you come by the lobby about eight-thirty? That should give me time to get changed and see to it, that my mother is taken care of."

"Fine with me," David said. "I need to make arrangements to get this car towed out of here and put in storage. I'll see you at eight-thirty."

David called the first tow company whose add caught his eye in the phone directory, *Jim's Towing and Storage*. Jim arrived in less than fifteen minutes with a flat bed service truck that David had ordered.

"I know this car looks like a piece of junk," David pointed to the open garage doors, "but to me she's a beauty."

"Don't worry mister. We won't hurt this baby. We'll take real good care her." As Jim bent down to hook up the tow chains he murmured, "Damn, I lived her all my life and never dreamed that old lady O'Ryan had this car stashed in her garage all this time."

Jim inflated the tires sufficient to allow the car to be moved. The winch on the truck groaned as it pulled the Chevy up and on the steel bed. Jim secured the car with chains and was finished and ready to move in about fifteen minutes. "Follow me out to my yard and we'll settle up." Jim was climbing into the cab motioning for David to follow.

David's experience at the junkyard was still vivid in his mind, but it did not overshadow the dinner he and Kathryn enjoyed later that same evening. The very thought of her brought a wave of sensual pleasure followed by gut wrenching pain. Even though he knew better than to get excited about something that was so far out of his reach, he couldn't help himself, her eyes drew him into her.

Last night he had been so anxious about going out to dinner with Kathryn that he almost forgot to get cleaned up. He was unprepared to stay overnight in Dumont. He stopped at the first gas station/mini market he could find and bought shaving cream, disposable razors, a toothbrush, and toothpaste. He found the not so clean washroom and took care of his personal business best as he could. As he combed his hair and tucked in his shirt, he took a long look at himself in the mirror. Not bad, he thought. He was fifty-seven years old, but he could pass for fifty if he had to. He was just a little short of six feet tall. At one hundred ninety pounds, he was in good physical shape. His face still showed several faint scars, courtesy of Vietcong incoming at Da Nang in 1967. Luckily, he did not lose his right eye despite a small piece of shrapnel lodged just below the eyeball. Other shrapnel wounds were nasty, causing the loss of one kidney.

The Dumont Holiday Inn was a carbon copy of Holiday Inns across the country. Acceptable, but unremarkable. The small lobby smelled like cheap disinfectant. It was eight-thirty and Kathryn was not in sight. David figured he had time to register for a room. You never know, it might come in handy and besides driving back to Chicago late at night did not appeal to him. The tall young girl behind the counter asked if he was alone. "Yes," he responded with a little irritation. What difference did it make to her if he was alone or not? "Will you be with us for more than just tonight?" she asked.

"No," David said wanting to get this formality over with so he could call his daughter and beg off taking the kids to the park tomorrow. Who knows what will be happening tomorrow? "Can you recommend a good restaurant around here where we can get a nice steak?"

The clerk recommended Irv's Chicken Shack, down the highway about three miles. "Don't be put off by the name" she said. "People come from all over to eat there."

No sooner had he finished registering and was handed a plastic card for the keyless entry system, when Kathryn walked up behind him and said, "Good evening David, I see you are prompt. I like it when people are on time."

David felt his face blushing. He turned, expecting to see a slightly altered version of the woman he had seen in the afternoon. She was every bit as lovely as he had remembered and she was flashing a smile Colgate would have paid millions for. He could feel his heart jumping in his chest.

What he saw was a woman in the prime of her life, glowing with femininity. She was dressed in plain white slacks and a lightweight rust-colored pullover sweater that did wonders for her figure. Her dark auburn hair was pulled back into a bun accenting her creamy satin complexion and expertly applied makeup. She was wearing just the right amount of cologne. Enough so you had to get close to really get the full impact, but not enough to overpower her other assets. Her eyes met David's and he felt a strange rolling sensation in the pit of his stomach. He felt like a teenager at his first junior prom.

He would call his daughter in the morning, no sense in wasting time.

When Kathryn heard where they were going she looked at him with a little smile, "Sometimes these little towns have a really great place to eat. But then sometimes they're not so good." She shrugged saying, "I am sure it will be fine and we will have a great time."

Once they got in the car and started driving, David's heart rate began to get back to normal. Before he could utter the rehearsed sentences he had practiced, she said, "Tell me why you were so interested in that old car? I know Chevrolets from the mid-1950s are favorite projects for people who like to customize cars, but convertibles were not popular as street rods." David was surprised to hear her mention the words "street rod" like she really knew what she was talking about.

He began by telling her about his experience as a young boy at the Beloit public swimming pool. "That car symbolized the American dream to me. I was thirteen years old that summer and just horsing around with friends. A new 1956 Chevrolet convertible, all black and chrome, pulled up next to the fence with two young couples in it. The girl sitting in the front seat was wearing a yellow sundress, she stood up and waved to me and I immediately fell in love. That scene left an indelible impression on me." David felt his face blush as he recalled the childhood dream and he was thankful it was dark inside the car. "The guy driving with that beautiful girl next to him always represented the image of 'Success' to me."

"I know I can never get back the feeling I had at thirteen, but you know what? I am going to give it a try. Actually, I am very excited about getting started on this project." He went on to described how he would go about restoring a classic car.

"I think it's a great idea you have," she said, in a soft voice that made David feel like he was the only person in the world. "I hope when you finish this project I will have the opportunity to see it. You make it sound like it's more than just a car. Did you actually ever get to meet the people in the car?" she asked.

"No, I never saw that specific car again. Convertibles were never popular in Wisconsin. They're cold and drafty in the winter. Actually, convertibles are not a practical car in any part of the country."

"I think we are coming up on Irv's Chicken Shack. I see the lights up ahead. I hope this is not a bust," he said more to himself than to Kathryn. Irv's Chicken Shack turned out to be an old sprawling roadhouse. The neon sign next to the highway had been freshly painted and all the letters were lit. That was a good omen. The parking lot was nearly full. The building itself was set on the bank of a small river with a deck extending over the water.

The dinner and drinks they shared last night were only a small detail of David's memory. The free flowing conversation, the exchange of personal information about each other, the intimate connection between two strangers was intoxicating. "My husband was a lawyer in a large maritime law office in San Francisco. His hobby was flying, and one day while flying solo, he had an accident, and was killed. That was nine years ago. Since then I have divided my time between London and San Francisco developing a small language-training course to be offered over the Internet.

"I was raised in Ireland, but attended boarding school in Switzerland and France. I much preferred sunshine to the gray overcast skies of Ireland. I attended a small private university in the south of France near Nice. I studied language and history with the intention of teaching school somewhere in Europe."

Kathryn told several funny stories about the time she spent in boarding schools. Evidently she was popular with the other girls and enjoyed playing practical jokes on the school staff. The major antic during this period was to sneak out of the dormitory at night and join the local lads at a dance hall.

They lingered over after dinner coffee until Kathryn said, "I really want to thank you for a very pleasant evening."

She looked and sounded like she meant it. "I didn't mean to bore you with the details of my life."

"It was my pleasure." David replied "Besides, I owe you for helping out with the bidding this afternoon." On the way out to the parking lot David asked, "What can you tell me about the history of the car? You mentioned it belonged to someone named Cynthia."

"I really don't know too much about it. Cindy, I think that's what everyone called her, was the daughter of Margaret and Timothy O'Ryan. Timothy's brother Thomas is my grandfather. The two branches of the family were not close. I think it was a case of being separated by long distances. Margaret was the last of the older generation and my mother is the only living relative, so she was named executor of the estate. I am sorry I didn't introduce you to her this afternoon. She would have enjoyed meeting you.

"Cindy disappeared shortly after she graduated from high school in 1956. I never did know the exact circumstances. I understand her father, the Judge, was very strict, so maybe she just simply left home. I really don't know why she left the car or why it was locked in the garage all this time. I don't think my mother knows too much about it either, but I'll ask her in the morning."

David thought about showing Kathryn the note he had found in the trunk of the Chevy, but then on second thought he would save it for another time. Perhaps he would uncover more interesting clues to Cindy's disappearance in the suitcases. Hopefully that information would provide a good reason to stay in contact with Kathryn.

"My grandfather, Thomas, started an import export business, specializing in machine tools, before the war. My father took over the business after grandfather passed away."

She did not elaborate on the reason her father moved his family to Dublin.

The drive back to the motel took only a few minutes. They pulled up to an empty parking stall shielded from the streetlights by several large trees. It was a few minutes before twelve o'clock. Going upstairs, alone, to his room was the last thing David wanted to do. Kathryn turned to him and said, "Now it's your turn. I know you lived in Beloit as a youngster, how did you get to California?"

David could not remember enjoying talking with someone as much as he had enjoyed talking with Kathryn. She was focused on him and he on her. There was a connection between them that kept the rest of the world shut out. He was glad for the opportunity to stay in her company even if it meant he had to talk about himself.

David was embarrassed thinking he had actually told her things about his life that he had not discussed with anyone for years, his boyhood in Beloit, his eight years in the Marine Corps, his two tours of duty in Vietnam. He had to include his marriage to Ellen and their two children Kelly and Chance. Chance had been killed fighting in Desert Storm. "Ellen and I never really hit it off after my second tour in Nam. We tried, but it just never was the same. Finally she found what she was looking for in somebody else...we were divorced in 1988."

They each looked at their watches and David got out of the car. It was quiet except for the crickets and the sound of light traffic on the highway. He knew in his heart, if given a chance, he would pursue her. This woman had captivated him body and soul. He felt his stomach turn and twist every time he looked into her beautiful eyes. David felt as though he had known her all his life.

As he helped Kathryn out of the car she took his hand and said softly, "Thank you for dinner and a wonderful time, I enjoyed it very much." She held on to his hand and looked into his eyes.

His internal chemistry was about to boil over. "I hope we can do this again sometime. I had a terrific evening. I really enjoyed being with you. Will I see you tomorrow?"

"I don't think so," her voice was soft and warm. "We are leaving for Chicago early in the morning. My father has to be in London Wednesday for a meeting with some customers and he likes to rest after a long flight. If you give me your phone number I will call you the next time I'm in California." She held on to his hands and pulled him close, leaning into him she planted a kiss on his cheek, and then pulled back slightly. David was a mass of nerves.

Impulsively he took her gently by the arms, pulled her close, and kissed her warm, soft, full lips. David could feel his knees shaking, every nerve in his body was energized. Her body pressed against his. He was afraid the bulge in his pants would betray him. Their tongues touched ever so slightly, tentatively at first. David wanted this kiss to last a long time. It did. He let his hands slide down over her hips and pulled her close.

Kathryn leaned back and took a deep breath. "I must go," she said in a whisper. "Leave your phone number at the desk." She turned and walked quickly through the lobby door and disappeared.

David stood motionless for a good five minutes. He could not remember feeling this intense about another human being in his entire life. His feet were rooted to the ground. He relived every event of the evening over and over in his mind and lingered a long time tasting the sweetness of the kiss.

Even now, lying on the cool grass, with the knowledge of the killing that had taken place out at Jim's, the memory of that kiss was vivid in his mind. He could feel her closeness. He could taste her lips. He had no idea of how he had found his way to his room last night. No woman had ever affected him that way. His stomach was in knots. He could not stop thinking of the woman that had come into his life, totally unexpectedly. Last night, he had lain awake in bed smelling her cologne on his hands as he tried to re-experience the feeling of their bodies pressed together. He had finally fallen sleep with the image of her face embraced by the soft candlelight as they dined.

This morning when he woke the sun was shining through the open window. It was nine AM. He had intended to get up much earlier, get out to the storage yard, and collect the articles from the trunk of the old Chevy. He called Kelly and explained what had happened and why he stayed over-night. She joked about him having a date. "Dad, you had better be careful. You are a prize catch. Women your age out-number eligible men two to one. Are you going to see her again?"

David smiled to himself, thinking you're damn right I will. I just have to be patient and avoid acting like a teenage jerk. "I may see her when she returns to San Francisco, that's her hometown. Don't start ragging on me just yet. Kathryn is a class act. Tell the boys I'll see them soon and we'll go to a movie or something." He hung up feeling like a million dollars.

David's stomach began to churn just thinking of what happened when he checked out of the motel. As he walked toward the front door the clerk called out, "Mr. Jordan, you have a message here. I almost forgot. I am sorry," she said handing a sealed hotel stationary envelope to David. He knew it had to be from Kathryn, no one else knew he was here. He had left his own telephone number and address at the front desk as

Kathryn had requested. He went back and asked if his note had been picked up. It had.

Reaching into his shirt pocket, he pulled out the source of his misery and re-read her note for the hundredth time.

> *Dear David,*   *13   June 1999*
>
> *I feel very badly I have to write this note, but I must. I did not have the courage to tell you last night. I realized you might think there is a future for you and me. There is not. There can never be.*
>
> *I'm engaged to be married. I should have told you right away, but for some reason, I hesitated and it seemed unimportant at the time. After we arrived at the motel, I knew our casual meeting in the afternoon had turned into something much more than I could cope with.*
>
> *When you kissed me, I knew we could not continue any kind of a relationship. I am sorry, I did not mean to deceive you.*
>
> *Kathryn*

He remembered sitting for a long time staring through the windshield at the blank motel wall. He read the note several times. He felt like someone had kicked him in the stomach, hard. Bang, bang, bang, he hit his fist on the dash. "Damn" he yelled as he slammed his fist into the dash again. Even now as he sat on the park bench holding the note the pain came back, ten fold. God, how dumb he had been to think he could win a prize like Kathryn. "See what happens when you reach too far, you dumb shit. You had no business with a class act like her in the first place!"

His note to Kathryn with his telephone number on it had been enclosed in the envelope. How could she change so quickly? They had shared an intimate closeness. He was sure she felt the same. He could not have been mistaken.

Her note proved she felt a connection, why would she bother to write it if she hadn't? Finally he calmed himself. He could not blame Kathryn. She had been caught up in the moment just as he had. He would not have volunteered his engagement had the circumstances been reversed. He wondered who the lucky son-of-a-bitch was.

For a moment, he contemplated abandoning the old Chevy project. What was the point if the girl was gone?

CHAPTER 4

Lack of a real breakfast was beginning to cause David's stomach to send empty signals to his brain. It was two o'clock in the afternoon and he wanted to call his daughter and let her know he wouldn't be home tonight. What he needed now was a cold beer and a hamburger.

David looked up and down Main Street looking for a place to eat. A flashing green neon light advertising "Murphy's Bar and Grill" grabbed his attention. Murphy's was located in an old building that had been updated by covering the original brick frontage with light green composition shingles. The one large window displayed a Budweiser sign along with advertisements for pool and sandwiches. The entryway was framed by cracked and chipped paint. The updating had failed miserably.

He was greeted by smoke and stale beer smell as soon as he opened the door. Murphy's was half full of bar patrons watching the Chicago White Sox play the Detroit Tigers on a huge television situated on the far end of the bar. David could care less. The last thing he wanted to do now was watch baseball. Settling down in a booth near the vacant pool tables he tried to figure out his next move. His brain was still in a state of disbelief. He had never personally known anyone to be murdered, except in Vietnam.

The place reminded him of a bar he stopped at occasionally near the waterfront in Long Beach. Not a lot of class, but plenty of atmosphere and good burgers.

He heard someone at the bar say, not too quietly, "That's him, the guy who bought the Chevy." Several bar stool customers turned and glanced at David and then turned back.

The waitress, wearing tight jeans and a "Murphy's" tee shirt came over and took his order. She was middle-aged and spreading out. Walking back toward the kitchen she said something to a faceless individual on the other side of the order window. Back behind the bar, she began talking quietly to people directly in front of the beer taps. A woman looked over at David and sized him up very carefully. He felt like the proverbial fish in a glass bowl.

When the waitress delivered his beer he decided to try to capitalize on his notoriety. He asked her name. "Brenda," she replied looking down at the name badge pinned to her tee shirt.

Ignoring his oversight, David said, "I'm the guy who bought the old Chevy from the O'Ryan estate. I asked Jim Ballantyne to move it to his storage yard yesterday evening." David made sure the people at the bar could hear him. "Did you know Jim?"

"Know him! Hell everybody knew Jim," she nodded her head toward the bar. "Jim was a local, he grew up here in Dumont. He used to come here several times a week. Darlene, his wife, worked here until she got pregnant."

Inviting Brenda to join him, he told her he was shocked at what had happened and wanted to know more about Jim and his family. "I'm really puzzled about my missing car. I can't imagine anyone stealing an old car like that, and committing murder at the same time."

Brenda did not sit down, but indicated with a thumb over her shoulder, "Barnet could tell you more about Jim than I can, they were buddies." She pointed to a young man at the bar in a black Harley Davidson tee shirt. Barnet turned as Brenda mentioned his name. He looked at David and turned slowly back to the bar.

David glanced toward Barnet and said loudly, "Can I buy you a beer?" raising his own mug and smiling. Barnet slowly got off his barstool, walked over, and sat down opposite David. He was not smiling.

Barnet looked to be well over six foot tall in David's eyes and very muscular in the upper torso. He sported a snake tattoo around his neck and the image of barbed wire around his right bicep. His dark hair was slicked back and he had a three-day growth of whiskers. His gray eyes focused on David.

David offered his hand saying, "Hi, my name is David Jordan. I'm terribly sorry about your friend, Jim Ballantyne." Barnet did not return the handshake. The distance between them suddenly widened and became very cold. David asked, "Had you known Jim for a long time?"

"Yeah, long enough." Barnet had a cold stare, never taking his gray eyes off David.

"Look," David said with a smile and leaning forward, "I am just interested in finding out a little information about your friend. I met him yesterday when I asked him to put the old Chevy in storage. He seemed like a nice guy with a wife and kid. Now, all of a sudden he's dead and my car is missing. I guarantee you I had nothing to do with Jim's death." He looked at Barnet for some indication of which way to go with the conversation. He found only a blank stare. "I would like to find my car," he said as an after thought.

Brenda served Barnet his beer. He took a long drink, wiped his mouth with the back of his hand and replied as if each word had been chosen, "Jim got himself in some trouble a while back. He spent a year and half in prison on a bum rap. The local sheriff set him up. He just got out about six months ago. Knocked up his wife right away. He was trying to make a living running a towing service. What did you want with that old Chevy, anyway?"

David felt very uncomfortable. He had nothing to hide, and yet this guy was making him feel guilty somehow. "I restore old cars as a hobby. I read about this Chevy convertible going on the auction block so I thought I would try to buy it. No secret, I am just a car buff. I was going to have it shipped back to California next week. I can't do anything about Jim's death. I am only interested in finding my car. Do you have any idea why someone would want to kill Jim or steal my car?"

Barnet was quiet and then lit up a cigarette. "If I were you," his voice had a quality to it that made the hairs on the back of David's neck stand up, "I would go back to California quickly, and look for another car. There should be plenty of old cars out there you could restore. You don't need to be nosing around here. I'm positive you won't find it around Dumont." He emphasized the word "positive." The tone of Barnet's voice was as cold as ice and the look in his eyes said that the conversation was over. He got up and walked to the bar without a backward glance.

Brenda brought over the hamburger David had ordered. He gave her a twenty-dollar bill and she made change out of her apron pocket. Eating the burger without tasting it, David noticed that Brenda had turned up the sound on the TV so that the sports newscaster's voice blotted out the bar talk.

Finishing his hamburger, David gulped down his beer, and headed for the door. Neither Barnet, nor his friends paid the slightest attention. His meeting with Jim's friend had not gone well. He felt intimidated by Barnet's brooding personage. Barnet had given David a warning and David was inclined to take it. He was not the type of person to confront people if there was a peaceful way out of a situation. Besides Barnet was less than half David's age and had muscles bulging out of his tee shirt.

David could take care of himself, at least that's what he kept telling himself, but something about Barnet sent chills up his spine. The way Barnet carried himself, his voice, his cold gray eyes, his air of invincibility, and his physical size all combined to create an image of fear. David certainly did not want a confrontation with the local tough. He got in his rental car and started driving.

David hated bullies and Barnet had bullied him. Now he had to get back in control of his emotions, forget what just happened. He wanted to use the time left in the day to find out more about Jim and the missing car. And then there was the note he had retrieved from the trunk of the Chevy. There had to be a long story there too, who in the hell has the initial B?

He decided to take a chance and go back to the old Victorian house of Kathryn's Great Aunt Margaret. Perhaps the housekeeper was there and he could question her about the car and possible links to the note he found in the trunk. The note was burning a hole in David's shirt pocket with curiosity. Kathryn had said the car belonged to a missing daughter. That would have to be the "Cindy" mentioned in the in the note. His mind tried to imagine a situation where a young girl, ready to graduate from high school, in possession of a new car, bags packed, boy friend waiting would suddenly leave it all behind.

Common sense told him to leave the murder investigation to the sheriff. For all he knew the sheriff may have found Jim's killer by now. It could be they found the car also, but he didn't have a good feeling about that prospect. He started to drive back to the junkyard and then thought better of it. The sheriff would consider David a suspect until he had checked out his alibi and there was no sense hanging around the murder scene increasing his visibility. He could find out more by talking to some local people.

What was the housekeeper's name? David tried to remember if he had ever heard it before, but he could not come up with it. He would just have to wing it. The Cadillac parked under the carport most likely had belonged to the deceased. She couldn't be driving at age 98, could she? Could it be the housekeeper's car? He parked behind it and walked up to the side entrance.

The door was open. David knocked and shouted, "Anyone home?" No answer.

He looked for a doorbell and found an old-fashioned pull chain hanging from the middle of the open door. He gave it a yank and it made an ungodly scratchy ringing noise. From somewhere deep within the house came, "I'll be right down, just a darn minute."

The black woman he saw yesterday, when he used the phone to call for a tow truck, came down the hallway from the kitchen. "You again, you want to use the phone? Help yourself." She nodded toward the kitchen.

"No. I would like to talk to you. I am trying to get some information about the car I bought. The car's history is really what I'm after. You know about the murder I assume?"

"Good lord yes. News like that travels fast in a small town." She looked like she was anxious to talk to somebody and looking for an excuse to sit down. She sat down heavily on a hall chair doubling as a storage locker and coat rack. "I have a friend who lives next door to one of the deputies. She called me early this morning before I was even awake. They even took that old car. What a shame. The wife being pregnant and all." She looked at David, "I don't know any more than what I just said. Besides, the sheriff was here asking if I knew anything about the whereabouts of Kathryn and her family. I had to give him their Dublin phone number."

"Could I have her phone number?" David responded automatically at the prospect of getting Kathryn's personal telephone number. "I need to clear up some information and I misplaced the phone number and address that Kathryn had given me. I've been in a state of shock since I found out about the murder." David followed the housekeeper into the kitchen and copied the address and telephone number out of the address book he was handed. He thanked her and then confessed he had not caught her name.

"Beatrice Canady, Bee is fine. Bee is what most people call me. Same as what Miss Margaret called me" shaking her head in disbelief. "Lord I miss that woman. She was the nicest person. The best I ever worked for.

"Your name was Jordan or sump'em like that, wasn't it?" she said. Her accent was from the south, but she obviously had lived up north for a long time.

"Yes, David Jordan," David sensed this was the opportunity he was hoping for. Bee seemed like one of those women who were just bursting to talk about something, anything. "I don't suppose you would have anything to drink around here? It's been a hell of a day and I could use a little something to take the edge off."

"Mr. Jordan, you be a man after my own heart. I been looking for an excuse to open one of them bottles of whiskey tucked in the back pantry. I'll be right back." For a big woman, she had no trouble shifting into the hurry mode. She disappeared to the back of the house.

On impulse, David quickly opened the drawer with the address book in it and opened it to "Philips." He copied Kathryn's San Francisco and London addresses and telephone numbers and put the book back just as Bee's footsteps could be heard coming down the hall way.

Bee appeared with a sealed bottle of Wild Turkey. "These bottles have been back there since before I came to work here. Miss Margaret occasionally would have a sip of whisky on ice before dinner. Whenever guest came we never served alcohol, unless somebody asked for it."

She took two glasses out of the cupboard and then opened the refrigerator door and placed a couple of ice cubes in each glass. She then proceeded to open the bottle of whisky and poured about two fingers of whisky in each glass. They touched glasses. Bee took a good long sip. The whiskey was smooth as silk. David was certain Bee was no stranger to Wild Turkey.

"How many years have you worked for Miss Margaret?" David began. Bee did not hesitate to give David a detailed summary of her nine years taking care of the "nicest lady" she had ever worked for. She loved the old lady and this was an opportunity to tell someone about her.

Two drinks later, David asked Bee about the car. He told her about the note he found. Bee looked down and then up obviously having a hard time deciding whether to answer the question. David decided to help her along and said he was interested in satisfying his own curiosity and she could count on him to keep his mouth shut. "Okay, but don't you ever tell anyone I told you. Miss Margaret swore me to secrecy, but I don't think that counts after a person passes on, do you?"

"No" David assured her. "When a person dies, promises die too" he lied.

CHAPTER 5

David was very careful to drive slowly on the way back to the motel. Three glasses of whiskey had just about put him on his butt. He had forgotten Wild Turkey was something close to 100 proof. Smooth as a baby's behind, but with a kick like a mule. He failed to notice an unmarked patrol car parked down the street from the old Victorian. It followed David to the Holiday Inn and then sped past the front entrance. The white Ford sedan made a quick u-turn, entered the parking lot and parked off to the side of the lobby behind David's rental car.

David was a little unsteady on his feet as he registered for a second night. The same desk clerk that was on duty last night had the duty tonight. She assured him it would be her pleasure to have him as a guest for another evening. David asked if there was room service. He knew the answer but thought he would try it anyway.

"No. There is no restaurant on the premises, but back in town there is a coffee shop open until ten tonight," she said with a practiced smile.

Driving back downtown was not what David wanted to do. Maybe some pizza would do the trick. Could he order a pizza and have it delivered to his room? "Absolutely. We have an excellent pizza shop, and they deliver right to your door. What kind would you like? I'll call it in for you."

"Just surprise me. Medium size and a couple of beers." David said as he began walking up the stairs to his room.

"I'll take care of it, Mr. Jordan," the clerk seemed glad for something to do on a Sunday evening.

David, fumbled with the plastic card key, and finally opened the door with a bang against the wall. Opening the window drapes wide, he allowed a breeze to enter the room loaded with moist, warm air. It was close to nine o'clock and he figured his daughter would be putting the kids to bed about now. He really did not feel like calling but he knew Kelly would be mad if he didn't. He dialed the number and Fred answered after the first ring, "Hey Pop, where have you been? We have been worried sick. We thought you were in an accident or something."

David did not care for the "Pop" tag Fred insisted on using, but he guessed it was okay. He much preferred to be called David. He liked Fred, but he was not his son and pop seemed too familiar.

David asked if Kelly could get on the extension and he would update them on his latest adventure. He told about his meeting with Barnet and how unfriendly he had been. Kelly and Fred were both interested in Cindy, the original owner of the car. They asked questions and David did his best to answer. After he hung up, he realized he had talked more about the young girl, "Cindy," than the murder at the junkyard. He did not tell them about Kathryn's note to him.

The pizza arrived just as David hung up the telephone. Miracles of miracles: the pizza was hot and the beer cold. They tasted good and David relaxed and sat back in front of the open window. His mind reviewed the story Bee had told him about the O'Ryan's and their daughter. It occurred to him it would make a good novel, or better yet a movie. David pictured in his mind a beautiful young girl eloping with her lover in a new car. Suddenly some kind of tragedy happens...he could not finish the plot because he did not know what had happen in real life. For some reason, it was becoming essential that he find out what happened to the real Cindy. David had always had a high curiosity level. Even as a child, he drove his father nuts with questions until he got the frustrated response "Go look it up in the library."

David decided he should keep a record of the story Bee had told him. Although his brain was a little fuzzy and his hand writing shaky, he managed to fill several sheets of motel stationary. Jim's murder, the missing convertible, the convertible's owner, the warning to get out of town and the prospect of being a suspect in a murder case all seemed to be tied together. But how? He wrote the questions but could only guess at the answers.

Bee had been full of information. The Wild Turkey helped her memory and encouraged her to forget the promise she had made to Miss Margaret. "By the time, I came to work for Miss Margaret, the Judge had been dead for over 27 years. Miss Margaret insisted that since she was born in Dumont, she would die in Dumont. Right here, in the house she lived in since infancy.

"She had married Timothy O'Ryan when she was thirty years old. They had one child, a daughter, Cynthia, born in 1939. Miss Margaret went to school in the East and came back to teach high school English and literature. She taught school full-time while raising their daughter. Her husband, the Judge, was a native of Dumont also. He and some other man were the only two lawyers in town. Her husband had a brother named Thomas. The two brothers had parted company a long time ago, long before he and Miss Margaret were married.

"Miss Margaret and the judge were both active in the Democratic Party during the Roosevelt years and after the war. I guess because of his work for the party, he was appointment to be a judge in 1948. Then he ran for Lt. Governor in 1956.

"Miss Margaret didn't seem to care one way or another what the judge did. She said he lost favor with his party for some unknown reason and was not placed on the Democratic Party ticket for the 1960 election. Two years later, on his way home one night he was killed in a freak car accident. She said,

'I have no idea what that man was doing out in the middle of the night during a thunderstorm. He ran off the road into a river. At least that's what the highway patrol told me.' I think there was more to that story, but she never got around to tell me."

Bee had been reluctant to talk about the daughter. However, once the barrier of the promise had been disposed of, it all came out. Cindy was a very pretty young girl. David was shown several pictures taken from Miss Margaret's bedroom wall, Bee was getting ready to pack them. One picture was of a beautiful young girl with long blond hair in a prom dress. The other was a group of cheerleaders and Cindy was by far the most attractive. Cindy looked more like she was in her early twenties then seventeen.

Bee's narration about Cindy, with aid from the whisky, rambled on and on but what David pieced together was a tragedy waiting to happen. The girl was beautiful, talented, outgoing and boy-crazy.

The Judge was gone a great deal of the time and when he was home he locked himself in his library reading official papers and writing letters. Cindy's mother, Miss Margaret, was busy with her schoolwork, correcting exams or engaged in community social organizations. Cindy was left alone for much of the time and she managed to find plenty of activities to keep her occupied in this small town.

"Miss Margaret regretted not paying more attention to her daughter, she blamed herself for much of what happened later. She did say that Cindy received good grades and the other teachers were reluctant to tell her what Cindy was doing in her spare time."

According to Bee, Cindy dated frequently with different boys until she met Billy during her senior year. "Then it was Billy every day, every evening and weekends. If they weren't together they were talking on the phone. Billy was 19. His name was William Sandoval and he lived with his mother in an old farmhouse outside of town.

"Miss Margaret said, 'Whatever Billy had, Cindy could not leave alone. She saw something in this young man's strength, character, and responsibility others including me, could not see'. The Judge got wind of the young romance and tried to put a stop to it. Billy was not the kind of young suitor he wanted for his daughter. No sir! It sounded like Miss Margaret didn't oppose the Judge on this subject." Bee had taken on the role of Miss Margaret, she sounded as if Cindy was her child.

"The Judge had several serious talks with Cindy. He tried his best persuasive techniques to convince her Billy was bad news. The Judge told her, 'Billy comes from a dysfunctional family. His father has been in and out of the county jail a half dozen times mostly for passing bad checks and brawling in the local bars.'

"Billy had dropped out of high school after his second year to work for the local Ford garage. He had a police record beginning when he was fourteen. He and a couple of his friends had broken into a farmhouse and stole guns and ammunition. Because of the farmhouse incident he had spent several months in county juvenile detention and placed on probation for three years.

"Miss Margaret said Cindy would not hear any of the bad things her father was telling her. The Judge had it all on paper, but Cindy would not even look at it. Instead, after one particular meeting, she swept all the papers off the Judge's desk. All Cindy could think of was how hard Billy worked to support him and his mother. He was a good mechanic and someday he hoped to open his own business.

"She had confided to Miss Margaret that she was in love with Billy. He treated her with respect. He treated her like a lady. Not like those other groping, panting, slobbering, boys she had dated in high school. He was smart, funny, charming, and very handsome, and she was going to marry him. No matter what her father said, she and Billy would be together."

It sounded like a B rated movie plot to David. For a while he thought Bee had been reading some of those cheap romance novels and was mixing truth with fiction. He hinted as much to Bee and she took offense. "Miss Margaret would never lie to me. She loved her daughter and wanted her to be happy. What I am telling you is the God's honest truth." Bee said it in a very loud emphatic voice pointing her finger at David. He decided he would not question her truthfulness again.

Bee continued, "Miss Margaret understood how a woman could love a man beyond reason. She spoke from experience. She did not marry the Judge until she was nearly thirty years old. Miss Margaret told me she had several suitors, before marrying the Judge. She had been around some. She lived in a small town, but she was not a small town girl. She traveled and corresponded with people from all over the country and Europe." As proof, Bee produced a large cardboard box of cards and letters of condolence from Miss Margaret's friends. "See there," she said. "There is more, I just haven't had time to make a list of the people who sent their respects. Miss Rebecca asked for the names so she could respond."

"What does Billy and Cindy stories have to do with the car?" David asked, he was getting a little fuzzy in the head from the Wild Turkey, but he wanted Bee to continue, but he wished she would get the bottom line before his mind got too numb.

"Everything," Bee said, emphasizing her words by banging her glass on the table. "The Judge gave Cindy the car as a bribe don't you see. He wanted to keep her away from Billy. That's how they met in the first place. The Judge taught Cindy to drive before she was 16 years old. He gave her an old Ford sedan to drive around town. It kept breaking down and she took it to the Ford garage for repairs. That's how she met Billy.

"The Judge figured he would buy Cindy the Chevrolet as an early graduation present and eliminate the need for her to patronize the Ford garage where Billy worked. Miss Margaret agreed that it seemed to work for a while. Cindy buttered up her father like only teenage girls can do and got his blessing to take a trip in the Chevy after graduation. She made plans with a girl friend to drive to New York City and spend several months with the Judges brother, Thomas, and is wife MaryAnn."

That seemed like a gutsy move to David. Letting two teenage girls' drive to New York City unescorted! He would never have let his daughter do that. And Kelly was a responsible young girl when she was 17. The Judge must have been desperate to get his daughter out of town and away from Billy.

Bee still had not gotten to the most interesting part of her story. She poured their third glass of Wild Turkey. David instinctively started to refuse, but he wanted to keep Bee talking so he took it and thanked her hoping he could somehow dispose of it without her seeing him.

"Miss Margaret didn't tell me the whole story in one sitting, but over a long period of time, several years in fact. Every so often, when the mood struck her, she would start talking about her daughter." This last part came as Miss Margaret was going over old pictures and letters, sorting things to keep and others to throw away. "She knew she didn't have long to live. She spent most of the last year writing down what she wanted to give away to her few relatives, friends and what she wanted to throw out. She left me that Cadillac parked out front. Can you believe it?

"It took her a long time to decide what to do with Cindy's pictures and letters. There are only four letters," Bee said with her eyes wide, shaking her head side to side.

"One day when Miss Margaret was sorting a box of old photos she started crying. I went to her bedside and tried to comfort her and she just sobbed and sobbed. After a few minutes, she calmed down and asked for a cup of tea. She sat looking out the window sipping the tea and finally began telling me what happened on that 'awful' graduation night.

"During the day, the Judge had lunch with Dr. James Whitworth. The doctor told the Judge about Cindy's condition. Cindy had not been feeling well the past few weeks and Miss Margaret made an appointment for her to see the doctor. Dr. Whitworth had been Cindy's physician since she was born. Miss Margaret didn't know if the doctor volunteered the information or if the Judge coaxed it out of him, but the real reason Cindy wasn't feeling so well was she had tried to force a miscarriage. She was pregnant. She had gotten hold of some concoction that was supposed to get rid of unwanted pregnancies. The drink, whatever it was, caused her to vomit and gave her a bad case of diarrhea, but that was all. She was still eight or nine weeks pregnant.

"When the Judge came home in the afternoon, he was in a dark mood. He was in the first year of his term as Lt. Governor and now his daughter had disobeyed him and gotten pregnant by that no-good Sandoval kid. That was what the Judge called him. He was afraid the scandal could prevent him from being nominated for Governor next term. The Judge ranted about that grease monkey Billy, and threatened to have him arrested for statutory rape.

"During his tirade, flowers were delivered at the front door. Several bouquets had arrived earlier in the day for Cindy. Miss Margaret put them in her room. Her graduation was scheduled for later in the evening. Cindy had been out driving in her new car and just returned when the roses were delivered.

"According to Miss Margaret, there was a terrible argument between the Judge and Cindy. The Judge accused her of being a whore, a slut and parading around town, sleeping with that damn no-good mechanic. Didn't she realize she had a wonderful future ahead of her? She had the looks, brains and a father who could help get her into any college in the country. 'She had the world by the balls', the Judge's very own words. He said, 'because you can't keep your pants on you've ruined everything and jeopardized my career as well.' 'Billy,' he said 'will end up in the state penitentiary and you would be on welfare with his kid.' Miss Margaret said the Judge was in a rage and slapped Cindy hard, knocking her down, she ran up to her room, slammed the door, and locked it.

"Miss Margaret said she was greatly upset at the Judge because she understood and sympathized with Cindy even though she wasn't very happy with Cindy's selection of boy friends. Without thinking she blurted out, 'Billy may not be the pick of the crop but by God, he's more of a man than you are', she told the Judge. I guess he was taken by surprise according to Miss Margaret, 'What do you mean by that statement?' That's when Miss Margaret told the Judge, 'You have no right to slap Cindy because you are not her father!'"

Bee could hardly get the words out fast enough now. This was the secret Miss Margaret had asked Bee to keep. "The Judge and Miss Margaret had been married for eight years before Cindy was born. At first, they tried to have a child, but nothing happened. After a few uneventful years, they both put aside the thoughts of children. They both had careers. Miss

Margaret was highly involved with the high school and he as the leading lawyer in the county and chairman of the county Democratic Party. Their marriage was in name only, and only occasionally in the bedroom. Miss Margaret didn't seem to mind telling me, she never felt ashamed of being unavailable whenever the Judge got ideas.

"Miss Margaret met someone special during her summer vacation of 1938 in Europe. The Judge had stayed behind and Miss Margaret traveled with several friends, visiting Paris and Rome. She went every year before the war. She met a man from Sydney who was working in the Australian consulate's office in Paris. He was widowed and had two children.

"They were drawn together by the invisible forces that bring couples together in Paris. The look on her face when she talked about that summer was a real treat. I could tell she was relieving it in her mind as she was talking. They couldn't resist being with each other. It was a simple case of the right person, the right time, and the right place. Soon they were inseparable lovers. Miss Margaret described their relationship as the most beautiful thing she had ever experienced. She never dreamed two people could be so close. She was in her late thirties at the time and had given up the thought of having a truly romantic relationship.

"When she was telling me about Randall Foster, that was his name, she got misty eyed and I could tell after all these years she was still in love with this man. Women can tell when another woman is revealing her true self. It's not like a man. A man will tell a lie and believe it hisself. A woman's eyes tell the truth. Miss Margaret was opening up to me and I believed every word.

"Miss Margaret told me she and Randall split from the group she was with on the pretext of wanting to visit a mutual friend. She didn't care if anyone believed her or not. They were all good friends and she could count on them to keep her secret.

"Randall and Miss Margaret spent the rest of the summer in the Alps, staying in a small inn at the foot of Mt. Blanc. She showed me pictures of the Inn and the mountains. Randall was very handsome. They were so in love they would spend whole days making love and talking the night through. Some times, they would forget to eat and have to go out and buy bread, cheese and wine late at night.

"She told of the day they parted as if it had happened yesterday. I cried when she told me." David could actually see Bee's eyes watering as she repeated what Margaret had said. "Randall knew war was coming to Europe. America and Australia would soon be fighting against Germany. England was in desperate need of experienced aviators to help defend herself against Nazi Germany. Randall was a reserve officer in the Australian Air Force. He had committed to lead a volunteer squadron of Australian pilots to fly for mother England. He was certain he would be in uniform by the coming fall.

"They made promises to one another like lovers do. After the war they would meet and decide what they should or should not do. They even agreed to meet at a specific inn in the Alps. Miss Margaret gave Randall her address and asked him not to write until he was sure he wanted to see her. He promised he would."

"Did Margaret tell Cindy who her real father was?"

"No, not then, not until Cindy was in New York staying with her aunt and uncle."

David had filled eight pages of hotel blank paper with his recollection of Bee's story telling. The last phrase he wrote was "Randall's promise was kept but not in the way Miss Margaret had hoped for."

CHAPTER 6

Standing and stretching, David gathered the papers together and numbered them so he could keep them in order. He could see that the parking lot below was nearly empty, except for six cars scattered around a space large enough for 40. It was dark and the lot was illuminated by several tall light standards. His attention was drawn to a white Ford sedan parked directly behind his rental Pontiac. There was a small antenna attached to the roof of the Ford. The car was obviously an unmarked police car and there was somebody in it. He could see cigarette smoke drifting out of the driver's window. The Wild Turkey and beer had put him in a stupor. Now, he needed his senses and he was having trouble focusing his eyes. Why were the cops watching him? Should he be upset or grateful they were doing their job?

He tried to imagine what the local sheriff was thinking. Of course, it was possible he had been the last person to see Jim Ballantyne alive with the exception of his wife and/or the killer. He had legitimate business with Jim and had no idea of why anyone would want to kill him. The sheriff was wasting his time watching him. How long had this been going on, he wondered. He had a hard time getting his mind in gear.

Finally, he decided there was nothing he could do about the cop sitting in the parking lot, so why sweat it? He finished the second beer, took two bites out of the next slice of pizza, and decided he had had enough. He flopped down on the bed and was sound asleep within minutes.

He woke early Monday morning, stared out the window, and watched the sun come up. The unmarked police car was still there. David took a long hot, shower and shaved with his emergency toilette kit he had purchased from the mini mart yesterday. He wished he had some fresh clothes to put on. He decided the first thing he would do this morning was to find some kind of clothing store where he could buy some clean underwear, socks, and a shirt.

David was on the verge of a hangover that could only be cured by a good cup of coffee. After dressing, he collected his few belongings including the notes he had written and walked downstairs to the lobby. The motel's continental breakfast was not much to look at but the coffee had been freshly brewed. Filling two cups, he put one in a little cardboard box along with a doughnut. He headed to the parking lot and the unmarked police car. The occupant was sleeping with his head in an awkward position. The sleeping driver was snoring so loud be could be heard several feet away. David placed the coffee and doughnut on the hood of the Ford.

Quietly, David opened the Pontiac door and got in. Now he wished for a silent starter. He turned the ignition key and as soon as the engine started he immediately put the car in drive and drove off. The Ford did not move.

The supermarket across the railroad tracks on the south side of town was open. Fortunately, the market had a skimpy clothing section. He bought a pair of packaged underwear, socks, and a cheap polo shirt. The unmarked police sedan was gone when David returned to the motel to change clothes.

Sherry's Coffee Shop was a bright spot in Dumont. Patterned after a national restaurant chain, the only thing lacking was a "Denney's" sign. David found a booth in the back near the kitchen that was empty. While he was eating and drinking his coffee, he went over in his mind the letter Randall had written to Miss Margaret. Bee had found it in a box of Margaret's personal correspondence and showed it to him.

Margaret told Bee she received it in 1944, eight weeks after it had been posted in Australia.

The letter was written on thin stationary paper, the type used for AirMail delivery during the war. It began with *"Dear Margaret, If you are reading this letter, you will know I will not be meeting you at the Valle d' Aosta Inn."* Randall wrote in a formal English style, bold and neat.

Randall had written the letter after he had been called to join his squadron in England. He expressed his love for Margaret and recalled some of the more intimate moments they had shared in the small inn. Randall stated several times, that Margaret was the most wonderful woman he had ever known. *"Our time together was the most precious time of my life. I know we will meet again in the next life. Only death could keep us apart on earth."* The letter was signed *"Love Forever, Randall."* He had given the letter to his sister and asked her to mail it if he did not return from the war.

The letter had arrived one afternoon in December 1944, just before Christmas break. Miss Margaret told Bee she nearly died of sadness and shock when she read Randall's letter. She stayed in her room for two days trying to cope with the grief. She told the Judge and her daughter, who was five years old at the time, she had a severe case of influenza and did not want them to catch it. Dr. Whitworth came and prescribed some sleeping pills and promised he would not tell the Judge she was suffering from depression, not a contagious disease.

Miss Margaret managed to hide her grief and still hang on to the memory of Randall. Bee said she moved into her own bedroom after the letter arrived and indicated the Judge and her never shared the same bed again. Margaret became totally involved with her teaching and the children at the high school. She tutored kids, chaperoned dances, and was active in virtually all school functions.

After Margaret retired from active teaching in 1965, she continued to tutor kids and offer advice to anyone who asked. She especially liked helping young people who wanted to become writers. She offered advice and a safe haven for girls in trouble. She was a woman of integrity and the young girls and boys put their trust in her.

Miss Margaret had an amazing memory. She was well into her nineties and she still corresponded with dozens of former students and friends. In later years she asked Bee to write for her because her hands shook so bad her handwriting was atrocious. Bee was constantly surprised by Margaret's ability to recall names, addresses and events.

With all the information Bee had given him, David was convinced, more than ever, he had the making of good novel.

CHAPTER 7

Sherry's Monday special breakfast consisted of hot cakes, eggs, and sausages. After finishing the cholesterol special, David decided he should find sheriff Woodford and see if he had made any progress toward finding Jim Ballantyne's killer. Maybe, just maybe, they had found his car? Also, he wanted to ask the Sheriff why the homicide detectives had not interviewed him yet. He didn't have to go far to find the sheriff. He was in Sherry's parking lot standing next to the unmarked police sedan talking and waving his arms in an aggravated manner. The occupant inside the Ford was slouched down in the driver's seat staring straight ahead. Finally the sheriff stood up straight, said something, and the Ford drove off.

David walked out the door just as the sheriff headed toward the restaurant. "Good morning, Sheriff," David said, in the most friendly manner he could muster.

"What the hell is good about it? You made a fool out of my deputy."

David tried desperately to hide his smile, "Your man made a fool of himself. I was being friendly and offering a working stiff a cup of coffee. What the hell was he doing parked outside my motel anyway?"

The sheriff swallowed hard saying, "You were told not to leave town and we just wanted to make sure you didn't. I'm short a couple of deputies and couldn't relieve Jackson last night. Let's go back to my office so we can discuss some details."

That was fine with David. He wanted to know what the status of the investigation was so he could go back to Chicago and be with his grandkids. He had just about given up any hope the Chevy would be found.

The substation was behind the city hall building just off Main Street. The sheriff got right down to business. "We verified your alibi. You were with Kathryn Philips having dinner at Irv's place until about eleven o'clock. We contacted her at a hotel in New York City. The motel clerk at the Holiday Inn vouched for you also. She said you went up to your room at about midnight. That still does not put you entirely in the clear because the coroner said Jim was killed somewhere between eleven-thirty and two in the morning. Jim's wife still has not been able to talk to us, or won't, depending on how you want to look at it. So, until she tells us who was out there last night, if she knows, I am going to have to ask you to hang around."

David said quickly, "I did not have anything to do with Jim's murder. I didn't even know the guy for Christ's sake. Surely you guys don't think I would have done it, do you?"

"No, I don't. But, until we can eliminate you altogether, technically you are still a possible suspect, but don't get your ass in an uproar. It's only a technicality. We have plenty of other options to look at. Jim was not your ordinary, upstanding citizen. He has been involved with people we consider to be a bad characters." The sheriff stopped and looked at David. He apparently wanted to say more, but didn't.

"Right now we want to get some more information about the car. We have the license number and vehicle number you gave Deputy Passmore, but those numbers are so old they won't help much. What we can't figure out is why they wanted that specific car. What is the value of it anyway?" The sheriff was sitting at his desk looking at a typewritten page from Passmore's notes.

David shrugged his shoulders, "I paid close to three thousand dollars for the car, but at this stage, it was probably over-priced. After it's restored, it might be worth twenty or twenty-five thousand or more, it's really a guess on my part."

Just then the telephone rang and the sheriff picked it up, "Sheriff Woodford here. Yeah, yeah, …no shit, great, I am on my way." He hung up almost breaking the hand set.

"Good news. Some kids spotted Jim's truck in a dairy barn out on the old Cooper place. I am headed out there right now do you want to go for a ride?"

David did not hesitate for one moment, "Sure," he said, but he was trying to remember where he had heard that name before. The old Cooper place. Then it came to him. The note, he found among the dried flowers in the Chevy's trunk, it read, "Meet me at the old Cooper place at twelve-thirty." Because the note was over forty years old, it was not worth mentioning to the sheriff. It had to be irrelevant,

Brushing aside the empty potato chip bag and empty Coke can, David climbed into the passenger seat of the sheriff's car. For a heavy man, Sheriff Woodford wasted no time scrambling into the driver's seat. He started the engine, turned on the flashing lights, put on his aviator-style sunglasses, hit the siren button, grabbed the mike, and told the dispatcher where he was going before squealing the tires as they exited the parking lot. In no time flat they were headed out of town on an unmarked county road heading due west, siren blaring. David was impressed with the sheriff's coordination. He decided this overweight, middle-aged, balding county sheriff would be the right man to have on your side if you needed a little law enforcement.

Once underway, the sheriff began to explain, "The Cooper place is an old dairy farm about five miles outside of town. The farm acreage was sold many years ago to some big agribusiness corporation. The farmhouse had been rented out for some years and then abandoned.

"The local boys use it as a place to take their girlfriends and do what young kids do. I don't think anybody has lived there for twenty years or more. A couple of local boys went out to do some target practicing this morning and shoot magpies, that's when they spotted Jim's truck. They called my office to report it because they knew it didn't belong there."

The Sheriff stomped on the brakes and made a right-hand turn onto an unmarked gravel road. The farm buildings were at the end of long tree-shaded lane set back into some low hills. David was hanging on the armrest as the sheriff went blazing down the narrow, rutted, tree-lined driveway. They entered the farmyard doing about sixty miles an hour and had to broadside the squad car in order to stop. Deputy Passmore headed for the bushes along with the two teenage boys.

As the huge cloud of dust started to settle, the sheriff stepped out of his police cruiser, took off his sunglasses and motioned for the deputy and the boys to come over next to him. David, Deputy Passmore, and the boys obediently gathered in a small group around Sheriff Woodford.

"Okay, boys, tell me what brought you out here." Deputy Passmore stepped forward with his notebook open and began reading what he had written down. The sheriff stopped him, "Let them tell me in their words deputy. Go ahead boys."

"We were just going to shoot some magpies with our twenty-twos. When we got here, we saw Jim's truck parked in the barn. We live a mile down the road so we ran back to the house and called your office." The taller of the two, had been doing the talking.

The sheriff asked the smaller one, "What's your name, son?"

"Bobby Haskell, we're brothers," he said, looking for support from the tall one. The sheriff was trying to be nice, but his size, badge, and gun caused him to appear bigger than anyone the boys knew. "We just live down the road. A lot of people come out here and shoot," he said in self-defense.

"I know that. You two are not in trouble. I just want to know all the facts. It's important. Did you know Jim Ballantyne was shot and killed last night?" Both boys shook their heads in the affirmative. "We need to know all you know no matter how small a detail you may think it is. You understand?" The sheriff was looking down at the two boys like bugs under a magnifying glass.

The boys, David and the two sheriffs started walking toward the barn. David looked around and saw the farmhouse had undergone several additions, but obviously had been empty for a long time. All the windows had been shot out and part of the second floor had burned. The outbuildings were all in shambles. The dairy barn was a huge structure, maybe 150 feet long, half as wide, and fifty feet tall. The barn had withstood the elements and time much better than the house had. Most of the support pillars were made from twelve-by-twelve timbers. It took several minutes for their eyes to adjust to the gloom once they entered the old structure. Light filtered through hundreds of bullet holes in the roof and rows of small windows along the sides of the building. A hayloft extended over half the length of the building. Milking stalls extended along each side of the barn. The old structure was so large it could easily hide several trucks the size of Jim's.

They saw Jim's flatbed tow truck parked off to one side. The sheriff told David and the boys to stand near the large double doors and not to go anywhere. He and the deputy began to look around, using flashlights. The deputy was taking notes as he walked.

David asked the boys if they had heard or seen anything Saturday night. They both shook their heads negatively. Then the youngest boy said, "Well, maybe we did hear a big diesel truck going west Sunday morning before we had breakfast."

The tall one interjected, "Hell, we hear diesels all the time going down the county road. They use it to avoid the state police when they open the weigh station on Highway 75."

"But I heard one Sunday morning, early," Bobby shot back.

Now the sheriff and the deputy were bending over looking at the floor of the old barn. The floor was dirt except in some sections where concrete had been poured. "Well, it looks like they loaded your car on a big rig and took it away," the sheriff said looking at David. "The tire tracks indicate the driver of a big rig came in through the doors on the south end and parked right here. He must have been here waiting for some time because of all the cigarette butts lying around. You boys don't smoke do you?" looking at the two teenagers.

"No sir," said the younger one. The older boy kept silent.

"Deputy, call the office and tell them we want Skip Jensen to bring his drug sniffing dog out here. Let's see if we can piece together what activity took place here last night."

The two sheriffs spent some time with their flashlights, following the tire tracks and making diagrams on a clipboard. David continued to talk with the boys and discovered they lived on a farm west of the Cooper place. They volunteered that older kids, with cars, come out here to drink beer and make out with their girlfriends. The three of them walked outside into the bright sunlight and David could see the barnyard was littered with empty beer cans and trash from the local fast-food restaurants. Several burned-out campfires were evident.

Mounds of trash were scattered in the old apple orchid. Several rusted car bodies, covered with vines and bushes, were lying about. Someone was using this abandoned farm for a trash dump. Brass cartridges and expended shotgun shells lay everywhere. It looked like a war zone.

The boys looked more nervous than they should, David thought. They hadn't done anything wrong, as far as he could tell. The sheriff even said they were not in any trouble. But the younger boy, Bobby, kept looking up to his brother who was too cool to be bothered with his little bother. David sensed something was not quite right.

"What time did you boys get here this morning?"

"About nine, I guess," said the tall bother.

"I didn't hear what you said your name was," David said looking directly at a gawky fifteen-year-old.

"Richard Haskell," the older one replied, without looking up.

"Did you see Jim's truck right away or did you get some shooting in first?" David asked.

"We shot two pies..." said Bobby before his brother elbowed him. Bobby stopped short and looked down. "Well, we did. Mom said we had to get out of the house for a while so we got three more after we came back here."

"Why did you have to get out of the house?" David asked. "It's okay. You didn't break any laws, but if you know something, you had better square up with the sheriff. I don't think he would be happy if he thought you two knew something important and didn't tell him. You can tell me first if you want to." David sensed the younger boy was dying to get something off his chest.

The boys looked at each other, the older one, Richard, scowled at Bobby and said through his teeth "Keep quiet. It's no one's business what happened at the house." Bobby looked like he was ready to burst, but David could see he was afraid of his older brother. Walking into bright sunshine the sheriff and his deputy exited the barn and walked over to the boys and David.

"It looks like someone, possibly the shooter, drove Jim's truck with your old Chevy on it, out here. Another truck, a big rig, it must have been a car carrier, was waiting here maybe since the day before. They backed Jim's truck up to the big rig, loaded your car on it, and left. They're some fresh car tracks in addition to the truck tires and many footprints. We think there were at least three people here last night. We're going to get the crime scene investigative team out here and really go over this place." The sheriff seemed to like being in the middle of an investigation and being charge. David had to admit Woodford was as competent as any big-city cop he had ever met.

"Now boys, I want you both to come with me and tell me again what you saw when you first came up here." Both boys' eye's got wide, and now the older brother looked a little pale. "Deputy Passmore, check with the office and find out when the drug dog is coming."

The deputy went to his car and started talking on the radio. Sheriff Woodford took the boys to his car and put them in the back seat. Leaning in through the open door he started questioning them. David couldn't hear what was being said. He hoped the boys would speak up, he was certain Woodford was not the type of man who would tolerate lying.

After about ten minutes of a very intense conversation the sheriff backed away from the squad car door and slammed it shut. The boys, still inside, were staring straight ahead.

The two officers talked quietly for a few minutes and then the sheriff turned to David, "I am taking these two boys home, you can stay with Passmore if you want or come with me." David's first inclination was to stay and keep looking around the barn but then he decided to go with the sheriff for no particular reason he could put his finger on. Thinking about it later David, felt as though some outside force was responsible.

Once in the car, the sheriff began driving at a reasonable speed. He explained that the boys had a problem at home when they called his office earlier in the morning. "They have a stepbrother named Adam Barnet." David's ears immediately picked up. "Adam went berserk when he overheard the kids on the phone telling my deputy they had seen Jim's truck in the barn out at the Cooper place. The boys indicated Adam was about to do serious harm to them when their mother came into the room and stopped it. She told the two younger boys to get out until Adam had cooled down."

Sheriff Woodford went on to explain he was well acquainted with Adam Barnet. He suspected Adam was somehow involved with Jim's murder and the stolen car. Woodford explained to David that Adam's mother was still in high school when he was born. "She didn't marry the father. I don't know who he is. She struggled trying to raise him and finish school, but in a small town like Dumont, it was difficult. She finally had to give Adam up for adoption when he was just a few months old.

"His mother married the younger boy's father, Herbert Haskell a couple of years later and moved on to the farm he had inherited from his folks. All was roses until Adam decided to find his birth mother when he was about seventeen or so. Naturally his mother was glad to have him back. Mother's love is the strongest bond of all. But he was trouble for us from the moment he came to town. He had a police record in

Minneapolis where his adoptive parents lived. I found out later, they were glad to be rid of him.

"He had a number of arrests up there for underage drinking, fighting, car theft, and finally dealing marijuana. His folks managed to keep him out of jail, but he was not thankful. They finally gave him an ultimatum: settle down and finish high school or get out and get a job.

"He got out. Somehow, he found out who his birth mother was and came to live with the Haskell's. We knew he was dealing drugs, but couldn't pin anything on him until he got greedy and started selling uppers and marijuana to the kids at the local football games.

"We caught him red-handed selling dope to kids after a game about four years ago. He had the stuff right on his person." The Sheriff rolled his eyes and shook his head, "Nobody said he was smart. He was eighteen at the time and served three years of a five-year sentence in the state penitentiary at Joliet. In the penitentiary, he made a big name for himself by bullying those around him and dealing drugs. He and Jim Ballantyne were in the lockup at around the same time. Ballantyne was in for car theft.

"After Barnet was out on parole, he got into a fight in a local bar here in town. He nearly killed a guy from out of state. He was still on parole and we would have tossed him back to Joliet but everybody in the bar said the other guy started it by pulling a knife. Adam claimed self-defense. So, we were stuck with him until he screws up again. We have been watching him and Ballantyne since they got out of prison. They hang around together and both of them spent time at Murphy's bar in town. That's why I want the drug dog out here so we can eliminate drugs or include it in our investigation. I'll put money on the fact the old barn smells like marijuana or coke. I think I could smell it myself. Couldn't you?"

David shook his head. He had smoked marijuana in Vietnam, but not since he had returned to the states. He hadn't noticed any marijuana smell.

The Haskell's lived on a picture perfect farm, surrounded by green fields of corn and soybeans, about a mile west of the Cooper place just like the boys said. The sheriff did not say a word as he pulled up under a huge oak tree next to the driveway. The boys were stone faced and silent.

The sheriff stopped the squad car and picked up the radio microphone. He radioed his office and told the dispatcher where he was. He swiveled around in his seat looking in all directions. The immaculate farmyard was picture perfect. Then he unfastened the little strap holding his sidearm firmly in its holster. David sat motionless, unsure of what the sheriff was about to do. Woodford got out of the car, turned to David, and asked if he knew how to use a shotgun.

"Sure. I've fired one before." He had no idea what the sheriff was getting at until he reached over and unlocked the clamp holding the military style pump action shotgun to the dash-mounting bracket. "Take the shotgun and stand by the car." Woodford looked at David and said in a very quiet but commanding manner, "If I get in trouble use it, it's loaded with double 00 buckshot. Then call for help on the radio, just press the button on the mike and talk."

Bobby was whimpering, and Richard was banging on the patrol car window. They shouted in unison from the back seat, "Let us out. Let us out." Both doors in the back seat were without handles and the dividing screen between the front and the back made a secure cell.

"You two keep quiet. Not one sound from either one of you," Demanded Woodford, Both boys stopped breathing.

David got out of the car and stood next to the front fender with the shotgun held tightly in both hands. He felt foolish. He had no idea if the shotgun had a shell in the chamber or not. If it didn't, should he jack one in? He decided to do it. The shotgun made a highly audible metallic clicking sound as a shell entered the chamber. His knees were shaking, despite the fact the temperature was in the mid-eighties. Visions of Vietnam came flooding back, the same sick adrenaline rush he had felt sighting in on enemy solders in the rice fields.

The sheriff walked up to the side entrance to the Haskell farmhouse and was met by a tall slender man of about fifty. The man walked out onto the porch and asked "What is it you want Sheriff. The boys in trouble?"

"Not these boys, Mr. Haskell. I came to talk with Martha's boy, Adam."

"Adam's not here Sheriff. He took off about fifteen minutes ago. Is he in trouble again?"

"Not yet. I just wanted to talk with him and find out what he knows about what happened over at the Cooper place last night." The sheriff stood at the foot of the porch steps looking up at Haskell, "His pickup is in back of the house. I saw it when we drove up."

Just then, Adam Barnet stepped out the door. "It's okay Herb, I just got back. What can I do for you, Sheriff Woodford?" His voice was deep and he emphasized the words "What can I do for you" so they dripped with false respect. Adam was dressed in Levis and a tank top showing off his muscular torso, complete with tattoos. He was unshaven and looked just as intimidating as when David had talked with him at Murphy's. "You got a new deputy, Sheriff?" Pointing a finger at David. "You always give your new men shotguns the first day on the job?" He had a half-ass smile on his face all the while looking straight at David with cold gray eyes.

The sheriff was just as intimidating. It was like two bull elephants squaring off over a disputed harem, "I don't trust you one little bit after the show you put on at Murphy's last year. You tried to kill some guy over a stupid pool game," the sheriff said keeping his eyes fixed on Adam and a hand on his military-style forty-five-semi-automatic. "What I want to know is, why did you get so upset with the boys here when they called my office this morning?"

"Ah, they were making a lot of noise when I was trying to get some sleep. You know how kids are Sheriff. No big deal. Why, what did they tell you?" Adam was smiling, looking into the back seat of the squad car.

"They said you tore the phone out of the wall and would have killed them if it hadn't been for your mother stepping in and stopping you." David could see the kids in the back seat cringe as Adam glared at them.

"I don't like having anything to do with law enforcement, Sheriff. I guess you know why. I just lost my temper for a bit, that's all. I have had my share of trouble with your office and unless you got something specific to talk about I'll be getting back to the baseball game I was watching." Adam turned and started to walk back into the house.

"I am sending the crime lab boys out here to take tire impressions from your pickup Adam. I think you were at the Cooper place last night where there was an exchange of stolen property. If you're smart you'll tell me about it now." The sheriff stepped back, reaching into the squad car, and picked up the microphone. He told the dispatcher to send the crime lab guys here first before they get started on the old barn at the Cooper place.

Mrs. Haskell stepped out on the porch and put her arm through her son's tattooed right arm. David could see where Adam got his looks. She was a big woman, tall, with well proportioned features.

"Sheriff, you are wasting your time. I was home in bed by ten o'clock, isn't that right, Herb?" Mr. Haskell looked a little pale around the eyes and said, "Sure, I heard you come in. He was here last night Sheriff. What happened at the Cooper place anyway?" Mr. Haskell avoided being specific about what time Adam actually came home. Fidgeting and jiggling the coins in his pants pocket Adams stepfather was nervous as hell.

"It was something having to do with the Ballantyne murder. I think your stepson knows about it. In fact, I think you were there last night, Adam."

"Prove it, Sheriff, or else get the fuck out of here." Adams face redden as his voice rose. "I am sick and tired of you and those other assholes in your department always hanging around my neck. I put my time in, I paid my debt, now leave me be." He took a couple of steps down toward the sheriff looking like a bomb ready to burst. He stopped and looked toward David and then back to the sheriff. "If you want me you had better bring some reinforcements Sheriff, and a warrant, cause that piss ant," looking at David, "is so fucking nervous he's likely to shoot his self in the balls."

Just then Passmore's squad car drove up and parked alongside Woodford's. The Sheriff gave orders to Passmore without looking at him, "Go over and check out the tires on Adam's pickup and see if they match the tracks we saw in the barn."

Adam shouted angrily, "You keep away from my truck. You don't have probable cause or a warrant." He started down the steps toward Passmore, and Woodford pulled his forty-five and leveled it at Adam.

"You take one more step, Barnet, and you're history. Now get down on the ground, face down, now!" The sheriff was shouting instructions at the same time indicating exactly where he wanted Adam to lay down.

Barnet, looking down the barrel of Woodford's forty-five, hesitated, glanced at David, then slowly knelt down with an anguished look on his face and took the prone position he was all too familiar with. The sheriff immediately stuck his gun back in his holster and dropped down with one knee in the middle of Adam's back. In one sweeping move, Woodford reached for his handcuffs and with his other hand grabbed Adams's left wrist. Adam let out a loud cry, "Don't let them lock me up again. Ma, I can't go back, Ma, stop him!"

Without warning Mrs. Haskell flew off the porch and landed on the sheriff's back yelling and screaming, "Let my son go, you bastard!" She grabbed the sheriff's hair with one hand and dug her fingers into his eyes with the other pulling back and screaming at the same time.

David was in a state of shock, not knowing what to do. The scene was unbelievable. Barnet rolled out from underneath the sheriff, pulled the sheriff's gun out of its holster, jumped up, and pointed it at Woodford. He yelled, "I'll blow your fucking head off Woodford, you are not putting me back in the stinking hole." He stuck the muzzle of the forty-five firmly up against Woodford's ear forcing his head to one side. Mrs. Haskell rolled to the ground and froze at the sight of Adam pointing a gun directly at Sheriff Woodford.

Deputy Passmore had dropped to his knee and drew his service revolver. David had raised the shotgun to his shoulder and pointed it directly at Barnet's head. Barnet yanked the sheriff to his feet keeping the forty-five jammed in Woodford's ear. "Drop it Passmore. You know I'm not kidding. The sheriff is a dead man if you try to stop me."

Passmore, realizing his boss's life depended on him giving up his gun, dropped it on the driveway gravel and raised his hands. Barnet turned toward the deputy thereby presenting David with a side view of himself and the Sheriff. Now Adam turned his head to look at David, "Drop it, piss ant." All of a sudden, there was an explosion. The shotgun bucked violently in David's hands. He could not remember deliberately pulling the trigger. It was a knee-jerk reaction to an unbelievable scene. He had his finger on the trigger and the gun just went off. Adam's head exploded and his body jerked violently away from the gun blast.

The sheriff fell forward. David thought for a moment Woodford had been hit also, but he had only been dazed by the shotgun blast and was not hit by any of the pellets. Mrs. Haskell was screaming "Adam, Adam. You killed my son, you killed him." She fell, sobbing and shrieking, on Adam's body. The top of Adam's head was ripped open oozing blood and brains. His body was twitching spasmodically in death throes.

David dropped the shotgun and stood still, frozen, not knowing what to do next. The sheriff tried pulling Mrs. Haskell off her son, but failed. He hollered to Passmore to call for the paramedics. He looked at David and then told Mr. Haskell to control his wife. The two boys in the backseat of the squad car were clawing frantically to get out. The sheriff stumbled over and opened the car door. Both boys piled out and ran over to their father who was holding onto his wife, who was holding Adam.

Sheriff Woodford walked quickly over to David, wiping some of Adam's blood off his face, and said, "I don't know what the hell you were thinking, Jordan, but I'm damn glad you did what you did, because I was a dead man. I knew no matter what Adam had in mind. He was going to use me as a shield and then he would kill me when I was no longer any use to him."

David's knees were shaking so violently he had to sit down in the passenger's side of Woodford's squad car. He could not believe he had fired the shotgun. He had not intended to. Or did he? It happened so fast. He had a perfect shot, but only for a second. Did his Marine Corps instinct take over? He had killed in Vietnam, but that was different, that was war. He had put that part of his life out of his mind, and rarely thought about it. He was thankful no one else was hurt. The sheriff had thanked him, so maybe he did the right thing by not deliberately thinking about it first.

God, he hoped he would not be charged with some kind of crime. His mind was going around in circles. Passmore came over and shook his hand. He said in a low voice, "You got more balls than I gave you credit for, Jordan. That was an excellent shot. The bastard would have killed the sheriff, you, and me, given a chance. You saved the taxpayers a ton of money."

Mrs. Haskell and her husband were sitting on the edge of the porch and the two boys were at her feet. Adam's body was lying motionless where he fell. A pool of blood had formed around his head. Passmore placed a blanket over him. The sheriff was talking on the radio to his office, telling them what had happened. He wanted the crime scene investigators out here and he wanted them out here now!

Herb Haskell took Martha into the house, the boys were close behind. David felt stronger and got up to stretch his legs. The sheriff told him to stay near the car. David felt like he had to piss really bad and started looking for someplace to relieve himself. He told the sheriff he was going over behind the workshop buildings to take a leak. The sheriff nodded, okay.

David walked fifty feet or so, rounded the corner of the neatly painted tool shop and immediately vomited.

CHAPTER 8

Killing another human being was not something David could take easily. He needed support and he needed it quickly. Deputy Passmore allowed him to use the police radio to the dispatcher's office so he could contact his daughter. He managed to keep his voice calm, but his legs were still weak. He told Kelly what had happened and she reacted with predictable disbelief, and concern for her father. Kelly and Fred were on their way to Dumont in record time. The boys would be staying with their usual babysitter, Mrs. Gould, who lived in the same building.

Mrs. Haskell' loud wailing could be heard plainly outside the farmhouse. The paramedics had arrived, but so far had not succeeded in quieting her. The crime scene investigation unit was setting up and beginning to collect evidence. The scene was straight out of a TV cop movie. David was sitting in the sheriff's squad car not wanting to get anymore involved than he already was. Two plain-clothes detectives identified themselves as Creighton and Bidwell. They asked David to go with them to the sheriff's office in Rockford, forty miles away, so he could make a statement. A stenographer would be available to prepare it for David's signature.

David protested, insisting his daughter and her husband would be here soon and they would be looking for him. Why couldn't they take a statement at the substation in Dumont or wait until the next day? Sheriff Woodford came over and settled it by saying David had had enough excitement for one day. The detectives could record his statement in his office and have it typed and brought by the hotel in the morning for him to sign. Bidwell did not like the arrangement and made no bones about not following policy. The Sheriff told him to can it and get a move on so David could be with his family.

The two detectives ordered David into the back of their unmarked police car and took him to the substation. They placed him in a small room, adjacent to the main offices. David could hear Bidwell talking with someone on the telephone. Apparently, he was still arguing with someone about not being able to take David to the main sheriff's station in Rockford.

Creighton brought in a small cassette recorder, set it up, and tested it to make sure it was working properly. David was thinking he should have a lawyer present before he gave his statement. After all he did kill someone and this is Illinois. According to the newspapers, there had been many problems with police testimony over the last six months resulting in innocent people being sent to prison. Several prisoners had been released from death row because police had lied on the witness stand and faked incriminating evidence. But those cases involved Chicago police and supposed gang members. This was a little town with local law enforcement. Not to worry, he decided.

David felt he had acted in self-defense and all he had to do was tell the truth. Besides, he had two credible witnesses, Woodford, and Passmore. Actually, he had the Haskell family also, but he was sure they would be prejudice in favor of Adam, especially the mother.

Bidwell entered the room without speaking and started the tape recorder. David answered the preliminary questions and then gave a long, thoughtful, verbal description about the events leading up to and including the shooting of Barnet. He said, as plainly as he could, he did not actually remember pulling the trigger of the shotgun or even thinking about it. "Everything happened so fast, I was faced with a life or death decision and my reflexes took over. I was positive my life and the two officer's lives were at risk." The two detectives left the room for a few minutes and when they returned asked David to repeat his story.

After the second interview, both detectives went outside to smoke while David visited the men's room. When they came back, they repeated the process a third time, taking turns asking the same questions as before. Only this time they used accusatorial phrasings to obtain an emotional response.

"When did you decide to kill Barnet?" "Did the Sheriff ask you to shoot that kid after or before he was down?" "Did the sheriff put handcuffs on Barnet before or after you shot him." Isn't true that Barnett had already dropped the gun when you shot him?" It was after eight o'clock in the evening, finally David stood up and said, "That's it, I have told you guy's the same fucking story three times and I'm tired. I know you have a job to do but this is ridiculous. I'm out of here."

He began to walk towards the door and Bidwell told him to stop. David turned and said in a very loud, agitated voice, "Unless you are going to charge me with something you don't have any reason to keep me here. I've told you the same story three times, that's enough!" Sheriff Woodford, who had been in the adjoining room at his desk, came to his rescue again and told Bidwell to back off and let David go. His daughter and her husband were outside waiting for him. The two detectives looked at each other and backed down.

David walked out of the sheriff's office and was immediately hit by camera floodlights. Half a dozen reporters with microphones began asking questions all at once. David's first reaction was to retreat back into the office. Sheriff Woodford standing behind David held up is hands and in a very loud and commanding voice, "All right boys, back off. If you' all will calm down, I will give you a briefing on what we know to date. Mr. Jordan has had a very trying day and he wants to be with his family. If he wants to make a statement later, he will let you know. Now come around here and I'll give you the facts."

Again, Sheriff Woodford saved David from an unpleasant situation. The sheriff herded the reporters and cameramen around to the side of the building under a large sign proclaiming: "Winnebago County Sheriff Sub Station, Dumont, Illinois, Leslie Woodford, Sheriff." The sheriff stood in the bed of a parked pickup. The reporters gathered around him like children. David did not stay to hear what was said.

Kelly ran up to him and gave him a big bear hug and a kiss. "Dad, my God, what have you been doing? I could not believe you actually shot some one. The sheriff told us how you saved his life. I'm so proud of you and glad you are okay. My brain is just not accepting the things the deputies were saying." She was talking a mile a minute while Fred was trying to get all three of them into the car.

David finally was able to get a word in edgewise and said, "Kelly, just slow down. I'll tell you what happened, but first I need some dinner and most of all I need a drink. Fred, just head south and let's go to Irv's Chicken Shack and have some dinner." Fred looked at David with a questioning look, but started driving around the parked TV vans. Soon he was headed out of town toward Irv's.

David collapsed in the back seat of Fred's Lincoln. He felt as though he had just emerged from a nightmare. The back seat of the Lincoln felt like a sanctuary, away from the police and TV crews. For a few minutes, Kelly was silent, waiting for her father to tell them about this wild story of him shooting and killing a suspected murderer. He wished he could close his eyes and drift away to some faraway place. It seemed like only a few minutes had gone by when they pulled into the nearly empty parking lot at Irv's.

"Let's get a table and order some drinks and I'll tell you both a story you won't believe," as they walked into Irv's. The hostess greeted them and took them to an isolated table, as requested by Fred. A waiter came over and took their drink orders. David looked at his daughter and Fred for a minute and then launched into a complete accounting of the day's events. During the storytelling, they had re-ordered their original drinks, and their dinner. Both Kelly and Fred asked dozens of questions until finally the story had been told.

After dinner David felt totally exhausted and drained. Fred picked up the tab and they headed back to the Holiday Inn. All David could think about at this point was taking a long hot shower and climbing into a soft bed. He needed sleep. They registered at the front desk and said their goodnights. David's room was on the second floor, Kelly's and Fred's was on the first.

The detectives had said they would be by about eight-thirty in the morning so David could sign a copy of his statement. He was still irritated by Detective Birdwell's cross-examination of him. It seemed like he was trying to find some way to blame David for the killing of Barnet.

Alone in his room, David shed his clothes and headed for the shower. The hot water felt like a cleansing solution. He had no idea how long he stood under the showerhead. Realizing his skin was turning red he figured he had been in there long enough. He toweled off, walked into the bedroom, and turned on the TV. A local station was repeating the late evening news broadcast. The newscaster was reading a story about President Clinton and the First Lady. David was not interested. He picked up the TV guide and looked for a channel he could watch and go to sleep with. Just then, the newscaster started talking about a killing that had taken place in Dumont.

Suddenly David saw his face on the TV screen. He was shown walking from Jim's mobile home, not answering any questions. The newscaster was describing Jim Ballantyne's murder and saying, "The man seen walking here was also seen this evening exiting from the sheriff's substation in Dumont. Sheriff Woodford identified the man as David Jordan. According to the sheriff, Jordan had been one of the last persons to see Jim Ballantyne alive Saturday night.

"This morning, again according to the sheriff, Jordan had saved the sheriff's life and the life of one of his deputies by killing a known drug dealer in a shootout on a farm near Dumont." The Sheriff's face loomed large on the TV screen as he described the showdown at the Haskell farm. "Adam Barnet was a suspect in the Ballantyne murder," he said. The sheriff also told how Mrs. Ballantyne was now able to describe two individuals who were present when her husband was killed Saturday night. One of the individuals was Adam Barnet. She could not identify the other man, except to say he was an older person.

David listened intently and wondered what exactly Mrs. Ballantyne had told the sheriff. He was not surprised Adam was one of the men present when Jim took his last breath. That would account for his serious objection to having anyone look at the tires on his pickup. It was obvious that the tire tread imprint left at the junkyard and at the barn on the Cooper place would match Adam's pickup. Who was the second person involved in the Ballantyne murder? Why did Jim's wife refuse to identify him? The sheriff had said there were three sets of footprints at the Cooper place. One set would be the truck driver's, one set Adams and one set must have been the unnamed third person.

David switched off the TV and lay down on the bed, staring straight up at the ceiling. The events of the day passed through his head like fast-paced video clips. Sleep finally came and David drifted off to a restless night.

When the telephone rang David sat up with a start. At first he could not remember where he was, then it all came back and he reached for the telephone while looking at the radio clock on the nightstand, it was four twenty in the morning. "Who the hell is calling me at this hour?" he asked out loud. "Hello, who is this?" David demanded, sounding like a Marine Corps drill sergeant. A long silence followed. David could hear music playing in the background. "Who is this?" he demanded again. He was really upset at the thought of some kid or some idiot playing games on the telephone late at night. How did they get his room number?

Finally after about thirty seconds a female voice came on and said in a tiny voice, "Is this David Jordan?"

David was getting really upset now. Was this some little kid or what? The voice was vaguely familiar. "Yes, now who the hell is this?

Another long silence, "It's someone...you don't know me." David stood motionless in the dark motel room.

"What is it you want from me?" he said in a softer tone.

"Please don't tell anyone I called. I know you shot Adam because you had too. But there is someone who wants you dead. I'm just giving you a warning. You should leave here as quickly as you can. Don't trust the sheriff's office." The telephone went dead.

CHAPTER 9

The sun had been up for two hours, and David had written ten pages in his new journal he now called "My Hellish Experience in Dumont." He included his meeting with Kathryn and their dinner conversation, omitted was any description of his emotional attachment, although he did include Kathryn's letter. He had no idea of who might read this manuscript, but he intended it to be as factual and as accurate as possible. He decided he needed to add this to the notes he made about Bee's recollection. This whole situation was getting more and more bizarre.

The warning message he had received last night kept surfacing in his head, "Don't trust the sheriff's office." That really put a wrench in the works. If he couldn't trust the sheriff, whom could he trust? There was no one else to turn to. He debated telling Kelly and he couldn't bring himself to tell the sheriff, not yet anyway.

David's engineering training came into play as he wrote. The descriptions of events leading up to and including the shooting of Adam Barnet were short and crisp: they contained just enough words to state the facts. David printed in a clear, unmistakable, technical writing style. The words were devoid of emotion. Pages and pages were added to the growing stack of notes.

It was close to eight in the morning when he called Kelly's room. "Hi Kiddo. It's time to get up and get some breakfast. You two sleep okay last night?"

"I've been up for hours," replied Kelly. "I went for a run already, thank you. This is a nice little town. Fred is just now getting up, the lazy bum. As soon as we both shower we'll meet you in the lobby at say, eight-forty five, okay?" She hung up without waiting for a reply.

David knew that Kelly liked to run at least four or five miles a day, regardless of where she was. At thirty-two she was in excellent physical condition. Not only was she physically attractive, but she had a high level of intelligence combined with a healthy dose of common sense. Chance, David's son had the same characteristics.

David was drawn back in time to the mid-eighties. Chance was also physically attractive and had the brains to become anything he wanted. Unfortunately, he had been caught up in the drug scene in his last year of high school and started running with a group of kids who were interested in things other than their studies. Chance got mixed up with a girl from a prominent family in Newport Beach who had a cocaine habit. She and Chance made the stupid mistake of buying cocaine from an undercover police officer.

Chance faced the possibility of jail time just as he was about to graduate from high school. David spoke with the prosecuting attorney, handling the case, and was able to find a compromise that satisfied the law and got Chance away from the cokeheads. David was sure Chance could not refuse the offer.

The prosecuting attorney agreed that if Chance would join the Marines and the Marines accepted him, they would drop charges. Convincing Chance and Ellen was a lot more difficult than David had imagined.

Ellen was against their son joining the Marines. She remembered, clearly, how desperately she needed David when he was in Asia fighting a war the country did not support. She remembered the time that David had been seriously wounded and how frightened she was. She did not want that to happen to her son.

Faced with jail time, Chance had no choice and he knew it, but the thought of joining the Marines was a joke. No one he knew was joining the service, let alone the Marines. He was not going to be one of the "Few Good Men." All of his friends would laugh at him.

During one of there "heated discussions", David looked his son square in the eye, took him by the shoulders, and said, "Do you think they will still be your friends when you get out of jail with an enlarged ass hole and prison tattoos?" Chance's face went white. Ellen shut up. The argument was won.

Chance was born to be a Marine. Much to his father's satisfaction and his mother's surprise, Chance's letters home were always positive with many colorful stories about his buddies, or the places he had been. He rose rapidly in rank and within three years had been promoted to sergeant, attached to a ground assault force. He had been stationed in the Far East for fourteen months and then transferred to the Marine barracks at Camp Pendleton in California.

When Iraq invaded Kuwait in Aug. 1990, Chance re-enlisted for another four years. The Marine Corps promised to send him to leadership school at the Marine Corps Barracks in Quantico, Virginia.

Iraq and Desert Storm interfered with the young sergeant's promised opportunity for further advancement. Chance was with the First Marine Division when the Marines breached the Iraqi lines and surrounded Kuwait City in February 1991. He was killed by friendly fire the night of February 27. That's what the young Marine Corps lieutenant said when he came to the Jordan's front door one day in March, of 1991.

David could not, and would not, accept the term "friendly fire." He insisted there was no such thing as friendly fire. "It should be called deadly fire from friendly forces." The Marine Corps did its best to provide as much information as possible about how the accident occurred, but David and Ellen were not interested in the facts. Their son was gone.

Ellen never said she blamed David for Chance's death, but it was obvious in her relationship with him. The glue that had held them together after the Vietnam War was gone. Their sex life had not been great and now it was only a memory. They divorced the following year.

During the divorce process, David learned Ellen had been having an affair with a doctor at the hospital where she worked. This bit of news was a real shocker for David. He had no clue Ellen was cheating on him, the affair had been going strong for over a year and half. Of course there were clues, but David had not been interested enough to notice.

David had to mentally push Chance's memory out of his mind and concentrate on business. He was due back on the job in Long Beach next Monday. He would have a terrific story to tell his friends at Hydraulic International Corp. (HIC). He wondered if any of the Los Angeles or Long Beach papers had picked up the murder and killing in Dumont. The local news had aired the sheriff's interview last night and this morning. David had not seen a newspaper since last Saturday.

He was dressed and walked down the stairs to the lobby when the desk clerk called out his name: "Mr. Jordan, I have a message for you." The clerk handed him a note on Holiday Inn stationery. "This message came in last night and the nightshift clerk took it." The note had contained instructions on how to retrieve a message from an answering machine. The number to call was preceded by the digits "011 171". David knew 011 was an overseas exchange, but did not recognize the 171-country code. He asked the clerk to look it up in the telephone directory and asked, "What time did the call come in?"

"The call came in at two-fifteen AM," as he looked through the phone book. "Ah, here it is, London Central, England," he said, smiling, proud of the fact he had found the information in just a few seconds.

Two AM local time was about nine AM London time, David calculated. Kelly wanted to know, "Who's calling you from London?" Fred was hovering nearby and said out loud, "That would be nine-fifteen AM London time."

David was trying to decide whether or not to wait until he could be alone and retrieve the message or do it now with everyone looking over his shoulder. He was sure it was from Kathryn. His daughter made up his mind for him. "Dad, aren't you going to find out what this is all about? Go over there and use the lobby telephone. We want to know who's calling you from London. Here, you can use my calling card." She dug quickly into her purse and handed it to him.

David knew when he was beat, so he walked over to the corner of the lobby, picked up the phone and dialed a zillion numbers before he actually got to the point where he entered the three digit code to retrieve the recorded message.

It was Kathryn's voice. David's heart skipped a few beats and his stomach knotted up. She sounded soft and warm. The connection was clear, Kathryn sounded like she was in the next room. He could hear her breathe.

"David, I didn't know how else to reach you, so I took a chance you would still be at the Holiday Inn. Please forgive me for leaving you the note. It was necessary. I hope you understand.

"I was so sorry to hear about the murder of the fellow who took your car in for storage. Sheriff Woodford contacted me last night. We spoke on the telephone for over an hour. Mrs. Canady had given him our London telephone exchange. He sounded like he thought you might have something to do with the murder at the junk yard. I hope I was able to convince him you and I were together most all of Saturday evening. I gave him all the details I could. Well…maybe not all of the details. Something's must be kept private." There was a long pause and then, "We had a wonderful time together. Please, do not be angry with me. Good-bye."

David wondered what Kathryn would think if she knew what had happened since she had talked to the sheriff. He would love to tell her about all the events of the past few days. She was so easy to talk to.

David sat motionless for a few seconds and before he could get up, Kelly was next to him saying, "Well, who was it? Was it the lady you told us about? The one you went to dinner with? She lived in Ireland, I thought."

"Yes. Now don't go flying to conclusions. She was just being polite." He was smiling at Kelly's curiosity. She had always been curious, even as a child. Fathers and daughters have a special bond, he loved Kelly more than he could possibly express. But this was a subject he was hesitant to discuss. "Kathryn called to tell me Sheriff Woodford had contacted her, and she just wanted to tell me and wish me well. That's all. Now let's go and get some breakfast. I'm starved."

CHAPTER 10

All three walked quickly through the motel lobby door and were met by detectives Creighton and Bidwell. "Hold on, Mr. Jordan, we need to talk with you." Sergeant Bidwell was doing the talking and not too politely.

"We were just on our way to get some breakfast, can't this wait for awhile? I can meet you over at the sheriff's office at ten o'clock," David said, being perfectly reasonable.

"We don't have time to fuck around, Jordan. We should have hauled your ass down to Rockford last night." Bidwell was nose to nose with David. All he could think of was how bad Birdwell's breath smelled. "If it hadn't been for Woodford butting in, we would have. Now let's go back inside so you can sign this statement."

The hair on the back of David's neck went up, "Why are you so pissed at me? You act like I'm the bad guy. You have been treating me like I'm a suspect. What the hell is going on anyway?" David was exasperated. He didn't like these two assholes, especially Bidwell. He had cooperated every step of the way and they were acting as though he was a low class petty criminal. The phone call he got in the middle of the night was looming larger and larger in his head.

Creighton stepped in and said, "Look here, Jordan, we need to get this part of the investigation finished. We have a million things to do today and this is first on our list. We want you to sign the statement you made last night. We had a stenographer stay late just so we could have this typed. Now it's ready for your John Hancock." He handed David several sheets of paper stapled together.

David looked at it and said he would not sign it until he had a chance to read it. Bidwell spoke up and said, "She just typed what you said in answer to our questions. No big deal, sign it and we're out of here."

"I wouldn't sign anything without reading it first." He was remembering what the female voice said on the phone last night. "Don't trust the sheriff's department."

"I said, I'll meet you at the sheriff's office at ten, and that's it. I'm going to read this first. If you want to follow us over to the coffee shop to make sure I won't get away, that's up to you." David turned to Kelly, took her arm, walked out into the parking lot, and helped her into Fred's Lincoln. The two detectives stood on the curb, scowling.

"Who put a bug up his ass?" Fred asked as he started up the car and drove the few blocks to Sherry's Coffee shop.

Kelly was outraged. She worked for several criminal defense lawyers and she knew what proper police conduct was and this wasn't it. "These two jerks are way out of line. I'm going to call my boss, tell him what is going on, and see what he says. Dad, it may be time for you to get some legal help here. Don't sign anything. I don't trust them."

That is exactly the way David felt. He did not trust them either. They sat in a back booth at the coffee shop and ordered breakfast. Kelly got up to go to the restroom, "I'm calling my office from the pay phone in the back." David began to read the typewritten papers Bidwell had given him. There were nine pages altogether. By the time David had finished the fourth page he slapped them down hard and said, "This is bull shit. They are trying to make it look like I fired at Barnet while he was on the ground and the Sheriff was sitting on him. They're setting me up for a murder charge or at least manslaughter. They have taken things I said out of context and not recorded some other facts. This is garbage." Several patrons in the restaurant turned and looked at David.

He could not believe his eyes. Why would they try to twist things around? Where was Woodford? Did he know about this? He was going to shove this so-called statement up somebody's ass.

Kelly came back to the table in time to hear David's angry words. "Carver, my boss, said, 'Do not sign anything. Don't say anything to the police or sheriff or anybody until he gets here'. He said you could be in a lot of trouble even though you did the right thing. He knows for a fact, the Illinois Attorney General's office was conducting an internal investigation in this county. He heard about it from an old school buddy two weeks ago when he was at the State Capitol."

"What kind of investigation?" Fred asked.

"I don't know, he didn't say, but he was adamant, 'Tell your Dad not to talk to anyone,'" She looked at David with eyes that said "please."

"Okay. That's an easy order to follow. I'm pissed, but I'm still hungry, let's eat. When will your boss get here?"

"Assuming normal traffic, about two or two and half hours." Fred spoke up. "I know Jeff Carver, he is first-rate, and he will give you good advice. He's probably one of the two or three top trial lawyers in the state." Kelly was nodding her head in approval.

For the first time David looked around the restaurant and noticed they were alone in a corner booth. The restaurant was half full, but no one had been seated near them. The other customers were talking in subdued voices. When the waitress came over to refill their coffees David asked why it was so quiet in here. She looked straight at him and said, "Some of us were friends of the Haskell's. Martha and Herb were customers here," she turned and walked up front and poured more coffee.

Now the cold shoulder treatment in the restaurant made a little sense. Adam may have been a nice guy to people he liked or supplied drugs to. Others were friends with his mother and stepfather.

They decided to stay in the restaurant and wait for Kelly's boss to show up. Kelly offered to edit the transcript. She was making a good living as a paralegal, writing legal documents and doing research so she felt she was qualified. David and Kelly went over each word, deleting some and making changes where necessary. When they finished, Fred offered to go outside and find a copy machine to make several copies, just in case it became important.

When they were alone Kelly took her Dad's arm and said, "I'm so proud of you Dad. I know what you did was terrible, but you did what you had to do, it was the right thing. You were very brave. Even the Sheriff's deputies we talked to last night said so. You always were my hero." She put her head on her dad's shoulder. David felt a surge of love and gratitude for his daughter. Girls were special, there was no doubt about it, and David would not trade his daughter's love for anything.

David decided it would be a good idea to call Bee Canady and ask her if she wanted to come down to Sherry's Coffee Shop and meet his daughter. When he wrote down Kathryn's telephone numbers in Bee's kitchen Sunday afternoon, he also took down the number of the telephone hanging on the wall.

Bee answered on the second ring. "Hello, O'Ryan residence."

"Bee, this is David Jordan, remember me?"

"Yes sir. My head still is throbbing. I hadn't drank that much in years." She was laughing. "What is it you want now? I heard about you and the sheriff getting into a gunfight with

Adam Barnet. He was bad news. Everybody knew he was
mixed up with Jim Ballantyne. I was sorry for you. It must have
been a terrible experience."

"Bee, I'm down here at Sherry's with my daughter. I
thought you might want to take a break and meet her." David
had felt a mutual friendship with Bee, she was a down to earth
type person and easy to like. He thought this might be an
opportunity to cement their friendship. He wanted to talk to her,
at a later time, about the old car and the young owner, Cindy
O'Ryan.

"Why, I would love to, Mr. Jordan, that's very kind of
you to think of me. I'll be right down as soon as I put sompen
decent on," she hung up.

David began telling Kelly more details about the car and
its owner, Cindy O'Ryan. He repeated the story Bee had told
him about how Cindy had disappeared shortly after the terrible
fight with her father. He mentioned that Mrs. O'Ryan had
received only four letters from Cindy the whole time she was
gone.

Fred came back with four extra copies of David's edited
statement. They all agreed to wait for advice from Carver before
making any decisions. The two detectives were standing next to
an unmarked squad car in the restaurant parking lot. They were
talking to someone in a sheriff's patrol car parked next to them.
Fred could not make out who it was.

Bee barged into the restaurant like she owned the place.
She greeted the cook behind the service window by name,
"Hello, Norman, how's your little boy? Is he still sick with the
chicken pox? I haven't had a chance to talk to Lana lately. You
tell her I'll call her soon, you hear?" The cook waved and
continued doing what cooks do.

David stood up and introduced Kelly and Fred to Bee. They pushed a couple of tables together. He was glad they had this whole end of the restaurant to themselves. Bee's voice carried quite a distance. Kelly, trying to be diplomatic, offered, "My father said you had done a marvelous job of organizing the auction and taking care of all the packing. It must have been a horrendous job considering how many years the O'Ryan family had lived in the house. How old was the lady before she died?"

"Well, your father is right. I've been working twelve hours a day, every day since Miss Margaret died over two weeks ago now. She was 99 years old, if you could imagine. She had a better mind than many youngsters do. She was a real lady.

"I know I'm working myself out of a job, but I know Miss Margaret would want me to take care of things the way she instructed me to. Miss Kathryn and her parents were a lot of help but they is gone now, so it's just me. The moving boys will be here tomorrow to take all of Miss Margaret's personal things to the storage building. Somebody from Chicago is coming next week to take all the furniture that didn't sell at the auction and then I be gone." Bee had a funny smile on her face as she spoke the last few words. She looked like she had resigned herself to an uncertain future.

David asked, "What about the house and all the stuff left in the garage? I remember a lot of boxes out there." In his mind's eye he saw bankers boxes lined up against one wall. The kind of box used to store office files.

"Those old files of the Judge's went somewhere in New York. Kathryn's father seen to that before he left. He called somebody from my kitchen phone Saturday night and told him or her to get a truck and come get all those files out of the garage and take them to some place in New York. I didn't get the name. Sure enuf, Monday morning a big ol' rental truck came down the alley. The driver gave me a piece of paper to sign and he loaded them boxes and was gone before I got back in the house.

"Say, Kelly, that's your name isn't it honey? Did you know your dad is a bad influence on people? Did he tell you what he did to me?" Bee had a smile on her broad face and proceeded to describe how David "tricked" her into breaking open the bottle of Wild Turkey. She claimed she never touched hard liquor except on New Year's Eve. David knew better, but he let her have her little joke on him.

It was apparent Bee was pleased to meet David's daughter and husband. He honestly liked the old housekeeper and wondered what she would do after the O'Ryan house was closed up and sold. He was assuming it was sold, but no one had actually said that. So he asked Bee, "Who bought the old house? Do you know the new owners?"

"No, I don't know who bought it. All I know is what Rebecca and John Millard told me. You know, Kathryn's parents, they are the executors. They say they had an offer for the house a week after Miss Margaret died. It was a good offer so they took it. Some realtor comes by and they all signed some papers, but I don't know the name of the person who bought the house. They talked like it was someone from a long ways away, because they kept saying how it was tomorrow wherever that person was."

"Where will you go after the house is closed?" Fred asked the next obvious question. "I don't have any close kinfolk around here and I'm so damn old now it would be hard to get another job. So, I'm going down to South Carolina and stay with my cousin till I figure out something. I got some money in the bank and the Milliards were real good to me so I don't reckon I'll have to miss too many meals," she laughed.

"Bee, I would like to have your address. Someday I may be in your part of the country and I would like to look you up. Maybe we could a have glass or two of Wild Turkey?"

Her eyes opened wide, "Don't you dare come down there and talk to me about having a drink. My cousin, Jasper Nugget, is a born-again Southern Baptist preacher. He would run us both out of town." Bee was laughing so hard, David thought she was going to pee her pants. "Here, I'll give you his phone number. You be sure and call if you get down my way. I have to get back to my packing. It was real nice to meet you all. Mr. Jordan, I hope you doesn't have any more excitement here in Dumont. Good-bye now." Shaking hands with Kelly and Fred she stood and gave David a bear hug, and walked out of Sherry's.

CHAPTER 11

Jefferson Carver was a no-nonsense type person. He was aggressive and obnoxious to a fault. He was also loyal to those who supported him. He had made a name for himself by defending some of the most unworthy characters anyone could imagine. Prosecuting attorneys hated him because he used every legal, and sometimes not so legal, tactics against them and was smug about it. He won more cases than he lost and the ones he lost were usually reduced to some relatively minor offense.

Carver was a partner in the law firm of Headley and Carver. The two partners had been together for over twenty years and now supervised a staff of twenty junior lawyers and paralegals with a small army of clerks and research assistants. Kelly was one of the six paralegals in the firm and one of the few who was not afraid of Carver. She would not put up with his intimidating, overbearing and womanizing mannerisms. Carver recognized the quality of her work and the two had reached an undeclared truce.

Kelly's confrontations with Carver were well known around the office. More than once she had stormed into his office and demanded he give her credit for finding a significant legal challenge that would allow Carver to nullify a prosecution's key bit of evidence against his client. His ego was huge and acknowledging a mere woman to share his accomplishment was an earthshaking experience for him.

Without openly acknowledging it, Carver trusted Kelly's work without question. He knew he had a good thing going with Kelly she was the best paralegal in the office. Now Carver realized he had an opportunity to repay Kelly for her hard work by helping her father. He knew police all over the country and especially in Chicago, were under the gun to reduce crime and record convictions. In their zeal to capture and prosecute the bad guys, the police made mistakes, or worse, manufactured evidence. In this situation, Carver sensed something rotten. Apparently Kelly's father was smack in the middle of an ongoing State Attorney General's investigation involving police corruption.

Jordan had killed a man in self-defense and the police were treating him like he was a murderer. Something was not right. Carver could smell blood, he was not going to let Kelly or her father down. He pulled up in front of Sherry's Coffee shop, at exactly eleven-thirty. His red Porsche stood out of place among the pickups and SUVs.

Kelly saw the Porsche and was out the door of the restaurant greeting her boss with, "I'm so glad you are here. I really appreciate your help, Jeff. I'm very much afraid for my father. These local detectives are acting like a bunch of barracudas."

"Okay, don't get too excited. I have talked to some people on the way out here and I have a good idea of what's happening. Let's go in and talk to your dad and then we'll see what we have to do. From what you told me on the phone and what I found out from the local DA's office in Rockford, your dad has nothing to worry about." Carver put his arm around Kelly and together they walked into the coffee shop. The two detectives had left the parking lot and now were back and looking over the Porsche.

Kelly introduced her father to Carver. David's first impression was that this is one slick S.O.B. I wouldn't try to put anything over on this guy on a bet. Expensive Italian suit, hand painted silk tie, well-shined loafers with tassels, Rolex wristwatch, and a diamond ring on his right pinky finger. He was a walking ad for GQ Magazine. If he were half as good at being a lawyer as he is at looking like one, David would be elated. The two shook hands and sat down. They still had the back half of the coffee shop to themselves. The waitress had not bussed the tables or brought more coffee. Fred went behind the counter and took the coffeepot back to their table.

Carver took a quick look at the statement the detectives had wanted David to sign. "You didn't sign this, did you?"

"Hell no. It's not correct. They left half of what I said out altogether."

"Good, now here is what I see we should do. I talked with the County District Attorney in Rockford this morning. As far as he knows there is no intention to bring charges against you," Carver said as he looked at David. "However, he is well aware of the State's investigation and wouldn't comment on any details.

I think we should talk to Sheriff what's his name, what is it, Kelly?" Carver expected an immediate response.

"Sheriff Woodford" Kelly and David responded in unison.

"Where are you guys staying? Is there a motel or hotel around here somewhere?" Carver asked.

"We are all staying at the Holiday Inn, you passed it on the way in. Unless you were flying," Fred said, referring to the red Porsche sitting in the parking lot.

"I want the three of you to go back to the motel and stay put. I'm gong to have a talk with the sheriff and get these two dickheads off your back. Kelly, I have your cell phone number, I'll call you and let you know what the next step is." Carver got up and asked Fred to show him where the sheriff's office was.

The three of them drove back to the motel in silence. Carver appeared to know exactly what to do. David felt better knowing he had someone looking after his interests. He asked

Fred to stop at the supermarket. He needed some more clean clothes.

Back at the motel, they sat around the patio and watched a couple from Canada play with their two preschoolers in the swimming pool. David had picked up a six-pack of beer and snacks the same time he selected a "new" wardrobe. He decided to tell Kelly and Fred about the phone call he received late last night.

"Dad," Kelly exclaimed. "Why didn't you tell us? This whole thing is getting ridiculous. You should have told Carver. He needs to know everything, he will be pissed when he finds out. I think I should call him now and let him know what you just said. It may make a difference in the way he talks to the sheriff."

Kelly walked into the lobby to use the telephone. Carver was waiting in the sheriff's office for Woodford to get back. He had been told Woodford was out on a call and was on his way back to town. He had been waiting for an hour and was not happy. He refused to talk to anyone else in the office, including the two detectives who kept checking on him from time to time.

Carver took Kelly's call on his cell phone and made a note on a legal pad he had in his briefcase. "You tell your dad, if he expects me to help him, I need to know everything." Carver was obviously pissed at not having been told about all of the events up to this point. Kelly said she would make sure her dad told him everything from now on.

Kelly could tell her dad and Fred were not going to be much company and she had no idea how long Carver would be in the Sheriffs office waiting, so she decided to take this opportunity to visit Bee and ask if she could tour the O'Ryan house. She asked Fred for the keys to the car. Following her father's directions, she found the house without difficulty, and parked behind the Cadillac under the carport.

Bee answered the door with, "Miss Kelly, what a surprise! Please come in. I is just finishing packing all of Miss Margaret's personal things."

"I just wanted to take a look around the house, if you don't mind. My father told me about how well kept this old house was. I just love old Victorian style houses, they have real character. We live in an apartment building and I miss not having more space and a yard for the kids to play in.

"You just go right ahead and look around. The house is mostly empty now, it looks very drab compared to when Miss Margaret was alive. She had some very nice pieces of furniture, everything she bought for this house was first class."

Kelly was looking at the beautiful walnut staircase running her fingers across the high-gloss finish.

Bee told Kelly to take her time and look around, she had to get everything itemized for the movers who were coming to pickup the remaining furnishings and Miss Margaret's things.

Kelly explored the whole house and marveled at how well maintained the floors and woodwork were kept. The bathrooms had been modernized, but still managed to keep the period look. The Judge's library reminded Kelly of a haunted house with its heavy drapery and floor-to-ceiling empty bookcases lining the walls.

"Bee, I'm leaving, but if it's okay I would like to see the garden."

"Go right ahead, the gardener is out there somewhere. Tell your father hello for me."

Kelly walked around the house and admired the neatly trimmed lawn and flowerbeds. The side of the house opposite the carport consisted of a large rose garden. Nearly all the rose bushes were in bloom, providing a heady atmosphere of color that melded with the hot and humid Midwest summer afternoon. A man was bent down in the middle of the rose garden, repairing a sprinkler head.

Kelly skirted the garden noiselessly and found the side door to the garage partially opened. She walked into the gloom and stopped after a few feet to allow her eyes to adjust to the darkness. So this is where the Chevy was found, she thought to herself. Pigeons were roosting in the rafters and making cooing sounds. She found a cord hanging from an overhead light fixture. The low-wattage, incandescent bulb did not provide much illumination, but then there was nothing much to see. The workbench had been swept clean and the boxes her father had mentioned were gone.

Switching off the light, she took a step toward the door and was startled by the sight of the gardener baring her path. "Excuse me. I didn't see you standing there. I was just looking around," she said, hoping this was not going to be some kind of confrontation.

"There seems to be lot of interest in this old garage lately," the gardener said, in a low husky voice. Dressed in a sweat-stained tee shirt, dirty work-trousers with grass-stained work boots, the gardener displayed his best machismo imitation.

"What do you mean a lot of interest? My interest is just curiosity. My father bought the old Chevy that used to be parked in here. Did you know there was a car in here?" Kelly asked.

"No. I was never in here. Mrs. O'Ryan or Bee never went in, as far as I know. But you are the second person today to be nosing around," the gardener said.

"Who was the other person?" Kelly's interest was piqued, she smiled and put her hand gently on the gardener's arm. Kelly was not above using her sex appeal to get what she wanted from men. And this guy could not keep his eyes off Kelly's breast. "Did he talk to Bee or did he take anything?"

The gardener smiled and said, "No, I didn't see him take anything. I think I've seen him around town once or twice. I drink beer with some of the guys down at Murphy's. I've seen him there. I think his name is Bill something. When he saw me he got back in his car in the alley and took off. I don't know what he was looking for. I told Bee but I don't know if she called the sheriff or not."

"Well, I'm going now. I told Bee I just wanted to see the old place. Keep up the good work. I'm sure the new owners will want you to keep the place looking like it does now," She made her way past the gardener who was still standing in the doorway. His eyes followed her, but he did not move.

Once outside the garage, Kelly headed straight for her car. She felt relieved to be out of range of this character. He looked like he would come on to her if she had given him half a chance. "Bill" was all the information she had to go on, she should have asked the gardener for a description. "Forget it," she said to herself, she was not going back to face him and give him any encouragement.

On the way back to the motel, Kelly saw Carver's Porsche back in the Holiday Inn parking lot. The Sheriff and her dad were talking through the open side window to Carver. She parked in the next parking stall and discovered Carver was headed back to Chicago. The sheriff shook hands all around, got in his car and drove off.

"The sheriff is going to rip some body a new asshole this evening." Carver said, smiling and apparently pleased with his interview with the sheriff. "When I finally got to talk to him, I asked what he was going to do about the phony confession his two detectives had conjured up. I'm certain he was not aware Creighton and Bidwell had tried to implicate your dad in some kind of scheme. After he read the copy you gave me and saw the corrections you made, he told the dispatcher to get those two in his office at once. They were outside, waiting, when I left. I wanted your dad to go over everything with the sheriff and me before I left to eliminate any confusion later. I didn't mention anything about the attorney general's investigation, I don't know if the Sheriff is aware of it or not. No matter, the district attorney and I are on the same page so your father can rest easy." Carver said Good-bye and told Kelly he would be looking for her first thing in the morning. He needed her to review some depositions for another case he was working on. "That man never quits," Kelly said to her father.

Kelly asked Fred if he minded driving back to Chicago alone so she could have a little quality time with her father. "Of course not. I need to get back early so I can get ready for tomorrow, I have to go to Milwaukee to see a couple of clients and I need to get prepared." Kelly gave Fred a kiss and he exited the parking lot following Carver's Porsche out of town. David gave his daughter a big hug. He was looking forward to having Kelly all to himself for a few hours.

A thunderstorm had been brewing all afternoon and finally it began to rain. Loud thunderclaps were heard and lightning was flashing in the north. David looked up and then at Kelly, "Let's go and get an early dinner and let the storm pass over before we head back to Chicago. It's almost five o'clock."

"Sure, just you and me Dad. Let's go to Sherry's, I'm not hungry for a big meal. Maybe just a salad and some fruit."

A light dinner was fine with David. They drove over to Sherry's in a downpour. Inside they joined a half dozen other diners sitting in the first row of booths. They asked the waitress if they could have the booth way in the back. She shrugged and took them to a booth next to the restrooms and back door.

The two discussed family matters over dinner, including what Ellen and her husband were doing. David's former wife had married the doctor she was having an affair with.

According to Kelly, Ellen was not happy and neither was the doctor. He had divorced his wife in order to marry Ellen and now the members of two families, including the principals, were unhappy with the results. David felt a little smug at the news of his former wife's woes, but hey, she deserves it, he thought. She had cost him plenty, emotionally and financially.

They talked about Chance and what he might be doing if he had survived the Gulf War. Kelly had been close to her brother until he got mixed up with drugs. They use to spend hours talking late at night about all kinds of things. They even discussed each other's love interests, very unusual for brother and sister at that age. That all changed during Chance's senior year in high school.

The storm was raging outside the restaurant. The rain was coming down in a torrent. The light inside Sherry's flickered several times. Lightning hit hard close to town and the thunder was deafening. David could see the waitress and the cook listening to a radio in the kitchen. He asked her if she knew what the duration of the storm would be. She said, "The weatherman was forecasting continued severe thunderstorm warnings for northern Illinois and the Chicago area." Kelly and her dad looked at each other.

"I don't think it would be a good idea to drive back tonight. Why don't we stay over and head back early in the morning? We could be back in time for you to fix the twins their breakfast," David said, as he looked out the back door of the restaurant.

"I guess you're right, Dad. I don't feel comfortable driving in weather like this. Besides, a hot shower and an HBO movie sound okay to me. At home I always have too much to do at night after I get the twins to bed or I'm tired and fall asleep before the movie gets started," Kelly responded.

The two of them ran for the car and headed for the Holiday Inn. The parking lot was empty except for a couple of vans with some lettering on the side David could not make out. They had checked out of the motel assuming they would be going home. The night clerk recognized David, smiled, and said, "Would you like your room back, Mr. Jordan?"

"This is getting to be a habit," David said. "Why don't you let us have a couple of rooms downstairs next to each other?" They registered and were given adjacent rooms halfway down the first floor hallway. David opened the interior connecting doors so the two of them could visit and still have their own privacy. Opening a bottle of wine he had purchased on the way to the motel, father and daughter sat at the window watching the lightning show. Neither seemed to mind drinking wine out of plastic motel glasses.

David got up and said he was going to continue writing in his journal and add the events of this day. "What are you going to do with a journal, write a book when this is all over with?" Kelly was muffling a slight giggle.

"As a matter of fact, I just might do that. I think there is a story in the old Chevy, I just have to get more information about what happened to the girl."

"Dad, I think you should." Kelly was suddenly serious. "You write well. I've seen papers you wrote for work and letters you've written. I am serious, you should do it. I can help you with the grammar and spelling, I am a pretty good editor. I do it for a living." Kelly had a hold of his arm and was smiling encouragement.

"We'll see. First things first. Right now, I want to get down all the facts and add my own comments, otherwise I won't remember the details. I'll get us a four AM wakeup call. That should give us time to get back in town." David gave Kelly a hug and kissed her forehead. "I love you, baby. I really appreciate your help and Fred's too." He walked into his room and partially closed the door behind him.

Sitting at the small desk in his room David began to write in his journal thinking about what Kelly had said. Could he actually write a book? Would anybody read it? He had always admired authors who could cause the reader to graphically visualize scenes from the words printed on a page. He wished he could put down on paper what he saw in his mind's eye. He poured himself another half glass of wine.

Although the thunder and lightning had moved south of town it was still raining outside. David decided to listen to the eleven o'clock news and was in the process of finding a local channel when he heard a tapping sound on the window. It sounded like a metallic object against the glass. Maybe the storm had knocked something loose.

David pulled back the curtain and was greeted by two small explosions and flashes of light. He was knocked backward, tripping over the bed. He felt a burning pain in his stomach. He instinctively rolled off the bed and onto the floor with a thud.

Kelly rushed in exclaiming, "What was that? Dad, are you hurt? It sounded like gunshots! Oh, God, you are hurt. Damn it, Dad can you hear me?" Kelly was bending over her dad and looking toward the window. The drapes David had pushed aside were back in place.

David could not believe he had been shot. He had experienced gunfire in Vietnam, but this was totally unexpected. His stomach ached and he felt a dull burning sensation deep inside. "Kelly, I need a doctor. Call 911. Get the sheriff here too." He had heard two shots. Had he been shot twice? He tried to get up so he could look at himself in the mirror, but when he used his stomach muscles he knew it was not good to be moving around.

He tried desperately not to lose consciousness. Kelly was on the telephone screaming at the dispatcher "My father has been shot I need and an ambulance now!" She kept repeating the room number and the words Holiday Inn.

A sheriff's deputy and the ambulance arrived simultaneously. David could see the paramedics but he could not understand their confusing commands to one another. The deputy was talking to Kelly and on his radio at the same time. The paramedic gave David a shot of something and he felt a warm sensation envelop his body. He closed his eyes, allowed his brain to shut out the pain, and drifted off to another world.

CHAPTER 12

The second day after he was transported to the Winnebago County General Hospital, David regained consciousness. The paramedic and ambulance attendants, who responded to Kelly's 911 call were quick to recognize the seriousness of David's wounds. He had been shot twice in the abdomen on the right side, just below the belt line. Because the gunman was standing at ground level, the bullets were angled upward. The gun used by the unknown assailant was a small caliber, probably a .22 semi-automatic.

The doctor on duty at the hospital emergency room had been in contact with the paramedics from the very moment they arrived at the Holiday Inn where David had been shot. The 40 minute ride to the hospital was made in a blinding rainstorm. On this day, Thursday, June 17, the sun was bright and hot. David turned his head slowly and looked out the window next to his bed. "Where am I?" he wondered. His stomach hurt like hell. He was connected to two bottles of clear liquid by tubes stuck in his left arm. David had no idea what they were for. There was no one else in the room.

The memory of the last night in the motel came rushing back. Someone had tapped on the window and when David opened the drapes two shots were fired and found their mark. David remembered Kelly's near-panic wails and the sheriff's deputy asking questions. The paramedic had given him a shot of something and it was lights out until this morning. It was morning wasn't it?

A nurse came in carrying a tray of instruments and medical paraphernalia. "Oh, Mr. Jordan, you're awake, I'll get the doctor right away. He's just down the hall." She disappeared and was back in less than 30 seconds. "Mr. Jordan, meet Doctor Vinod Al-Khatib, he has been taking care of you since you came into the emergency ward Tuesday night. He spent all night in surgery with you."

"I'm sorry you didn't get any sleep, Doctor. I didn't get the last name." David said, with a thin smile on his lips.

"Oh, I got plenty of sleep Mr. Jordan. Its Al-Khatib, pronouncing his own name carefully. I slept here at the hospital. How are you feeling? You have been unconscious for almost two whole days. I was very concerned about the blood loss. We had to fill you up again." The doctor said, smiling and exhibiting a large gap between his two front teeth. He was very happy his patient was awake and responding to verbal input.

David could see the doctor was from the Middle East and spoke English as a second language. He had a dark complexion and was small in stature. "Tell me Doctor, what kind of shape am I in?

"We have good news and bad news to tell you Mr. Jordan. The good news is you did not lose your right kidney. It was already missing in action." He smiled, according to your daughter you lost it in Vietnam. Beautiful girl, your daughter. Very concerned about you. The bad news is your lower intestines were perforated in four places. We had to do some pretty amazing repair work to allow you to eliminate body waste normally from the original orifice. We are monitoring your white blood count frequently for any sign of peritonitis. As far as I can tell right now, you will not have any negative results after the healing is complete. Of course we must be concerned about scar tissue, but it should be minimal."

David was relieved to hear good prognoses for his injuries. "Where is my daughter?" David looked to the nurse for an answer.

"She was here earlier." The nurse responded, "I'll try to find her for you, she left her motel phone number."

"How many pints of blood did I need?" David asked the doctor.

"Four or five, I believe." He was scanning through the medical chart that had been hanging at the foot of the bed. "Yes, four the first night. We were afraid you would go into shock before we got you stabilized. You had several nasty wounds inside your belly, Mr. Jordan. You are a lucky man." He patted David on the shoulder, "I have to finish my rounds, but I'll be back before I'm off duty. If you need anything just call the nurse. They are good people here." The doctor turned and walked out of the room.

David thought about what the doctor had said. It sounds like he would be back to normal before too long, thanks to modern medicine. He was concerned about the four pints of blood he had been given. AIDS was what David was afraid of. But it was over with, if he got it, he got it. He knew these days the blood supply was checked thoroughly before being administered to anyone, but the fear was still there.

David's thoughts went back to the night before last, and the instant he had been shot. Who was behind the gun? And why? What had he done to piss someone off so bad they wanted him dead? He needed to talk to the sheriff and find out what Woodford could tell him about his assailant.

Kelly ran into the room. "Dad, I'm so glad you are awake, I was so worried. Thank God, I prayed the whole time," Kelly was hugging David's neck, crying and laughing at the same time.

"Take it easy, Sugar. I am going to be okay. The doc explained it all to me. How are the twins and Fred? Are they getting along okay without you?"

"Their downstairs in the waiting room. I made them wait until I could see for myself you were awake and okay." Kelly was wiping her eyes. "I'm going to tell the nurse to let them in for a few minutes."

The twins ran to David's bedside and grabbed his hands. David felt tears welling up in his eyes. He hadn't realized how much he loved these identical faces. Fred was standing at the foot of the bed smiling broadly.

After lunch, David took a long nap. He was weak and unable to eat anything solid. His gut ached. The nurse came and changed his dressing. For the first time he saw that good doctor had cut an eight-inch incision to make the repairs he was talking about. He had cut out some of the old scar tissue and made a new, much more precise, incision. No wonder he had a stomachache.

Sheriff Woodford was waiting for the nurse to leave so he could talk to David. She collected her supplies and equipment and left the two men alone. "Well, David, you certainly get involved with the locals when you come to town. I think everybody knows who you are. You're a celebrity of sorts."

"A celebrity out of sorts, if you ask me. I guess this must be my fifteen minutes of fame, wouldn't you say, Sheriff?" David asked.

"It's been a lot longer than fifteen minutes. There have been TV cameras and reporters hanging out here since Monday. Fortunately, the hospital security won't let them in. Tell me, David, just what did you see the night you got shot? I've been waiting to hear what you saw."

David began, "I could not see who it was Sheriff. The light was on inside the room and it was pitch dark outside. All I could see was my own reflection. I heard a tapping sound. I thought the storm had knocked something loose around the window so I opened the drapes to take a look and "bam-bam" that's all I remember. The next thing I knew, my gut hurt, I knew I had been shot and it was serious. I woke up this morning and that was it. Here I am." David nodded "Now it's your turn."

The sheriff had his pocket recorder out. Now he clicked it off, stood up, and turned toward the window. "We found two empty shell casings outside of your window. They match the one we found at Jim Ballantyne's mobile home. They come from a small caliber twenty-two semi-automatic.

"Kelly said she heard shots and came running to your room. She thinks she heard a car drive off with the tires spinning on wet pavement. When we examined the parking lot after the rain had stopped, we couldn't find a thing except the two shell casings. We know the shooter found out which window was your room by calling the desk clerk and asking for you. A man's voice said they had a delivery to make and the clerk gave out the room number. It's against the house rules to give out room numbers.

"The young girl on duty last night lost her job. She was pretty shook up, but she didn't follow procedures and someone got hurt. We didn't think you were going to make it for a while. Anyway, the delivery was two bullets.

"The shooter counted off the windows from outside the building and bingo, he had your room." Woodford was looking out the window again. "I am not satisfied with this setup. People across the street in the apartment building can see in here. For some reason, David, you are ground zero. I'm going to beef up the security around here as well. Now the word is out you are still alive someone may try to finish you off."

"Oh, that's real good news, Sheriff. Now that really makes me unhappy as hell!" David said.

"Don't worry, I'm bringing in extra help so we can keep an eye on Kelly and her family as well. The shooter may be thinking Kelly and Fred know your secret as well.

"I just don't get it. What is it, you know or saw, that makes somebody so desperate to keep secret that they are willing to commit murder?" The sheriff was clearly without any clues. "I keep going back to the old Chevy. Whoever killed Jim also wanted the car. Erika, that's Ballantyne's wife, said her husband was arguing with Barnet and an older guy about the car. They could have had any number of junk cars to choose from or even some late models in storage, but they took the '56, Why?" The sheriff was looking at David but talking to himself.

David was interested in what the sheriff was saying, but God he was tired. He could not keep his eyes open any longer. Sleep was creeping up on him.

"Sheriff, what's the next step?" Kelly had cornered Woodford the minute he exited David's room. "We want to move Dad to our place as soon as possible. So we can be close to him. The doctor says Dad will require hospitalization for at least ten days."

"Kelly, I know you would like to move your dad, but his life is in danger. The shooter is still out there. We don't know who this person is, although we have a suspicion. Until we find him, even you and Fred are in danger, in my opinion." Woodford looked at Kelly emphasizing his last remark.

"You don't know that for sure Sheriff. We could put Dad in an ambulance and take off without anyone knowing where we were headed. I'm sure we could find a hospital near our apartment in Chicago where Dad could recuperate."

Woodford started walking over to the nurse's station. "I don't think the doc is going to let you move your dad any time soon. In the meantime, I am going to have him moved to a more secure room here." The sheriff spoke to the nurse sitting at the front desk. He told her he wanted Mr. Jordan moved to an interior room facing the courtyard. A room where he would not be next to the window. "I am going to arrange for a deputy to be stationed outside his door. Kelly if you do decided to try to move him, let me know ahead of time, so we can make arrangements. I've got to go now and get back to work."

"Thank you, Sheriff, for your concern, but as soon as Dad is able I'm going to move him."

"Oh, there is one thing I didn't mention to your dad. We put both detectives Creighton and Bidwell on administrative leave. I can't discuss the specifics with you, but you can tell your dad maybe the caller was right about warning him not to trust the Sheriff's Department." He looked down at his shoes and shook his head, "I guess there is always the ten percent that screw things up for the rest of us."

Kelly took the sheriff's arm as they walked down the hallway toward the exit. "Do you think they had something to do with Dad getting shot?"

The sheriff looked dejected and said, "I sincerely hope not, but in this country we see more and more cops turning bad and taking payoffs from the drug pushers or pushing drugs themselves. Drugs corrupt countries, people, judges, lawmen, everyone, and I don't see an end to it. The state attorney general is investigating my department and those two guys are on the list."

"What list?" Kelly said.

"I said more than I should Kelly. Just take my word for it, if those two, or any others are dirty, they will answer to me and to a judge. Now, I have to go. We have a line on the guy who we think pulled the trigger and shot your dad, and I don't want to miss a chance to bring him in."

The new room was exactly the same as the old one with one large exception, no windows. Kelly thought it was very antiseptic and told the nurse so. "This is what Sheriff Woodford ordered,"

Kelly's father was still sleeping. She left to go downstairs hoping to find her husband and boys, and talk about where they were going to stay. There was a sheriff's deputy sitting outside her father's door. She spent a few moments talking with a very young, obviously new Deputy Sheriff, Albert Coleman. After introducing herself she asked, "How long have you been a sheriff, Albert?"

"About three months ma'am," Coleman said. "I heard all about your father. Everybody in the department thinks he is a hero. I won't let anyone hurt him. Don't you worry."

Just as she was about to leave the floor, a florist deliveryman exited the elevator carrying a large bouquet of flowers. Kelly overheard the man ask for Mr. David Jordan's room number. I hope Fred remembered to order flowers, she thought to herself.

Kelly turned and followed the deliveryman into her father's room. The young sheriff guarding the door stopped the flower deliveryman and inspected the flowers thoroughly before taking the bouquet himself and setting it on the dresser. David was still sleeping. Kelly signed the receipt. She reached for the small envelope attached to the bouquet and pulled out a card, it read:

"David,

You cannot imagine how terrible I felt when Bee called last night and told me you had been shot. I hope and pray you will be up and around in no time. I asked Bee to keep me informed of your condition. I hope these flowers make your day a little brighter.

Kathryn."

Kelly read the note several times and placed it back in the envelope. Her father had not said too much about this mysterious woman from England or Ireland or wherever she was from. What he did say about her caused Kelly to feel there was a lot more to the story than just a casual dinner date. The flowers proved it.

Kelly was aware her father had dated several women since her parents divorce. He had not confided in her about his love life, if you could call it that. It probably was more of biological need to be close to someone of the opposite sex.

Kelly's family traveled to Southern California at least once a year. During these visits, David had introduced Kelly to several women, whom he called, "Close friends." Kelly knew her dad was attractive to women, but he had refrained from forming a permanent relationships since the divorce. These liaisons seldom lasted more than a month or so and seemed to be nothing more than random pairings.

Kelly made a mental note to question her father about Kathryn when he was in better health. His immediate health was her primary concern now. How fortunate, the gunman had shot her father in his right side, the side with the missing kidney. What a disaster it would have been if the bullets had hit the left side.

CHAPTER 13

David woke Thursday morning feeling much better than he had the previous day. His right side was painful, but he was not as groggy as he had been. The bags of liquid were still dripping into his arm. David assumed it was his breakfast. He closed his eyes and pictured a plate full of waffles, sausage, eggs over medium, and a pot of hot coffee. Then he spotted the flowers.

The large bouquet was out of reach on a small table next to the bathroom door. It was beautiful. Kelly and the twins must have picked it out. Something sparked in David's head and his curiosity led him to believe he could get up and retrieve the small envelope. He tried to sit up and swing his legs down to the floor. His gut reacted with sharp pains. Not too bad, he could stand it. He had endured worse, much worse in Nam. If he could just take two steps, he could retrieve the card. He needed to start moving around anyway to keep his joints loosened. There was jest enough slack in the intravenous feeding tubes to allow him to take the two steps and pull the envelope out of the bouquet.

Back in bed and out of breath David rested a moment and then opened the envelope. It was from Kathryn. His internal emotional thermometer rose twenty degrees instantly. He read and reread the note a half dozen times. "She cares!" he said aloud, "There is no doubt about it, she cares!"

All the pain suddenly vanished. He felt like dancing around the room. God bless Bee. He wondered what other news Bee had passed on to Kathryn. Was Bee programmed to contact Kathryn on a periodic basis? Had Kathryn interrogated Bee to find out more about him? No, of course not. Kathryn was too sophisticated for that type of direct action. She could have called to discuss the business of transferring the house to the new owner. That's it. Bee would have volunteered the information about David without Kathryn asking specific questions.

Relaxing for the first time since he had been shot David closed his eyes and visualized Kathryn's face and figure. She was beautiful. He daydreamed of meeting her in different of settings. Now he knew for sure she had feelings for him. He let his mind wander without restraint. The fact Kathryn was engaged did little to slow David's imagination.

A hospital orderly appeared with a dinner tray and placed it on the rollaway hospital table. He helped David sit up and placed a couple of pillows behind his back. Removing the cover from the main dish he asked, "Do you want some decaffeinated coffee now or later?"

David looked at the meal in front of him and lost his appetite. Everything was soft and mushy. He assumed the doctor did not want him to eat anything that would cause any possible internal stress. What the hell, he thought. He needed the food value to help him heal as soon as possible. He could eat whatever they placed in front of him if it would help him get out of here.

The evening television news was on when Kelly and the twins came clamoring into the room. "Grandpa we went swimming all afternoon," both of them said at the same time. David hugged both boys and then Kelly. These kids are bright, well behaved, mischievous, and all boy, he thought. "As soon as I get out of the hospital we are going to a baseball game." They made him promise.

"Fred had to go back to Chicago to tend to business. So the twins and I are staying at an all-suites hotel not far from the hospital. As soon as the doctor allows it, we are moving you home."

"That can't be soon enough, I need to get out of here and get some decent food."

A nurse barged in exclaiming, "Mr. Jordan, you are on TV." She grabbed the remote, and switched to a local station. "They are on commercial right now but when they come back they are going to interview Sheriff Woodford. " He caught the man who shot you!"

All eyes were turned toward the wall-mounted TV. An anorexic model was pushing some kind of invisible makeup, "No one can tell you are using makeup," she crooned. If it was invisible, why wear it? David wondered. Then a news commentator came on. "Sheriff Woodford announced today his deputies have captured a man they suspect of shooting David Jordan last Tuesday in Dumont. Mr. Jordan was with Sheriff Woodford and another deputy when Jordan was forced to shoot and kill a suspected drug dealer, Adam Barnet, on a farm near Dumont. The following night Jordan was shot twice in the stomach by an unknown assailant while standing near the window of his motel room." The camera switched locations to Sheriff Woodford standing outside his headquarters in Rockford.

The sheriff read from a prepared statement. He told the TV crew his deputies had located a man named William Sandoval whom they believed to be the man behind the attempted murder of David Jordan. Sandoval was located in a boarding house in the downtown Rockford area. Woodford credited his deputies and praised the cooperation from the Rockford police department. Sandoval was arrested without incident. The TV cameras focused on a slender, balding older man being helped into a waiting patrol car.

"Hooray," shouted Kelly. "They got him. Now we can all breathe easier."

"Did you hear who he said tried to kill me? It was Billy Sandoval!" David was looking at Kelly in utter amazement. "It's Cindy's boyfriend." Kelly had a blank look on her face before David continued, "He wrote the note I found in the trunk of the convertible. That is incredible! Just amazing!" David fell back in his bed, shaking his head in disbelief.

"Dad, maybe it someone else with the same name. Even if it is, they got him. And he's locked up so we can relax a little."

David felt a huge surge of relief pass through him. He wanted to talk to the sheriff and find out all the details. He and Kelly hugged and the kids joined in. Several nurses and Dr. Al-Khatib came in and joined in the general celebration. Finally the head nurse ushered everyone out and said, "It's time for Mr. Jordan to get ready for a good night's rest. You all can come back tomorrow."

Kelly approached Dr. Al-Kahtib in the hallway, and asked, "How much longer do you think my dad will have to be in the hospital?" She told the doctor she could arrange for a full-time nurse, if David could stay with her, until he was well enough to travel back to California.

Dr. Al-Kahtib looked down the hall for a minute and then replied, "If David keeps improving at his present rate, I will discharge him on Monday. Mrs. Elliot, you must promise me you will keep your father resting, without physical exertion, for another two weeks. I will give you the name of a physician in downtown Chicago I want David to visit next Wednesday. If you personally take care of him, I see no need for a full-time nurse."

Kelly hugged the doctor and gave him an air kiss on the cheek. She promised to do everything the doctors and nurses told her to do, and she would personally take her dad to see the local doctor. Kelly stuck her head back in her dad's room and gave him the good news. "I'll see you sometime tomorrow morning dad. What do you want me to bring you besides the newspaper?"

"Two chocolate doughnuts and a cup of real coffee," was the hopeful reply.

After his "sponge bath" David managed to eat a bowl of chocolate cookie ice cream. He then surfed all the channels on TV for a few minutes and then decided to go to sleep and dream of Kathryn riding in his '56 Chevy convertible. It was around twelve o'clock when David woke with a start. He set up in bed, sharp pains immediately told him not to move so fast.

He had been dreaming about the afternoon he shot Adam Barnet. He could hear the explosion from the shotgun as it bucked in his hands. The lightning flash of gunpowder, the image of Adam's head exploding would forever be imprinted on his brain.

He tried not to think of that afternoon, but tonight it all came back with a roar. The most vivid and grotesque scene was when Adam's mother threw herself down on Adam's dying body and began that awful wailing. The look she gave David was full of anguish and hatred.

He was sweating and the sheets on his bed were damp. He had killed in Vietnam, but this was different. He could not recall the face of any Vietcong he had personally killed, and he was glad. David knew Adam Barnet's face would stay in his memory for a long time.

CHAPTER 14

David's recuperation at his daughter's apartment in Chicago was one of the more enjoyable experiences of his life. Kelly's motherly instinct was in full bloom. She begged off taking on any long-term assignments from work so she could take care of her dad. Kelly cooked, cleaned, and hovered over David like his own mother would have. He loved every minute of it. It had been a long time since he had been smothered with love and attention. He let the twins wait on him and in return played their games and read books to them. Fred was a little put out because he was not getting the attention he felt he deserved. He was gone most of the time on sales calls so David soaked up as much attention as he could get.

He was due back to work on the 26th of June. He knew he would not be in top shape by then, he would have to contact his boss at HIC. The day David was discharged from the hospital he faxed a copy of the news article explaining the whole incident at Dumont and sent an e-mail to his boss requesting a medical leave of absence. To David's utter amazement and disbelief he received a reply on Kelly's fax machine two days later denying his request. David read the terse statement from his employer to Kelly:

Dear David,
We regret to inform you we cannot grant you a leave of absence at this time. We are in critical negotiations with our largest customer, Bell Helicopter, and we need your input to complete the manufacturing department's plan for implementing the terms of the new contract. Report for work as scheduled.

Shirley Chamberlain,
Personnel Administrator

David nearly had a relapse as he read the fax aloud. "That son-of–a-bitch! He didn't even have the nerve to answer my fax personally. He had Shirley do it for him. What a shitface. We don't need a written plan to handle the new contract. We already have a well-defined manufacturing process and all we need is his authorization to hire the number of people required to make the damn parts! He knows that. He's forcing every manager to write a plan and include production numbers that are impossible to meet so he can come back after the fact and chew everyone a new asshole for not meeting the plan." David was so angry Kelly had to physically set him in a chair and calm him down.

Kelly reacted with equal disbelief. How could her dad's company act so irresponsibly? Her father had worked tirelessly for twenty-four years as a loyal employee. He was the most productive manufacturing manager the company had ever had. She took the fax out of David's hands and read it herself. "He can't do this. There must be some kind of law, which protects people, when they have a legitimate medical excuse. I am going to check with the office, I know somebody up there will have the proper words for your reply. You are going to respond aren't you Dad? You can't go back to work now!"

"You're damn right I am. First, I'm going to call Shirley. She's a heads-up lady. I know she will fill me in with what Becker has been up to lately." David began punching numbers into the telephone. Working his way through the ridicules automated answering machine, he finally reached the office of the personal administrator, "Shirley, this is David. I got your fax today. What the hell is going on back there? Doesn't Becker realize I'm in no condition to work for a while?"

After a brief silence on the other of the phone, "Good morning David. Glad to hear you are recovering from your wounds. Now, what is your question?" David hesitated and smiled at Shirley's sarcasm.

"What is Becker thinking?"

"David, your fax laid on Becker's desk for two days. Everybody in the plant keeps asking about you. The newspaper account of your situation is on every bulletin board. I didn't know anything about the fax until this morning when Becker stormed into my office, threw it on my desk, and screamed, 'Don't grant anyone a leave of absence or vacations or time off for any reason until after we get the Bell contract.' He stormed out and that was it. All vacations and leave of absences have been canceled since last Monday.

"The guys in marketing tell me the negotiations with Bell have been going badly. The word from the corporate office is, if we don't get this contract they will find a new plant manager. You know Becker, he can't take the pressure. I'm sorry David, you know I had to do it, right? I need this job. I have too many years in now to screw up."

"It's okay Shirley, I know who runs the show there. I don't blame you. But I do need the name of the vice president of legal affairs in the South Bend corporate office. Fax me his name and phone number. I'm going to make some waves. Thanks for your help, Shirley."

David knew exactly what he was going to do. "Kelly, ask your buddies down at the office to generate a response to Becker on your firm's letter head."

A one-paragraph reply went back to California late in the afternoon. David sent copies to the South Bend headquarters of Hydraulic International Corp. Other copies went to every manager and supervisor at HIC. That evening, David played Monopoly with the twins, ate dinner, and went to bed early. He slept the night through without waking once.

The next morning Kelly got the kids off to summer school and then tended to her dad. "How you feeling this morning, Pops?" she asked, as she fixed his special breakfast of soft-boiled eggs, toast, juice, and coffee.

"Where did you and Fred get this 'Pops' business? Sounds like a candy bar or something."

"Oh Dad, it's just a nickname that seemed appropriate. We have to call Fred's father 'Grandfather Elliot.' The kids hate going over there, they don't have any fun. They can't touch anything, make any noise, or even watch TV. I'm afraid they will break something and he really gets mad if they don't address him by his proper title. We all love you Dad, what would you like to be called?"

David quickly changed his mind, "Pops is okay. I just hadn't heard you use it before." David started eating his breakfast content to cut his loses. Maybe 'Pops' wasn't so bad after all. He had met Fred's father at Kelly and Fred's wedding. He was a salesman who sold janitorial supplies to public schools. He was a dull person with a dull job and a bad attitude.

Physically, David was feeling a lot better, he was at the point in his recovery to have enough mobility to risk the possibility of re-injuring himself. The pain in his stomach was bearable without painkillers. The incision on his right side was healing nicely. This scar would be much neater and thinner than the one that was cut out. The incision made by the Navy doctors in Vietnam, looked like it had been made by a dull knife and sewn together with fishing line.

A thundershower the night before had cleared the air and David decided to sit out on the balcony and enjoy the sunshine before the temperature climbed above eighty degrees. He closed his eyes and daydreamed of Kathryn. "She cares." he said to himself. He had read and reread her note that came with the flowers when he was in the hospital. He read between the lines, she cares no mistake about it. He did not have a formal plan to bridge the distance between them. There was one huge obstacle. Kathryn was engaged to be married. He didn't even know the name of lucky guy. The name didn't matter anyway. He needed to make a plan to see her again without appearing to be overly aggressive. He would have to be calculating so as not to give her the impression he was chasing her but giving her just the right amount of attention so she would keep him on her mind.

David's brain switched to the old Chevy and the investigation being conducted by Sheriff Woodford. Billy Sandoval was in jail. He knew that this Billy Sandoval had to be the same Billy Sandoval that was Cindy's boyfriend. The mystery of the convertible and its missing owner begged to be solved. The fact that Cindy's old boyfriend had tried to kill him was almost impossible to believe. Now he had more reason to contact Kathryn.

He had no way of knowing if a motive had been established for Billy's attempt on his life. He needed to know why he had been shot. The only thing to do was call the sheriff after lunch and find out the latest information.

In the back of David's mind, he could not get the Chevy's owner, Cindy, out of his mind. Why had she disappeared? Was she still alive? Apparently, Miss Margaret had heard from her several times over the years, but, according to Bee, there were only four letters. David wondered if those letters still existed. What secret did Cindy take with her? Was Billy involved in her disappearance? Instinctively, he knew there was a story here. Wouldn't it be great if he could devote the time and energy to find Cindy and interview her? Maybe interview Billy in jail. More discussions with Bee and Miss Margaret's family. Interviewing Kathryn's, parents would certainly be in order.

Suddenly, the picture of the future came clear to David. He could write a book about the old Chevy and its owner. It would not be a biography, but a novel based on real events. He liked writing, arranging and rearranging sentences, and trying to use the least number of words to convey a meaning. He had written hundreds of technical procedures, memos, business letters, but never anything fictional. It would be fun to try. And who knows, he may find a way to see more of Kathryn and somehow prevent her from getting married. What a terrific plan, he thought. David daydreamed several different scenarios, all of which put him and Kathryn together at the end. "What have I got to loose?" he asked himself. "Nothing," was the answer? His job was finished. He knew he could not work for Becker anymore. But first, David would make life so miserable for that spineless bastard he would have to take him back, and then he could quit on his own terms.

Almost twenty-four hours to the minute after David's reply, Kelly's fax machine began printing a message addressed to Mr. David Jordan:

"David Jordan

Your request for a thirty-day medical leave of absence has been granted. Please forward <u>all medical records</u> to this office as soon as possible. You will be required to obtain a company appointed physician's release before you return to work.

Shirley Chamberlain,

Personnel Administrator

"Thanks Kelly," David exclaimed. "Tell the people at your office I really appreciate their input. It did the trick. I would love to have seen the look on Becker's face when he got the call from the corporate legal office. I'll bet he is still firing e-mail messages to everyone, trying to cover his ass."

"Dad, you still have got to face him when you go back to work. You may have a job, but Becker will make your life miserable. What are you going to do? You still have a few years left before you can retire."

"I have a plan. Becker will be so glad to get rid of me he will put me in for early retirement and/or a large severance package. In any case, I think I will be financially secure for a few years until I get my book published." He glanced away sheepishly, he had not intended to mention the book until later.

"What book? Are you going to write a book about your near-death experience?" Kelly gave her dad a questioning look.

"Actually I'm thinking about writing a book about the Chevy. We talked about it before. You offered to edit it for me. I have a good feeling there is an unusual story associated with the car. I want to investigate the background of the people involved and write about them. It will be a novel, maybe a mystery novel, or possibly a romance story."

"Dad, do you think you could write a romance novel? Mom will laugh her head off when she hears that," Kelly said, as she covered her mouth and stifled a laugh.

David felt defensive, but held himself in check. Stage acting, he said, "Your mother never was able to bring out the true romantic nature of my personality, so I will have to use my imagination, but don't think for a minute your old dad doesn't know what true love is all about."

CHAPTER 15

David actually looked forward to the flight to California. Staying at his daughter's apartment with her twin boys and salesman husband left very little time for private thinking. Kelly was a great nurse/mother/daughter and he appreciated everything she did for him, but it was time to be getting back to reality. Recovery from Sandoval's two gunshots was remarkably uncomplicated. It was painful to do sit-ups, but David knew he would be able to go to the gym and get back into his routine within a few weeks.

The fact he had been shot by Billy Sandoval, Cindy's boyfriend of forty- plus years ago, was astounding and unbelievable. In addition the car Billy and Cindy planned to elope in was stolen. It was just too much of a coincidence. The whole affair at Dumont took on some kind of a Hitchcock movie plot atmosphere, unbelievable.

The Chicago doctor recommended by Dr. Al-Khatib, had given David a clean bill of health and sent a medical statement to his boss at HIC. David made an appointment with the company doctor back in Long Beach for the next morning, July 27. He anticipated a quick check up and he would be back to work by ten o'clock in the morning.

United flight 992 from Chicago to Long Beach was smooth as glass. The Long Beach Airport is served by only a handful of flights during the day. Parking is a snap compared to Los Angeles or Orange County Airports. David sat at a window and watched thunderheads forming over the farmlands of Iowa. He felt confident he had a plan for the future, it gave him hope. Hope that he would somehow be able to form a permanent relationship with Kathryn and write a best-selling novel at the same time. Daydreams. What would life be without dreams? Boring, David concluded.

He wanted to get back to his small apartment in San Pedro and open it up to the sea breeze off the Pacific. Actually, it was an old stucco duplex that sat on a hillside with a panoramic view of the city of Long Beach and its harbor below. The coastline of Southern California extended to the southeast.

After Ellen and David divorced in 1988, David deliberately looked for a place to live on the steep hillsides of San Pedro. HIC was located not far from the Long Beach Naval shipyards and only four miles from his apartment in San Pedro. He liked the town for its ethnic diversity, quirky neighborhoods, and killer views of the Los Angeles and San Pedro harbor. San Pedro's importance as a major fishing port had long ago passed into history, leaving behind remnants of a fishing fleet, shipbuilding dry-docks, and an outdated Fort MacArthur Army post.

Sitting near a window of the 757, drinking fresh coffee, his mind went back to yesterday and a visit from Sheriff Leslie Woodford. The sheriff had called early, before eight o'clock. He wanted to make sure David was still at his daughter's place and was feeling up to a visit. "Of course," David responded, "I want to know what's going on with the investigation. Did you find my Chevy?"

"No, but we have a lead. I'll fill you in when I get there."

David had made plans to fly back to Southern California the next day and he was glad for the visit. He had spoken with the sheriff several times over the past few weeks by telephone, but the sheriff refused to provide any details. "It's an ongoing investigation and I can't talk about it right now," was his standard reply whenever David asked specific questions.

Billy was in jail. The judge had refused to grant bail because of Billy's long criminal record, he considered him a flight risk. So one of the bad guys was locked up, two others were dead, what else or who else is involved? David could only speculate, obviously others were involved, the trucking operators for example. How about the people supplying the drugs from down south? Don't forget the buyers on the West Coast and of course the two detectives that had given David such a bad time.

The sheriff walked into Kelly's apartment wearing civilian clothes. David was totally surprised at seeing Sheriff Woodford dressed in khaki shorts and a Hawaiian sport shirt. Woodford was a big man and in his sheriff's uniform was intimidating. Now he looked like he just stepped off the beach. "Are operating under cover Sheriff?" asked David smiling and trying not to laugh.

"Believe it or not I am on vacation. To Hawaii, that is. The last couple of months have been hard and I have not had a day off since Memorial Day. What do you think of my shirt? Will I pass for a native?"

"Sheriff, you would stick out like a sore thumb no matter where you were. But in Hawaii everyone who isn't brown or Asian sticks out like a sore thumb, so you should fit in nicely." David was laughing. Not so much at the sight of a big man in a loud shirt, but rather at the sudden feeling of relief he felt and the camaraderie he sensed. "Are you leaving today? Are you going alone or are you taking someone?" suddenly David realized he didn't even know if the sheriff was married or not. What a jerk he had been. He had spent hours with the sheriff and never asked the question, the sheriff never volunteered any information about his private life.

"No, I'm not taking anyone. I'm figuring on meeting someone interesting once I get there. My plane leaves in a couple of hours, so let's go over the details of the Sandoval case. Maybe your daughter could make some coffee. I'm about three cups low right now."

Kelly disappeared into the kitchen and hastily made a new pot of coffee, not wanting to miss anything the sheriff had to say. She thought of recording the conversation on a small recording device her husband used to dictate sales reports she typed for him. She grabbed the device from the kitchen counter, switched it on, and stuck it down her shirtfront into her bra. She checked herself in the mirror fluffed her shirt out a little and walked back into the living room. Her father and the sheriff were standing in front of a large picture window overlooking the Chicago skyline.

Kelly insisted they sit down while she poured coffee. Woodford began by saying Sandoval had shut up like a clam and refused to say anything. "He knows we have enough evidence on him to send him up for three life terms. The district attorney will probably ask for the death penalty. He has prior felony convictions to boot. In situations like this, most x-cons will spill their guts because they have nothing to loose and it's a chance to get everything off their chest or get even with someone. They may even get a reduced sentence. They think they may help their case if they give the cops what they want, but Sandoval is holding back, I think has something up his sleeve. He also has a lawyer from East St. Louis who is a popular defense attorney for the local drug dealers in that part of the state.

"The attorney's name is Ramon Ruiz. He tried to make a deal with our DA. It turns out Sandoval had connections in my department. In return for reduced charges, he would point his finger at a deputy who was being paid to look the other way. You probably knew the State Attorney General was conducting an investigation in my department based on a tip from some drug informants. Christ, they even bugged my phone at the house." The Sheriff shook his head in disbelief.

"Anyway, the short version is this. I personally talked to Sandoval late at night one evening. He is tough, but when I explained the facts of life to him, he changed his mind. The guards in the jail and at the state penitentiary belong to the same union as I do so he began to get the picture. He gave up two names."

David butted in, "You going to tell me its Creighton and Bidwell. Am I right?"

"Bidwell and someone who sits on the dispatcher's desk. Creighton was just along for the ride. Bidwell had something on him, I haven't found out what it is yet. Creighton was forced to keep his mouth shut. As it turns out, the Attorney General had him pegged as well, so the next day we busted the three of them."

"So why did Sandoval try to take me out? I still don't get why he thought I was some kind of danger to him," the whole picture was not clear to David.

"This is the way I figure what happened." Woodford edged closer to Kelly and David. "Bidwell put him up to it. He was pissed because you got in the middle of a very nice operation he had set up. He was working on a nice retirement package by arranging transpiration of undiluted cocaine to the West Coast via car transporters. He knew this little setup was history after Billy shot Jim Ballantyne during an argument. He had to cover his ass. You took care of Barnet for him, but Bidwell needed to get rid of Sandoval to eliminate the one remaining link to himself.

"He gave Billy Sandoval your motel room number and ordered him to take you out. Sandoval was afraid Bidwell would have him charged with a parole violation and he would spend the rest of his days back in the slammer. Bidwell was planning to frame Billy and instigate a situation where Billy would be killed during a police raid. That would have eliminated an essential witness, but Billy gave up without a fight, unexpectedly, there was no gunplay when we made the arrest.

"Bidwell was pushing Billy all along. Actually, Billy tried to go straight after his last stretch in Joliet. But Bidwell found out what Adam Barnet and Jim Ballantyne were doing with junk cars and he wanted part of the action. They had a deal with a West Coast buyer who dealt cocaine and owned a car lot on the side. They would load up late-model used cars, some times late model wrecks, with the dope they brought in from New Orleans, and transport it to California. Before long, Bidwell was top dog because of his position in my department, and he could offer protection. He used Billy as an enforcer, which apparently worked well because he sure put Jim Ballantyne in his place when they argued over your Chevy.

David thought about what the Sheriff just said and then asked. "So why did Bidwell try and get me to sign a doctored statement?"

"Initially, he thought he could make you out to be the bad guy in Barnet's death. That would take the spotlight off him and the drugs. He hadn't counted on Carver showing up and getting you off the hook. His plan never would have worked anyway, because I would have seen through his scheme as soon as I saw your statement."

Kelly refilled each coffee cup and the three of them toasted each other. "Now for the big question, Sheriff. Where the hell is my Chevy?" David was on the edge of his chair anticipating some good news about the car that started this whole mess.

"Remember the business card you gave me with the phone number? It had the name of a car carrier on it. You said Jim Ballantyne gave it to you. That was when I got mad because you didn't remember to give it to me the day before."

David nodded, "Yeah, I remember. How could I forget? You made me feel like an ass for not coming up with that information sooner."

"Well, it was too late to find the truck in Illinois, but we looked up the phone number in the reverse directory and found the trucker's house in the outskirts of Chicago. He was gone, of course, but the police found a name and California address for a used car lot tacked up next to his workbench in the garage. We contacted the police in LA. They waited for him to show up and when he did they welcomed him with open arms and handcuffs. There was your Chevy, plus four other cars that had been picked up across the country."

"Well, where is it now? Can I pick it up when I get back to California?" David could not believe his luck. The cops had actually found the Chevy.

"Sorry, David, but things are not that easy. The Chevy was loaded with cocaine stuffed in the door panels and in the gas tank. The other cars were clean, but yours was going to some guy in Hollywood who collects cars and deals cocaine to the local movie people." The sheriff looked at his watch and began to get up. "I've got just forty-five minutes to make my flight.

"David, this is the name of the detective in LA handling the case out there. He can tell you about your car." The sheriff handed David a piece of notepaper with a LA police sergeant's name on it. "There is a law on the books allowing the police to confiscate personal property's associated with illegal drug activity. Your old Chevy was loaded with coke and it was worth more money on the street than a thousand new Chevrolets would be.

"I've got to get going David. I want to thank you again for saving my life. I really mean it. I know it's hard to accept the fact you killed somebody, but what you did was the right thing. I knew Barnet was going to pull the trigger. All I could think of was being shot with my own gun. You did good." Woodford shook David's hand, almost crushing it in his big hand.

CHAPTER 16

The Boeing 757 landed in Long Beach airport shortly before 11 AM. The flight had been uneventful and David gained a couple of hours flying east to west. He took a cab and was soon in San Pedro. God, it felt good to be back on his home turf. His apartment was hot and stuffy, but otherwise just like he left it, slightly messed up, complete with dirty dishes in the kitchen sink.

He spent the rest of the day cleaning and washing clothes and getting ready to return to work. David did find time to call the detective Sheriff Woodford had told him about. The detective was out so all he could do was leave a message. David called his second-in-command at the plant to find out what was going on and try to get a head start for tomorrow

Manuel (Manny) Diaz had worked for David for over ten years. He was a terrific machinist and inspector. David had brought him along and had encouraged him to take as many night school classes as a man with a wife and five kids could. Manny had the type of personality commanding the respect of people working around him. His parents emigrated from Mexico during the early sixties, raised seven children, and instilled an enviable work ethic in all their children and especially Manny, the oldest.

Manny spoke excellent English with Mexican accent, but his written language skills were lacking. For this reason, David knew Manny was limited in terms of promotions. The corporate policy was that management level personnel and their prospective replacements had to have a college degree. Performance and ability were nine times more important than a person's alma mater, as far as David was concerned, but the corporate office in South Bend made the decisions and he couldn't alter them.

When he made Manny General Forman in charge of the entire machine shop, Becker nearly had a stroke. "The man has no education, he never completed high school, he can't write a memo without making a dozen mistakes. You keep advancing this guy, but you know he can never be your replacement." Becker was red in the face and out of breath by the time he finally ran out of gas and sat down, but not before he threw the four-page employee review form down on his desk in front of David.

In the end, after an hour of listening to Becker whine about corporate policy and making David promise to find someone else to put on his replacement list for the coming year, he signed the review.

The first evening David spent at home was devoted to sitting at his computer and compiling his journal notes and organizing all the information he knew about Kathryn and her family. He made a large spreadsheet and taped it on the wall. On it he detailed what each person had told him concerning Cindy O'Ryan and Billy Sandoval. He began to outline various possible scenarios regarding the relationship between the two main characters in his book. He felt that this project was going to be fun. First, he needed to get Cindy's story, and Billy's. Both were going to be difficult as far as David could see. He had no idea where Cindy was or whether she was alive. Billy was in jail and probably would not want to talk to David, the man he tried to kill. That problem was down the road. Tomorrow it was back to reality and HIC.

David was at Dr. Andrew Haddock's office at 9 AM the day he was supposed to report to work. His appointment was for 9 AM but so were the other twelve people in the waiting room. He sat back and replayed the conversation he had with Manny yesterday afternoon.

"We will be so glad to see you back on the job boss. Becker has been terrorizing the work force, yelling and scheming at every opportunity. I think the man is crazy, I really do. He has caused havoc in every department. Becker doesn't know a damn thing about engineering or manufacturing, but he is good at counting numbers. If we miss a deadline or our productivity numbers are short, he comes unglued.

"The third-quarter profit projections are not going to be met and we know the boys from headquarters will be in Becker's office for a visit. We're all hoping he'll get the ax.

"The marketing department is still wining and dinning the corporate buyers from Bell Helicopter, so we figure the new contract has not been signed. Other than that, everything is wonderful!"

Manny was straight and to the point as usual. David was mentally preparing for his first staff meeting when the doctor finally made an appearance in the small examination room David had been sitting in for forty-five minutes. To David's surprise, the doctor was holding a copy of the medical report from his Chicago doctor and appeared to be actually reading it.

"You are a lucky man, Mr. Jordan. How do you feel?"

"I feel great. Can I go back to work now?" David was hoping for a quick exit from the small closet sized-examination room he was in. He noticed the doctor was wearing Levi's under his white lab coat and loafers with no socks. Not the uniform David expected of a doctor.

"No, not just yet. Take off your shirt so we can see what kind of work the doctors back east did for you."

Dr. Haddock spent the better part of thirty minutes examining David and asking a lot of questions. He asked David to perform several different kinds of physical exercises just to make sure he could move without pain. "Okay, Mr. Jordan. I'll send a medical release document to your personnel administrator and you can go back to work."

"But I need it today. Can't you give it to me so I can hand carry it with me?"

"It will be on Mrs. Shirley Chamberlain's desk before you get back to the plant, I'll fax it." Dr. Haddock smiled and walked out of the room.

David stopped for a cup of coffee at a corner Stop-n-Go market. He wanted to walk into Becker's office carrying a cup of coffee and act as nonchalant as possible. Becker did not like people drinking coffee in his office because the cups made little round circles on his imported mahogany desktop.

David walked in the lobby, stopping momentarily at the front desk to say hello to the young receptionist, Christina. She had a chest on her that wouldn't quit and a smile from ear to ear for David. She got up from her desk and gave him a big hug and a smooch. David felt his face redden, but it was worth it. God, what he wouldn't give to spend one night with her, it might kill him, but it would be worth it.

He walked down the hallway to Becker's office trying not to be noticed by anyone in the marketing department. He wanted to get past the confrontation with Becker he was sure was going to happen. He held his finger to his lips as he walked past Becker's secretary and knocked on the solid oak door and walked into the dimly lit lion's den. Becker was staring intently into his computer screen. His face had a slight greenish glow.

"Hello Stanley," David said, as graciously as possible. "The doctor gave me a clean bill of health. Shirley has the medical release papers."

Becker looked up with a scowl on his face, hesitated and then said, "Welcome back, David. We have all been very concerned about your health. You have become a hero to all of our employees." Becker walked around his desk, reached for David's hand, and shook it hard. "Have a seat, I want to hear all about your adventure. Did you actually shoot that man? The stories in the paper made it sound like a scene from a movie. Sit down, relax, and enjoy your coffee." David could not have imagined a more cordial welcome from Stanley Becker. The legal people at headquarters must have scolded him severely. David made a mental note to send a letter to Kelly's lawyer friends in Chicago and explain how their one paragraph letter had turned his boss into a pussycat.

An hour later David emerged from Becker's office. He had intended to give Becker the short version of his experience in Dumont, but the boss kept interrupting with questions. When he wanted to be, Becker was a good listener, he could pick up on details that escaped most people's attention and ask pertinent questions, often times putting the speaker ill at ease. However the events that occurred in Dumont preventing David from returning to work as scheduled, were irrefutable.

At the end of David's story, Becker received a phone call and excused himself. He stood and thanked David for stopping by and filling him in on his unbelievable "cops and robbers tale." He advised David to ease back into his job. "Take a tour of the plant and get reacquainted with what has been going on since you left, and we will discuss our current plant status in detail during tomorrow's staff meeting. See you at eight sharp tomorrow morning, David. Nice to have you back. Oh, why don't you grab a copy of the minutes of last week's staff meeting from my secretary? And please close the door."

David exited the office and stood in front of Liz Bryson, Becker's secretary. "He was actually pleasant to me. I didn't expect it. What's going on, Liz?"

She looked around, and then said softly, almost a whisper, "He had Charlie Beritz for breakfast before you got here. Mr. Becker's appetite for raw meat was satisfied about seven this morning." she said, with a look of resignation on her heavily made up face. "There wasn't hardly anything left of poor old Charlie."

Charlie was the engineering manager. He and Becker had been at war with each other since Becker had been transferred here, as plant manager, from headquarters. Charlie had been with the company for twenty-two years and was set in his ways. He insisted on thoroughly testing any new product or modification to an old product before releasing it to manufacturing for production. He wanted all the bugs worked out and the manufacturing process qualified first, before production was ramped up.

As far as Becker was concerned, Charlie was costing the company its competitive edge because HIC could not meet the delivery times demanded by the customer. He wanted the design phase, qualification testing, manufacturing process development and quality plans all conceived, finalized, and implemented concurrently.

Charlie could not accept Becker's compressed time schedule for new products. David often wondered why Becker didn't fire Charlie and hire someone who would answer 'yes' to the boss. They never agreed on anything of substance. The staff meetings often ended up in shouting matches between Becker and his stubborn engineering manager.

David knew Becker was right about needing to speed up the new product development time, but Becker did not have the leadership skill to make it happen and Charlie would not move any faster if his life depended on it.

David had lunch with Manny and a couple of the people from marketing. The plant was behind schedule on two new product lines and the Bell contract was far from in the bag. David could see there was no light at the end of the tunnel. Becker had held several plant meetings during the last thirty days in which he cajoled all employees to work harder, faster, and spend less overtime doing it. He did not provide the means or a plan for achieving his goal. He merely was cracking the whip without the carrot. The audience's reception to his demands was less than cordial. A smattering of applause was all he got and that came from people who were not listening and were hoping for their shift to end.

David's decision to resign had been reinforced several times over. From his perspective he could see Becker was getting ready to take over the engineering department and was actively taking charge of the marketing department as well. The pressure from corporate headquarters was on. They wanted to boost profits, and no excuses were allowed. He knew the manufacturing department would be under scrutiny and tomorrow's staff meeting would be a killer, perhaps in more ways than one.

CHAPTER 17

On his way home after his first day back on the job, David stopped at a small beer bar, ordered a cold draft, and listened to bar talk about the Dodgers. On the overhead TV screen he could see they were playing the Giants in San Francisco, the score was 3-3 top of the ninth. A sea breeze was blowing in the front door and out the back, taking smoke and the stale beer smell with it.

David had spoken with the people in his department and most of the other managers and supervisors. He had a good idea of what action needed to be taken in order to get productivity back on track and he was prepared to offer his plan at the staff meeting tomorrow morning.

David decided he would layout his ideas in the staff meeting instead of discussing it first with Becker as protocol dedicated. Then he would wait for Becker's verbal attack. He knew Becker would shoot down his ideas because they were not his. The root cause of most of the plant's problems was caused by Becker's inept efforts to motivate the shop personnel, and his constant meddling in the internal affairs of departments he knew nothing about. David's plan for improving the plant's performance directly contradicted some of Becker's edicts.

After the meeting, David would walk into Becker's office, and present him an opportunity to get rid of the large thorn in his side. David was sure Becker would jump at the chance to rid himself of the criticism David had presented. At least that is what David envisioned would be Becker's response.

Two year's salary would be nice, including the year-end bonus. A lump sum payment of his retirement account and David would be willing to go quietly off into the sunset. Oh yes, and company-paid medical insurance.

He was daydreaming again. However, he had every reason to think he could pull it off. He would expose every two-bit idea Becker had come up with and counter it with a plan that had the backing of the other managers. He could count on all the managers except Shirley in the personnel office and the accounting manager. David knew accounting would side with whoever seemed to be winning the argument at the moment and side with them. Shirley had only a few months to go before she was sixty-five and he knew she was counting on a retirement check. She could not afford to take a chance in losing even part of it.

David tapped the answering machine "play" button as soon as he walked into his apartment door: "This is Sergeant Skinner, LAPD. You called and left a message to call you. I'll be in the office until eight or nine tonight if you want to get a hold of me." David mixed a light beam, Jim Beam Whiskey and Diet Coke, picked up the phone and walked out on the patio and sat in the shade of an overgrown acacia tree. From his patio, he could see the entrance to San Pedro harbor and the cargo ships heading out to sea and coming in from Asia. It was a quarter to seven when he dialed Sergeant Skinner's number.

A low, almost inaudible voice answered, "Hello this is Sergeant Skinner." There was a lot of background noise. The sergeant sounded like he was in a crowded bus station with a loud speaker in the background.

"This is David Jordan, I got your name and number from Sheriff Woodford in Rockford, Illinois. He told me you could help me find my Chevy convertible." David waited a long time before a reply came.

"Mr. Jordan, what I have to tell you, you are not gong to like, but it's the law and there isn't anything I or you can do about it. Your car was confiscated in the course of an illegal drug operation. It was found to contain twenty kilos of cocaine. That's a damn fortune to you or me.

"I know from talking to Sheriff Woodford you are not involved in the drug operation, but the car was. The manifest we found in the cab of the truck indicated the car had been sold to Harvey Driscoll. All the cars on the truck, what's its name, Central Illinois Trucking, that's it and the truck itself have been impounded as physical evidence. The driver has been arrested and charged with interstate transportation of a controlled substance with intention to distribute and possession of stolen property", Sergeant Skinner paused.

"Sergeant, tell me how to get my car back. Who do I have to see and where do I have to go?"

Sergeant Skinner continued as if David had not said a word. "The drug delivery was being made to a movie producer in Hollywood, a Mr. Harvey Driscoll. He has also been arrested and is in jail trying to raise five-hundred-thousand-dollar bail. His car collection, his condominium, and its contents are now government property. My advice to you is to get a lawyer and contact the district attorney's office. I can't do anything for you. Sorry Mr. Jordan, good-bye." The phone went silent.

David mixed another drink leaving out the Diet Coke. He was pissed. What kind of government would confiscate the property of an innocent citizen and not give it back? Now he supposed he would have to hire a lawyer to find the damn car and then wait for it to come up for auction and buy it back. What bullshit. He could prove he owned the car, if anybody had thought to ask, and it had been stolen. He had absolutely nothing to do with the illegal drugs and yet he was now a victim.

He thought about contacting Kelly's boss at the law firm, but decided against it. Carver would charge him for his services this time. David guessed he could end up paying more in legal fees than he paid for the Chevy in the first place.

After his second light beam, David cooled off. He certainly did not have any sympathy for people dealing in drugs and it was okay with him if they lost everything they owned. But why couldn't there be some way for innocent people to regain their property without having to pay for it again?

Maybe he should contact a local attorney and have him talk to the DA and see if there was a way to get the Chevy back. He called Kelly's number in Chicago and got her answering machine. He left a message asking her to check around and see if she could recommend a local attorney in Long Beach he could trust.

David deliberately pushed aside the problem he encountered with the LA police and began to think about trying to find Cindy. He reviewed his notes and journal entries. If he could get his hands on those four letters Bee had referred to when she was telling him about Cindy that would be a good place to start.

He found the phone number Bee had given him. She was going to stay with her cousin Jasper Nugget. David would have to wait until tomorrow to call because the area code was in South Carolina and three hours time difference. Another possibility he just now thought of, Cindy might have stayed in contact with a high-school chum. He could nose around Dumont and see if he could find a classmate or two. What David really wanted to do was go to Ireland and interview Kathryn and her parents.

Wouldn't that be great? Ireland. Maybe stop over in London, see all the places he had heard about. He had never traveled outside of the United States since coming back from Vietnam. He didn't even have a passport. He had plenty of frequent flyer miles racked up from traveling around the country on behalf of HIC. Tomorrow he would go to the post office, apply for a passport, and begin to do a little research on Ireland.

The more David thought about it the more the idea made sense. He could fly to Chicago, drive to Dumont and look for a classmate. Try to set up a meeting with Billy Sandoval. Continue on to South Carolina and talk to Bee. Fly on to Ireland to interview Kathryn's parents, and have fun in London, maybe with Kathryn. What a great idea.

The next morning David's alarm went off at five o'clock. He was up and dressed in his shorts, tee-shirt, and running shoes. He didn't want to start running yet because he didn't think his gut had fully healed, although he felt no pain. He went out the side door and began walking uphill. His intention was to walk briskly for about an hour and then get ready for a big day at the plant. As he walked, he mentally reviewed the five major points of his recovery plan he would present at the staff meeting. That was the easy part.

David walked into his office at 7 AM sharp. His secretary, Kay Drew, and a few of the other women in his department, had cleaned up his desk and hung a big "Welcome Back" banner across the back wall. They were glad to see him and were eager to help get him familiar with the latest rumors. David listened with interest as he was brought up to date on who was doing what to whom and who was left out in the cold. Office politics and the rumor mill were the highlight of Kay's day. Fortunately, she could also run the manufacturing office almost single-handedly. After his second cup of coffee, David was ready for the staff meeting.

David took a single sheet of paper with him as he entered the conference room. The other staff members were all seated and were busy organizing various pieces of paper and material they planned to present when requested to do so by His Highness, Stanley Becker. They were all there in their places, Shirley Chamberlain, Personnel Administrator, Christopher Lasarrus, Accounting Manager, Lloyd Driggs Q.A. Manager, Doris Weiss, Purchasing and Material Manager, Elizabeth Claypoole, Customer Service, Oscar Amorelli, Contracts and Sales Manager, and of course, Charlie Beritz, Engineering Manager who was looking none the worst for wear after his verbal battle with Becker yesterday.

David knew he could count on Becker being five or ten minutes late. As predicted, Becker entered the softly lit conference room in a rush apologizing for being late saying, "I couldn't get Wallace off the damn phone." He unloaded a ream of papers and his lap top computer on the table. He carried a laptop around because he was unable to make a decision without first pretending to review half a dozen files. He was referring to Amy Wallace. Amy worked for the Vice President of Finance for the entire corporation at South Bend and she was always working on some special assignment for him. Becker would use any excuse to look busy and important, and be late.

Suddenly, one of the rumors David's secretary had related to him this morning came to mind and it had to do with Becker. Apparently, someone had seen him with a woman, not his wife, preparing to go sailing at the Newport Beach Marina. They appeared to be very friendly as they huddled in the stern of his thirty-six foot Catalina sailboat. Could Becker's reference to Amy have anything to do with that? Becker was a womanizer and had been warned, two years ago by the Vice President of Human Resources, to keep his hands off women at the work place.

David had met Amy at a training session in South Bend last fall. She was a good-looking divorcee in her mid-thirties. She had blond hair, wore blouses that always seemed to have the top two buttons unbuttoned. She insisted on wearing young girls skirts displaying her well-shaped, long legs. If it was to her advantage, she did not hesitate to flirt with anyone. She was easy to remember.

Becker was talking with Shirley about something in a low voice, so David said, "Excuse me for a few minutes, will you please? I forgot something." He walked out of the conference room and picked up a phone from an empty desk down the hall. "Kay, this is David. Please do me a favor, call South Bend, and ask for Amy Wallace. Tell her I want to make a comparison of our manufacturing budget with the budgets of the other plants. Ask her to fax the information to me right away. If she is not in, find out where she is and get a telephone number and I will call her myself later. Thanks, Kay. Oh,… call me in the conference room after you have made the call." He hung up and walked back to the conference room.

If his hunch were right, he would have the hammer to ensure that his retirement negotiations with Becker would go smoothly.

CHAPTER 18

Stanley Becker settled comfortably into the leather armchair at the head of the conference table. The mirror like finish on the oval shaped table reflected the faces of the people seated around it. Track lighting could be adjusted to suit Becker's mood, from soft and seductive to a glaring spotlight on a victim or speaker. Hidden in the ceiling was a computerized multimedia projector. An old-fashioned direct transparency projector stood in the corner. Becker insisted everyone use the computer when presenting graphs, spreadsheets, and other visual data.

Becker sorted his papers, blew his nose, drank from a glass of ice water, and continued to waste everyone's time. "Okay, where do we start today? You all know our manufacturing manager is back with us. I am sure you read the newspaper articles plastered on the bulletin boards describing David's experience with the criminal element. I guess we don't have to waste time on that. Chris, why don't you go first and report on the July numbers so David can see where we are and what his department must do in August to make up for our losses in July," The finance manager was very animated and talked with his hands. The numbers were not good. The plant had not made its shipping quota for four months in a row. Normally David would be racking his brain trying to figure out how to make up for lost productivity, but not today. He sat back and smiled at Becker.

Next was Shirley with a brief account of personnel terminations and hiring. The purchasing manager droned on about the high cost of raw materials and how she beat the suppliers into submission and got the rock-bottom price. Elizabeth Claypoole from the customer support department reported the customer satisfaction ratings were the lowest in the corporation, but she made no reference to what caused the low ratings or what was being done to improve them. Oscar Morelli was out of town on a sales trip and no one had been appointed to sit in for him, which pissed Becker off and he made a big deal out of it.

"You all need to make sure you have a competent back-up in your department. I want them to sit in for you at these meetings and make decisions for you when you are out of the plant." He was looking at David. Manny had sat in for David at every meeting during David's absence. Manny was very happy to see David back so he could retreat to the relative safety of the shop.

Lloyd Driggs, Quality Assurance Manager, was one of the few people Becker listened to. Like David, Lloyd was a former Marine and was capable of standing his ground when required to do so. His report was brief. The quality of outgoing products was acceptable by any measure, if we could eliminate the customer complaints about late shipments our record would be a lot better. Driggs ran a tight ship, had a good crew working for him, and provided a good dose of common sense to the highly imaginative plans put forward by Becker.

Becker turned to Charlie Beritz and said, "Your next Mr. Engineer."

Charlie stood up, "You've taken over the engineering department Mr. Plant Manger, so why don't you tell the rest of the staff about it and let's get on with it."

Becker rolled his eyes up toward the ceiling and said, "I was hoping you would explain our plans for the future, Charlie. But if you're not willing to, I will." He spent the next half-hour detailing how he was going to reorganize the engineering department so it would be more efficient. The plan would leave Charlie isolated in a minor role as Engineering Documentation Manager. The plan would be implemented in September after extensive group meetings, furniture moving to accommodate the reorganization, and general disruption of the organization. The reorganization was nothing more than a Band-Aid, ignoring the real problem of obsolete thinking and outdated technology.

"David, I know this is your first full day back and I see you didn't bring any manufacturing reports with you. Is Manny going to come and report for manufacturing?"

"No, I will make my own report, thank you." David stood up and moved over to the podium in the corner of the room. He turned on the direct projector. He knew Becker hated it when people deliberately ignored his multimedia projector. David fiddled with the controls and focusing until it was just right.

"This will be short and sweet. A formal report detailing my plan for production improvement and future growth will follow, all of you will be copied." The telephone in the back of the conference room rang with a soft tone. Shirley moved to answer it. David paused because he knew it was for him. Shirley nodded toward David and held out the receiver.

"I hope it's important," Becker snapped.

It was Kay. She spoke quickly, in a low voice, knowing the information she conveyed was of more than a passing interest to David. "David, Amy is here, or rather in Newport Beach. She's staying at the Newporter on Jamboree Drive. Did I tell you Mrs. Becker is in Europe attending a seminar sponsored by the French Government and Aerospatiale?" She gave him the telephone number and room number where Amy was staying. He made note of it on the single piece of paper he carried into the conference room. "Thanks Kay." He hung up smiling.

"As I was saying," David slid the paper under the projector lens, "everyone will be given a copy of my plan, including Dustin Nagle." Nagle was Becker's boss back at corporate headquarters. He slid the paper up so the first paragraph was visible. The word Newporter, handwritten, was visible in the upper right had corner.

"Why are you bringing Dustin into this?" Becker was clearly irritated.

"Patience Stanley, you will see in just a minute."

David proceeded to launch into his plan. Speaking confidently, he described the problem areas and his solution for a remedy. Becker was red in the face after the first solution. He was writing ferociously on his note pad and at the same time opening and pounding, his notebook computer with his fingers.

The solutions David offered directly countered Becker's weak-kneed, crack-the-whip attempt to wring out a profit from the demoralized factory population. Becker had not allowed for market fluctuations or anticipated new product development by competitors.

The plan was straightforward and encompassed most of the thoughts the other staff members had discussed over the past few months. The most notable, and probably the most rewarding solution was for Becker to take a long vacation and when he returned to refrain from interfering with the day to day operation of the plant. If all five points were followed, the plant could be on schedule by the end of the year. David was confident of the results. Chris Lazarus was nodding in agreement as were the other staff members.

Becker stood up and shouted, "Jordan, I want to see you privately. The rest of you, get out." Becker waved his hand. The room emptied as if it were on fire.

In his loud and high pitched voice Becker sputtered, "What in the hell do you think you are doing? I am the plant manager and I will interfere with any department or any person

I think needs interfering with. And what is that phone number and room number all about?" He was now standing over David, who had remained seated. The veins on Becker's forehead stuck out and he was just short of physically grabbing David by the collar.

David hesitated, enjoying this moment. For once in his life he was in total control and he liked the feeling. "All right Becker, this is what I want." He pulled out a folded sheet of paper from his inner jacket pocket. "Early retirement. Effective immediately. My terms are listed here and they are not negotiable."

Becker looked at the paper shoved in front of him. "Two year's pay plus bonus? What the fuck are you talking about? Are you crazy? I can't do that, wouldn't do it even if I could! Who the fuck do you think you are, making demands on me?" His voice rose higher, as he spit out the words.

"I'm just a guy trying to make ends meet." David replied, "You, on the other hand, make a living off the backs of people who bust their butts and you take credit for it. You don't have a clue how to manage people. All you can do is kiss ass with Nagle and the other corporate big shots. But, that's beside the point.

"You can get me out of your hair by arranging for my retirement. I know it can be done because I've seen it done for others. Nice retirement packages are common as dirt for the corporate office and now, I want mine."

"Well, you're not going to get it. With the performance you put on this morning, how could you possibly think I would do anything out of the ordinary for you? In fact, you are terminated as of now. Whatever back pay you have coming, if any, is all you're going to get." Becker was yelling. He turned and started to walk out of the conference room.

David stood and said in a loud voice, "Amy said you two had a great time sailing last Sunday. Was your wife along?" David looked directly into the eyes of a cornered animal. Becker's face turned white.

"I know you've been fucking her. She's staying at the Newporter all week. Your wife is in Europe living high on your expense account. Very convenient. I will lay odds Amy is putting her hotel bill on her expense account also. Wouldn't her boss love to know what company business you two are engaged in?"

Becker sat down with a thud. He looked at David like he had just been confronted by Mike Wallace and a 60 Minutes TV camera in the parking lot.

David knew he had his man down and now he was going to rub his face in it. "You are a sorry sack of shit, Becker. I have a complete report detailing my solutions for improved plant performance ready to fax to Dustin Nagle. Attached to it, are the sailing activities you and Amy find so enjoyable. Your wife's on the distribution list. If you think I would hesitate for one fucking minute to expose you for the incompetent shithead you really are, you are greatly mistaken." David was standing up now and looking down on Becker. What he saw was revolting.

Becker's hands were shaking, he was short of breath, tears were forming in his eyes. He blew his nose and wiped his face with his embroidered handkerchief. "You're blackmailing me. You will never get away with it."

"On the contrary, you'll never get another job in this business after this news item hits the press, and neither will little Miss Amy Wallace. I'll have the pictures scanned onto the company web page."

"You have pictures?" Becker had aged ten years in the last few minutes. He sighed with resignation. David did not have pictures, he threw the bait out on impulse and hit pay dirt. "All right. All right." Becker, deflated like a kids balloon, offered, "You have to give me some time to work it out. It's not something I can do with a memo to the finance department."

"Amy works in the corporate finance department, why don't you ask her to help?" David asked quite innocently. "You have until Friday of this week to announce my retirement."

David stood up, reached for the list of demands Becker had crumpled, smoothed the paper out on the table, placed it back in Becker's hand, and walked out.

CHAPTER 19

It had been two months since David was the guest of honor at his retirement luncheon on September 10th. He missed his friends and the people he had worked with for many years, but now his life seemed to be starting over, full of hope and adventure. He did not regret for one minute bailing out of a company that had provided a paycheck all his adult life. Under the circumstances, he would have quit, or been fired, long before he would have been eligible for retirement.

David had succeeded in getting exactly what he wanted in terms of an early retirement package, including a nice medical insurance plan that would last indefinitely. Amy Wallace was instrumental in making all the arrangements. Apparently she had arranged this type of retirement package before and knew just how to go about it: getting signatures of approval without causing embarrassing questions. She knew how to avoid ugly legal hassles with other employees.

David spent the last few weeks getting ready for his trip to the East Coast and Ireland. He told Kelly he would be staying at her place before and after he visited Dumont. He would spend a few days with her and the twins before heading to South Carolina to visit Bee.

The arrangements with Rebecca and John Millard had been a little difficult. At first, David tried to call long distance. He asked the person who answered the telephone for Kathryn. After he identified himself, the person said in a voice that sounded rather irritated, "She is not taking calls presently," and hung up.

"Not taking calls." What the hell does that mean? Is she there or not? Or was she not taking calls from him? Or was she on the toilet? David puzzled over the response for a long time. After some thought, he decided to write a formal letter requesting an appointment with Mr. and Mrs. Millard. It seemed better to make this a business request rather than a personal visit. Kathryn had already made it known she did not want to pursue any relationship with him.

David sent the letter to Dublin, Ireland on September 7th, receipt requested. In the letter, David explained he was fascinated by the history of the old Chevy convertible, which was currently lost in the government's bureaucracy. Nevertheless, he felt there was a terrific human-interest story behind Cindy's disappearance. His intention was to write a book based on her disappearance and the life of Miss Margaret.

In the letter, he promised to use fictitious names and places in order not to cause any embarrassment to the family members. He provided his personal references and emphasized his past writing accomplishments, although technical in nature.

Three weeks later he received an answer: "Yes, we will agree to a meeting with you, Mr. Jordan. The subject of our discussion would be our family history, relating to my Aunt Margaret O'Ryan. However, you may want to save the expense of making a long journey by jotting down several questions and posting them. We would be most happy to respond in a timely manner. Signed, Mrs. John Millard." In the letter, she suggested the second week of November as being convenient. After November her and her husband would be traveling and unavailable.

"Well, in November, Mr. Jordan would be traveling," he hoped, in search of Cindy, David said to himself.

All the travel arrangements had been made and David was on his way. He felt like a new man. The old life was behind him and a new adventure was about to take place. Well, not all was peaches and cream. He received a letter from his wife's attorney, reminding him he owed half of his retirement settlement to Ellen. His opinion of the letter was demonstrated by the flushing sound it made going down the toilet.

He fantasized moving to Europe and out of reach of Ellen and her attorney. Mexico might be better, he always thought highly of the Mexicans and loved Mexican food and beer. He could write anywhere. He did call the person who figured his taxes every year and asked for information about moving his bank account offshore. He would do anything, short of going to jail, in order to keep Ellen's hands off his money.

The first stop was Chicago and a rental car. What a hassle. There had been heavy thunderstorms over Detroit and Cleveland. The Chicago O'Hare airport was stacked up for hours. Incoming planes couldn't land and outgoing planes couldn't take off. People were packed in the waiting rooms, bars, and restaurants.

David's plane had been two hours late when it landed and then another hour waiting for an open gate. The mad rush exiting the aircraft comprised mostly of angry, frustrated, salesmen trying desperately to get to the rental car desk so they could make their last sales call. David decided to forget about the car for now and take a taxi to Kelly's place and worry about finding a rental car tomorrow.

The twin boys, Danny and Steven, jumped into David's arms when he opened the door to the fourth floor apartment. "Grandpa, Grandpa, we've been waiting for you," they said in unison, "Your going to stay in our room, and you can read to us. We got a new video game you can play."

"Dad, I hoped you could make it here by dinner time, but I suspected the plane was delayed because of the weather. I saw the weather forecast on TV. I saved some lamb chops for you. You want me to warm them up?" Kelly was hugging her dad and talking so fast David didn't have time to say anything.

It felt good to be with family. He hadn't realized how much he missed the closeness.

Kelly warmed David's dinner. After he finished, Fred came in from a late dinner meeting with clients and he and Kelly quizzed David about how he had engineered his early retirement. The boys were playing Nintendo in their bedroom.

David took some pleasure in relating how he had maneuvered Becker into a position he could not wiggle out of. Of course, the Amy Wallace affair had a lot to do with the success of David's plan. As it turned out, Mrs. Becker had known for some time about Becker's extra-curricular activities. She sued for divorce from France and was taking Becker for everything he owned. David knew the feeling.

The next morning David called the rental car agency down the street from Kelly's apartment and by 10 AM he was on his way to Dumont. He had planned to call Sheriff Woodford when he got a chance. He might be able to introduce him to Cindy's classmates, if any were still around. It was mid-afternoon when David drove down the main street of the small town. He had checked into a nondescript motel on the north side of town. He could not bring himself to stay at the Holiday Inn. The memory was still fresh in his mind of the night he was shot.

The North Star Motel had nine rooms, all were available this night. The price was right and a person could walk from the motel to the main street business section. Actually, the place was very comfortable and clean. The woman who rented the room remembered his name from the TV news broadcast and asked him if he was back on police business or what?

"Please don't say anything to anyone else. I'm just here to tie up some loose ends, personal business. I would really appreciate it if you would keep my name out of any conversation you might have," David asked, with all the sincerity he could muster at the same time slipping an extra twenty-dollar bill across the counter.

After David settled into his room, he walked the four blocks to the city library. He approached a heavyset, matronly librarian and asked her to help him find the 1956 yearbook for Dumont High School.

There were only three other persons in the library besides David. He sat in a far corner and tried not to be noticed. He found Cindy's picture among the senior graduating class. The biography under the photo read, "Cynthia Louise O'Ryan, Nickname: Cindy, Ambition: To be really, really sophisticated, Says: Hello to all the guys. Member of the Dumont High School Science Club, Thespians, Cheerlead squad, Girls Club. Ambition: To be a movie star."

Following the vital statistics were a list of all the school activities Cindy had participated in and the offices she held. Judging by the number of times, her picture appeared in the yearbook, Cindy was a very popular girl. She managed to be photographed with various teachers and members of the football team. She was homecoming queen two years in a row. Cindy and a tall lanky boy named Ron Canfield were voted best personalities.

One item in the yearbook struck David as odd: Cindy was pictured with Mr. Carl Warren, the math instructor, as he presented her with a trophy for taking first place in the district science tournament. She had maintained a 4.0 grade point average in mathematics, according to the caption. In David's high school experience, only nerds excelled in mathematics. David read the caption under the photograph several times, letting that fact soak in. Bee never indicated Cindy had been a scholar. The image of the Judge's daughter certainly didn't project a scholarly young lady, quite the opposite in fact.

Cindy appeared to be involved with all kinds of outside activities, theater, cheerleader, girls club, dances, journalism, and boys. Boys would be crazy over a gorgeous young girl like Cindy.

David looked for Billy Sandoval's name among the seniors, but did not find it. He took the three proceeding years of high school annuals down from the shelf in the reference section of the library. He found Billy's name listed under the sophomore class picture of 1953. He was not listed in any of the following yearbooks. That meant Billy was one year ahead of Cindy, if he had stayed in school. According to Bee, "Miss Margaret said Billy quit school and went to work in the Ford garage."

David wrote numerous comments in his journal and photocopied the entire senior class of 1956: eighty-six classmates. After he returned the books to the reference section, he stopped by the librarian and asked if by chance she had lived in this town a long time. She was a woman of indeterminate age, somewhere over fifty years of age.

"All my life, why do you ask," she looked squarely at David in the same manner as a schoolteacher would look at a student who asked an imprudent question.

"I'm doing some research on a woman who lived here some time ago and I was wondering if you lived here at the same time?"

"I was in the fifth grade in 1956. That is the year you are interested in, isn't it?"

"The person I'm doing research on graduated in 1956. Do you happen know if anyone who graduated in that class still lives here?" David could see in her eyes her level of curiosity was raising.

"Well, if I knew the name of the person you were interested in, perhaps I could give you some useful information."

David decided to hold off, and not mention Cindy's name right away. "I've got an idea." He laid out the photocopies of the '56 senior class. "If you would look at these and tell me if any of these classmates are still in town that would be really helpful."

"Are you a police officer or FBI investigator? I really don't think I should be giving out information like that."

"No, I'm not a policeman or an FBI agent. I'm just trying to find someone and return something to them they lost many years ago. I'll tell you who it is, if you tell me if any of these people are still living here." David was trying to be pleasant as possible, even flirting, in hopes he would get her to cooperate.

After a lengthy pause, "All right. I guess I don't see any harm." The librarian started with the top of the alphabet. She related what she knew about the names she was familiar with, many names were skipped. David took notes, without comment, until she had finished all eighty-six names. Twelve were known to still be living in town or on farms near Dumont. All she said about Cindy O'Ryan, when she came to her picture was, she was very popular, "My brother dated her for a while. I remember because she came to the house several times. My father made remarks about 'that girl'. It seems she had a bad reputation. I think she left town right after high school."

"Thank you for your help, I'm David Jordan and I'm trying to locate the where bouts of Cindy O'Ryan.

"I knew who you were as soon as you walked in. You're the man everybody is talking about." the librarian displayed a knowing grin across her face.

"Well, so much for privacy," David was resigned to the fact that he would have to stop playing amateur detective and be upfront with the librarian and other locals in town. He told her he had found personal items in the Chevy that were valuable and wanted to return them.

"That's the gentlemanly thing to do. What kind of items are you talking about?"

David knew that what ever he said would be spread all over town by the time he returned to his motel room. "Their were personal items in the car that I don't want to talk about in public. Being a woman, I'm sure you understand."

She offered that her brother lived in Chicago and maybe he would agree to talk to David. "I can't give you his phone number, but I will call him and ask if he is willing to talk about Cindy. You can stop by tomorrow and I'll let you know what he said."

David drove out to Irv's Diner and had a couple of drinks at the bar before ordering dinner. Eating steak in the bar allowed him to watch Monday night football.

After dinner, he took a cup of coffee out on to the deck overlooking the river running behind Irv's. The night was cool. The trees were showing their fall colors. David's thoughts were on the dinner he and Kathryn had enjoyed at this restaurant a few months ago. He wondered if Kathryn was still engaged. Somehow, he knew she had not married. Maybe wishful thinking on his part, but David liked to think he could sense she was waiting for him to save her from a loveless involvement. A Prince Charming that's what he wanted to be. Farfetched, yes, but how would he ever know unless he tried? He would follow his plan and take what action was necessary or settle for what was possible.

Kathryn's perfume, the color of her hair, the warmth of her touch, her lips, were vivid in David's memory. It was like she was here, standing next to him. He could feel her presence. How could a human being feel such strong emotions after such a short meeting? David did not understand how or why, Kathryn had captured his heart and soul. All he could do was accept reality. And the reality was, he was in love. He had to carry out his plan regardless of how long the odds were against him.

The weatherman had predicted heavy rain and for a while it looked like he was going to be wrong, but now a steady drizzle turned into a cold hard November rain. Back at the motel, he turned up the thermostat, poured a little Jim Beam in a glass with some ice, and looked up the twelve names he got from the librarian. The local phone book encompassed six small towns within a fifteen-mile radius. He wrote the telephone numbers and addresses in his journal. There were eight boys and four girls on the list. The librarian even knew the married names of the women. In the morning, he would start interviewing Cindy's classmates.

CHAPTER 20

The next three days were spent talking in person and on the telephone to the twelve people the librarian had identified for him. They all remembered Cindy except one man who said his memory was getting so short he was having trouble remembering what happened yesterday.

Cindy's personality was emerging much the way David had imagined it would from what Bee had told him. She was very attractive, mature for her age, as some of the women put it. The men were more frank, "physically mature my ass, she was really stacked, like one of those pinup pictures." One of the boys claimed to have dated Cindy and said she was very aggressive sexually. He claimed she practically raped him one night after a football game. He said he avoided her afterward because he just couldn't handle that much girl.

One member of the football team said she was the hottest thing to ever hit Dumont. He had sex with her as early as their freshman year. He claimed she probably did the whole football team at one time or another. It was hard for David to separate fact from fiction. Much of what the men said sounded like teenage boasting.

A woman named Joan said she had been a cheerleader with Cindy. They were friends since grade school. "Cindy was always flirting with the boys, but I don't think she ever slept with any of them as far as I knew. She never said she did. Cindy was smart, but hardly ever studied and she still got very good grades. She could do complicated math problems in her head."

Another woman said she was a friend of Cindy's until she stole her boyfriend away in their junior year. They never spoke again. Cindy never apologized. This classmate said that

Cindy spent a lot of time with the math teacher, Mr. Warren. She took all of his classes and even went to his house for special instruction? This ex-classmate suggested there were more than math instructions going on.

"You could just tell there was something special between them. She would stay after class just to ask questions that I knew she knew the answer to. She just wanted to be near Mr. Warren. He was kind of cute. But, jezzes, he was married and his wife had a new baby."

The most interesting information came from a man who now ran the local grocery store. His name was Donald (Danny) Parker. Danny was a math student in the same class as Cindy in 1956. According to Danny, Cindy could solve the most difficult problems. She really was a math genius in his mind. She also was teachers pet."

"What ever happen to Mr. Warren. Has he retried? Does he still live in the area?"

"Carl Warren left town the summer after we graduated. I really don't know what happened to him. We kind of thought something was going on between those two, you know what I mean, but we never had actual proof. There was some gossip about why he left town, especially since it was not to long after Cindy left. You know," Danny hesitated for a moment trying to bring back memories, "now that I think about it, she was fooling around with some kid who had dropped out of school. I don't remember who he was, he was an outsider. Her leaving, sudden like, seemed funny. The story went around that her father took her back east to get her away from… Billy, yeah that was his name Billy something or other. Some people said she was pregnant. She never came back to Dumont as far as I know. Then I think her father, the Judge, died after she left. No, that is not right. He was Lieutenant Governor, he died in the early sixties. There was something funny about that too, but I can't remember what it was."

David sat in his motel room writing in his journal. He tried putting together all the bits and pieces of information about Cindy he had been given. He felt like a police artist trying to make a sketch of a suspect from eyewitness accounts. The picture was beginning to become clear, but major pieces were still missing. Bee said Cindy was pregnant, but why would she leave town and never come back. It could be that she felt ashamed and never wanted to face family and friends. But on the other hand, this was her home, her mother and father lived here, her boyfriend was here. If she was pregnant why didn't she stay with the boy friend? There had to be more to this story.

David called Sheriff Woodford early in the afternoon and made plans for lunch on Friday. He was looking forward to seeing the sheriff and being brought up to date on the trials of Creighton and Bidwell. What he really wanted to do was arrange to see Billy Sandoval. He wondered what the sheriff would say about visiting someone who had tried to kill him.

"You want to do what?" The sheriff could be heard clear across the parking lot. "I don't think that's a good idea," the sheriff said, with a mouth full of Dairy Queen cheeseburger. The two men had met in the parking lot and decided to eat outside on the metal tables under the patio cover. "You can try to see him in the county jail, but it's up to him if he will allow the visit. His lawyer may not allow it. We cannot force him to confront you. Exactly what is it you plan on doing or saying? His trial has been postponed until after the first of the year. You'll have a chance to confront him in the courtroom."

"I don't want to confront him, I just want to talk to him about his past life with Cindy O'Ryan. I know it may seem strange to you, but I don't feel any real animosity toward him. I know he tried to kill me, and what he did caused me a lot of pain, but I have bigger goals in life than wasting time trying to extort some kind of revenge from a small-time criminal. He has enough trouble with the courts. They'll inflict more pain on him than I could get away with."

"Did you ever find your Chevy? Was that L.A. cop any help?" Woodford asked

"Not exactly. I hired a lawyer out in Long Beach to recover it for me. But you know how bureaucracies work. The LA police confiscated all the cars, and the truck they were on. They claimed the guy in Hollywood owned them. You know the guy, the one who was taking delivery of the drugs. Well anyway, by the time my lawyer got involved, the car was not where it was supposed to be. The cops have a huge impound lot somewhere out in Van Nuys. According to my lawyer, cars disappear out of there just as fast as they come in. He was not impressed with the security there.

"He did manage to find some paperwork indicating it had been shipped to a staging area near the Burbank airport. Evidently, that's where they auction all the cars and personal property collected as a result of drug arrests. The car was not there or it could not be found among the thousands of cars on the lot.

"By this time, my lawyer was into me for twelve hundred dollars, so I told him to stop. It was just not worth the effort and there was no guarantee of success. I'll find another '56 some day when I'm ready for it." David looked off into space for a few seconds. He did not let on how much he wanted that particular '56 Chevy.

"What's happening to your detectives? When is their trial coming up?" David asked.

"They both are out on their own recognizance. The judge felt they were trustworthy. Can you beat that? No priors. They're rotten cops and the judge says, 'We're going to trust you to stay in the county.' They didn't even have to post bail. The system sucks. Anyway, we keep an eye on them both, but it's hard, we don't have enough people to do our job without having to tail those two creeps every day." David could tell Woodford was getting worked up about the situation. He felt a little uneasiness in his stomach. He had not counted on those two being out on the street. "What about Sandoval? They didn't let him out, did they?"

"God no. He won't see the light of day ever. His lawyer can't even get him to discuss his case. I guess he thinks it's hopeless and he's resigned to spending his last days in jail. Chances are he won't see you either, David." The sheriff got up and put on his hat, cinched up his gun belt, "David, I'll pass the word down at the county jail, you want to see Sandoval, but don't be surprised if he refuses.

"Oh, I almost forgot. Word around town is the new owner of the O'Ryan house is coming in from Australia next week to sign the final papers. One of the ladies over at the bank told me about it. She works in the escrow section and they have been handling all the paper work."

David immediately thought of the affair Margaret had with the Australian aviator in Europe. "Did she give you a name?"

"No. She couldn't tell me, or wouldn't tell me is more like it. Something about bank confidentiality rules. Banks on both sides of the Pacific are handling the transaction. After the deal is recorded I'll find out a name and let you know.

"So long David, I'll be in touch when we start trial." Woodford got in his patrol car, called into his dispatcher, and wheeled out of the parking lot.

David checked out of the North Star Motel and drove the forty miles to Rockford and the county jail. All the while he was driving, he was thinking of an opening line to begin a conversation with Billy. Everything he thought of sounded theatrical, phony or both. In the end, he figured he would say whatever came to him and improvise.

The county jail was an old brick building dating back to pre W.W.I. Armed guards were prominent all over the place. There was no pretense to make the building feel warm and pleasant. The entrance was crowded with people coming and going. Visiting hours were 2 to 4 PM.

A black female clerk behind the bulletproof glass said, without looking up, "Name please?"

David stood motionless for a moment, not knowing how to respond, "Whose name do you want? Mine or the person I want to visit?"

The woman looked up from her computer terminal and looked at David as if he had something hanging out of his nose. "If you had read the goddamn sign you would know it's the prisoner's name I want. And then I want your name and identification and thumbprint," She was nodding in the direction of a sign hanging from the ceiling listing the rules for visitors.

Responding in kind, to a surly clerk in police uniform, probably was not the wise thing to do David decided. So he answered as polite as possible. "I want to see William Sandoval and my name is David Jordan." David pushed his driver's licensee into the sliding drawer under the thick glass. The woman behind the glass keyed the information into the computer. She slid out a form with a place to make a thumbprint. David complied without comment.

"Go sit down. We will call you when you can go into the visitation room."

David looked around for the men's room. He found one and pushed open the swinging door. The stench was overwhelming. Two of the four stalls were taped closed, the other two must have contained decomposed dead animals, judging buy the smell. The urinals were gross, one about to overflow. Two characters standing next to the only window were watching David. He kept an eye on the two figures huddled close together, they kept staring at him.

"It's hard to piss when someone is watching," David said in the direction of the two.

"Hellfire, you ain't got nothing I want to see," said one of the men as he dropped a cigarette butt and stomped on it. They both turned their backs to David and began talking about how fucked up somebody named Jesse was. David didn't bother to wash, he wanted out of there fast.

The reception room was crowded and noisy with kids running around, babies crying, a TV set in the corner tuned in to a soap opera. It was thirty minutes before his name was called and he hurried over to the officer standing next to the visitation door. He passed through the metal detector without setting it off. "Booth number fourteen," the guard said as he opened the door for David to enter.

The visitation room consisted of a long row of booths separated by six-foot tall partitions. The visitors, two at a time, could sit side by side and talk to the prisoner via telephone. They were separated by bulletproof glass. David's palms were sweaty and he felt very uneasy. He was grateful for the protection offered by the glass and armed guards.

David walked down the line of partitioned booths, his stomach churning. Not knowing what to expect, he had to force his legs to move. At number fourteen, sat Mr. William Sandoval. David felt the urge to turn and run, but he held firm. He pulled a chair out and sat down. Billy did not look like a killer. In fact, despite the yellow jailhouse jumpsuit he was wearing, he looked like a businessperson. The lines on his face reveled his sixty-one years. His hair, mostly gray, was combed straight back and he was clean-shaven. David could tell Billy was tall and slender even though he was sitting with his hands on his knees chained together. He watched David with dark eyes, never once looking away. They both reached for their headsets at the same time.

"You are the last person I would expect to come here," Billy said. His voice was crisp with no noticeable accent or emotion. "What is it you want? I'm pretty busy these days."

"I have several questions I want to ask, if it's not too much trouble." David swallowed, "First, why did you take the old Chevy from Ballantyne's storage yard?"

"Is that what's on your mind?" Billy laughed and said with a sarcastic little grin on his face, "My friend on the West Coast collects cars, old cars, I wanted to give it to him for a birthday gift." He looked around to see if anyone was listening. The armed guard standing about ten feet directly behind Billy seemed to be in a trance.

David was feeling more at ease, because it was clear Billy Sandoval was just a man and not anybody special, maybe even a little stupid considering he had spent a good portion of his life in prison. "Did you know who the car belonged to when it was new?" he asked, moving a little closer to the window.

"I have no clue. Does it matter?" Billy was staring at David not offering one clue that he was the same man the gardener had seen snooping around O'Ryan's place. David was positive Billy knew exactly where the car came from and who it belonged to.

"It belonged to Cindy O'Ryan. She put a few hundred miles on it before her father, Judge O'Ryan, locked it up in the garage. Did you look in the trunk when it was at Ballantyne's?"

Billy sat still, hardly breathing. Finally, in a lowered voice, "No, I didn't look in the trunk. What was in there?" He had lost his menacing look as he searched David's face. David sensed Billy was apprehensive to hear what he had found inside the trunk. He had caught Billy completely off guard. Holding up the small envelope and card next to the glass Billy's eye focused on the words. The muscles in his temple tighten and his eyes narrowed. He read the card and sat back as if slapped. David could swear he saw what little color there was drain from Billy's face. He turned away, saying nothing. After a few seconds he turned back staring at David, "What is it you really want?"

"I know you and Cindy were boyfriend and girlfriend back in 1956. I know she was planning to runaway with you after graduation, but something happened preventing that. I want to find out what that was and I want to find Cindy."

He explained his plan to write a book based on Cindy's life, if he could find her. David was sure the concept of being a character in a book never really sunk into Billy's head. He never acknowledged it. He seemed almost dazed by the fact someone had dug up the past he had buried in his mind a long time ago. After a long silence, Bill Sandoval began talking, and didn't shut up until the guard told David he had to leave because visiting hours were over.

It seemed to David, that Billy was glad for the opportunity to tell his story to someone who would appreciate how he had once tried to make a better life for himself. The most amazing thing about the whole interview with Billy was the total lack of animosity between them. Billy told a story David had no trouble believing because it fit in with the rest of the information he had gathered. After the visit, he walked out to his car and sat for over an hour recording Billy's recollections in his journal.

David knew a great deal of what Billy told him already, but it was good to have it confirmed by the party involved. He could hear Billy's voice as he wrote the words.

"She was the best thing that ever happened to me," his face brightened noticeably when he mentioned her name. "I knew Judge O'Ryan considered me dirt under his feet. Cindy and I talked about it all the time. The Judge was heavy into politics and didn't want Cindy doing anything that would cause a scandal. The Judge tried everything to get Cindy to stop seeing me. He even bought her a new car, the convertible, as a bribe to stop seeing me. Cindy and I were in love. It was the real thing. I believed her when she said she would never let me go.

"After the Judge bought the convertible, we got together on a regular basis. My mother had a cousin who was a teacher at the high school, he helped us get together after school and sometimes in the evenings. He taught math and was helping Cindy with her schoolwork. We would meet at his place."

"Would his name be Warren?"

"Yeah, how did you know?"

David told Billy about the math contest and Cindy's four point grade point average in math.

"I knew she was smart, but she never acted like it." Billy was quite emphatic "We were in love, but I never touched her. I respected her too much to risk it. We were saving that for when we could be together for good."

Billy's voice sounded hopeful when he started talking about the planned trip to California. "We were going to drive to the West Coast. Cindy always wanted to see the ocean, I knew she really wanted to get into movies. I wanted to work behind the camera. I read every book I could get my hands on about photography. We even made some home movies." Billy stopped reminiscing for a moment and sat straight up. "Did you find the film in Cindy's car?"

"Yes, I saw some rolls of film in there when I found the card. But the car is gone now I have no idea where it is." He told Billy how the L.A. police had confiscated the car.

"That figures, the fucking cops are stupid. You can't trust 'em."

"Tell me what happened that night Billy. I know you two were planning on leaving for California."

"I don't know! I never heard from her or knew where she went. I was pretty upset about it. I had saved some money from working in the garage and we planned to elope right after graduation night. I sent her flowers with a card, that card, telling her where to meet me. Later in the evening, I drove down the alley in back of her place and put my suitcase in her car, hers was already there. So I knew she was keeping her promise to go with me. I planned to meet her at the old Cooper place where we spent a lot of our time together. We had made great plans, we were going to Hollywood." Billy actually looked happy, his face was glowing and his hands emphasized his words.

"On graduation night, I waited in the dark at the Cooper place until 6 AM. Cindy never showed up." He looked away for a few moments, "Finally, I couldn't stand it any longer, I went back into town, to the O'Ryan's and knocked on the door. Mrs. O'Ryan came out and told me Cindy was gone and wouldn't be back. I had talked to Mrs. O'Ryan a couple of times in the past, but she had changed. She seemed cold and afraid to talk to me. She shut the door in my face."

When Billy was telling this part of the story, David could see the hurt in his eyes. Mrs. O'Ryan told him the Judge took Cindy to Chicago where they would catch a train for New York. The Judge had arranged with his brother for Cindy to stay and go on to college. Mrs. O'Ryan would not give out any address or names. Instead, she insisted Billy forget Cindy and go on with his life.

"Some of the rumors around town were that she was pregnant and her father took her to New York to have the baby. But I knew that was a lie. She couldn't have been pregnant. I knew Cindy well enough to know, that regardless of what the Judge wanted her to do, she was her own person and if she wanted to come back to Dumont or contact me she would have, but she never did." There was hurt and anger in Billy's eyes when he repeated, "She never did call, or write, or come back for me." A look of despair overcame Billy. "I know her dream in life was to be a movie actress, but I guess she never made it, I never saw her in any."

The weeks, months, and finally years that followed were hard for Billy. He worked but could not get ahead. He got caught stealing money from his boss and was fired. It was downhill from then on, in and out of jail, a series of low paying jobs, never married, alcoholic, dealing drugs, and hardened by life in the penitentiary.

A couple of years ago a detective from the sheriff's office started muscling in on Adam Barnet and Jimmy Ballantyne's drug transportation business. David was surprised

Billy brought up the subject of the Sheriff's detective without being asked about it. Perhaps Billy sensed this would be the only way for him to get his side of the story out into public knowledge.

Whenever the drug transportation business needed a little muscle to help things along, or needed protection, they called Bidwell. He in turn would call Billy. That's how Billy got his money, doing Bidwell's "security" work. The night of the murder at the wrecking yard was bad news from the start.

"The transport truck was ahead of schedule, Jim Ballantyne didn't have the cars ready. Barnet had the drugs in his truck and had to get rid of them. Everything was going wrong. They got in an argument about which car to take and that's when Bidwell called me to go out there and get those two assholes moving. I had been drinking all day and I wasn't in the mood to take any crap from those two punks.

"I delivered Bidwell message with a little extra emphasis and Jim got pissed. Jim told me to get the fuck off his property. I never did like him. He was nothing more than a smart-ass junk man, so I did what I felt I had to do to shut him up. It was a stupid move, shooting Jim, with his wife and kid in the house.

"I threatened to kill the woman's kid if she talked and gave the cops our names." Billy looked down at his hands, "I wouldn't have." But I knew she would talk eventually. Hell, Jim's wife knew Barnet and me, we had been out there a bunch of times. My life isn't worth much, so I couldn't have cared less. I never tried to run, I had no place to go. My life was pretty well fucked up a long time ago. I knew it was over.

"Some how Barnet and me finished loading the dope in the old Chevy and pulled it up an on the Jim's service truck. All the while Jim's wife was hollering out of control. I thought

Barnet was going to whack her. Barnet had a short fuse and you never knew when he was going to go off."

David thought to himself, "It must have been Jim Ballantyne's wife, that called me in the motel. She warned me about not going to the sheriff's office for help. She knew her husband and Barnet were working with someone in the Sheriffs department."

He had to ask Billy the question that had puzzled him from the night he was shot. "Why was I considered a threat to you or Bidwell. I was merely a bystander in this whole mess. Killing me would not have helped either one of you."

Billy did not acknowledge David's question. Instead, he continued to tell his story in a matter of fact manner. "I really don't know what Bidwell's motives were. He told me what he wanted and I knew unless I did what he said, he would find a way to put me back in prison. I really could not go back, I can't, and I won't. I will stall and use the system to stay in county jail for as long as I can. Maybe something will come up and help me, but I am not going back to Joliet. It's' a hellhole."

"Bidwell threatened to have me picked up on parole violation unless I took you out of the picture. If I didn't do what he said, I'm sure he would set me up for a fall. He could fake a confrontation, kill me, and claim self-defense. Plant some dope and a gun on me, no problem, I'm gone.

"He gave me your room number. Besides, you wasted Adam and our nice little business was suddenly gone. Nothing personal." There was almost a hint of a smile across Billy's lips.

The guard that had been daydreaming suddenly came to life and moved forward. "Come on Sandoval. Its time to go back home."

Billy stood, rattling the leg irons. He had a melancholy look on his face as he turned to leave, then he looked directly at David and said, "If Cindy and I had gotten together, I know we could have had a good thing going. I could have had a life, but for whatever reason she chose not to come back. If you find her, tell her I waited a fucking lifetime."

CHAPTER 21

David had one more person to interview regarding Cindy O'Ryan before he could fly to South Carolina and visit Bee Canady. Eric Mann was the brother of the librarian who had been so helpful to David in Dumont. She had arranged for her brother to talk to David at his home, a single-family, brick, tract home in Oak Lawn. A Eric had retired from teaching school after thirty-two years.

"I really appreciate you taking the time to see me." David began the conversation. Both men were seated in the small living room. Eric's wife was serving coffee. David wished he could get her out of the room so Eric would be a little more open with his answers. "As I told you on the phone I'm interested in finding out the history of Cindy O'Ryan. I'm trying to get background material for a book I'm writing. Your sister told me you had dated her in high school, so I thought you might be able to shed some light on why she disappeared right after high school."

"Sure, I dated her a few times, but that was all. We never went steady or anything. I believe it was in the summertime, probably before our junior year. We went to a few movies together. We double-dated with my buddy and his girl. Nothing special. Just the usual kid stuff." Eric shrugged.

Mrs. Mann butted in, "I don't remember you saying anything about her before." Her voice was sweet but her look said something else. Silently, she seemed to be saying, "Eric, I can tell when you're not being truthful, you know."

Eric continued with a description of the old drive-in theater in the neighboring town the kids used to congregate at. "Cindy always wanted to go to the movies. She knew all of them, which actor or actress starred in them, the rumors from Hollywood, things like that. She was pretty much a regular girl." He went on to explain Cindy was very popular and it seemed like she did not have much parental supervision. Her dad was a big-shot politician, never home, and her mother was a schoolteacher and local socialite.

David could see he was not going to get any useful information from Eric with his wife sitting there, so he decided to cut this conversation short. "Did you ever hear anything about Cindy that would cause her to leave town suddenly after graduation? There was some speculation about her being involved with one of the school teachers and maybe being pregnant."

Eric had a pained look on his face for only a second and then said, "No, I don't remember anything like that. I hardly talked to her except for the few times we dated that summer. Sorry I can't be more help."

David thanked them both and began to leave. Eric moved to walk him to his car, Mrs. Mann started to tag along. Just then, a dog started barking loudly in the back yard. Eric turned and said sharply, "Go shut the mutt up before the neighbors complain again." He turned and walked out the door with David. "That damn dog of hers drives me and the neighbors crazy.

"Look, I couldn't say much with my wife sitting there, but Cindy was one hell of a girl. She had a reputation for being easy, I am sure you know what I mean. One night my buddy and I took her out to an old farm outside of town. We had a few beers and she got real friendly. We both screwed her. I remember it well because it was my first time. It was not her first time.

"Her reputation was well known around town and my parents objected to me dating her. She sure was good looking and smart. I didn't have much to do with her after that. I don't know anything about her being pregnant. Wouldn't surprise me though. We didn't use any rubbers and she didn't object."

Eric's wife came hurriedly out the front door clutching a shawl around her shoulders and stood along side her husband. "Do you have any idea where she disappeared to?" Eric was speaking to David. Mrs. Mann seemed eager to find out more about this previously unknown girlfriend of her husbands.

"No, so far I have not been able to track her down."

"Will you send us a copy of your book when it's published?" Mrs. Mann said smiling.

"Of course, I'll let you know when it gets published."

David drove off smiling to himself, Eric will have some explaining to do before that household gets back to normal. David wondered why a girl with all the talent and good looks would be such an easy lay. What was it that caused her to screw every boy she came in contact with? Boys tend to exaggerate their sexual conquests, but even considering that, it still put Cindy on her back more often than not.

Cindy's math teacher seemed like a good prospect for further investigation. David had tried to find out where he moved after he left Dumont by asking various people around town, including the librarian, who searched the public records but found nothing. After all, it was over forty years ago, what did he expect? The original high school building had been torn down and rebuilt. David decided he would write a letter to the high school administration office and ask if the teacher's records from 1956 still existed. If so, he wanted to know where Carl Warren moved.

He called Bee and told her he would fly down to South Carolina on an early morning flight.

"Where is Easley, South Carolina? I don't think I ever heard of it."

"We live not far from Easley, I'll you tell how to get here. It's near Greenville. Just take Highway 123 east to Easley. We is about ten miles outside the town of Easley next to a country church." She gave directions using landmarks that sounded easy enough to follow.

"How is the weather down there Bee?" David was getting tired of the Midwest fall weather. He was used to Southern California and, it's almost, perfect climate.

"It's okay. Some rain now and then. You can put away your overcoat, you won't need it down here. It's about eighty degrees right now." Bee knew exactly what the November weather was like in Dumont. Warm weather was music to David's ears.

He flew to Greenville after changing planes in Atlanta, rented a car and drove the twenty miles or so to Easley. Bee was living with her cousin, Jasper Nugget, in a house furnished by the church. He was anxious to see Bee again. She was a good-hearted woman and the source of much of the information that David needed.

Bee greeted Him with open arms. "Aren't you a sight for these old eyes? Come on in and make yourself comfortable. Jasper, I want you to meet David Jordan, he's the fella I've been talking about." Jasper was a big man. Over six-feet tall and close to three hundred pounds, David could imagine him at the pulpit, very impressive. His voice carried across the street, even when he talked in a normal tone of voice. He was about the same age as Bee, somewhere in his late fifties or early sixties.

They sat down in what had been the living room, but now the walls were covered with bookshelves and family pictures. This was the preacher's office. They settled into a large overstuffed sofa and easy chair placed in the center of the room. Jasper was asking about the flight and making small talk. David was wondering if there was a Mrs. Nugget. Bee brought in some iced tea.

"Now, you got to tell me all about that shooting out at the Barnet farm and how you got shot too." Bee threw up her hands, "Lord have mercy. You looks good, everything must have healed up good. How do you feel? They said you was in critical condition. You looks fine now." Bee was sitting across from him with an expectant look on her broad face.

"I'm fine now. All systems go."

As he described the events leading up to the night he got shot. David realized he was going to have to tell Bee and her cousin all the details of his exploits or he would never get Bee to discuss Cindy. It was getting late in the afternoon when Bee said she was going to start supper and they could all move into the kitchen where David could carry on with his story. "By the way, David, you are staying here tonight. I put clean sheets on the bed out on the sleeping porch."

David told his story, Bee cooked and Jasper listened. The dinner was a good solid, meat, and potato dinner with homegrown vegetables. Afterwards, Jasper led David outside to show him the remains of his vegetable garden. Jasper was an expert gardener, raising more vegetables than he and Bee could possibly consume. "What do you do with all the extra veggies? Do you sell them locally?" asked David.

"Oh no, I trade some to the church women in return for canned goods, fruit, and other things I need." Jasper's smiling emphasized "other things." "Sometimes, someone will butcher a hog or a cow and bring some packaged meat over in return for a flat of tomatoes or bunches of carrots or something else eatable. Of course, we always get plenty of chicken in trade. God has been good to me, I got everything I need right here on this patch of ground.

"It was a blessing when Bee came to stay here. My wife Emma passed away two years ago, the church women took good care of me, yes sir, but I like having someone around to talk to when I feels like company." He smiled and added with a wink, "She sure know how to cook and take care of a man, yes sir."

David felt like he did not need any more information than what Jasper just revealed, regarding this relationship, but he couldn't help asking one question, "Jasper, you wouldn't have a little drink of something around here would you? I always like a little after-dinner drink, just to take the edge off."

A slight smile curled on the very ends of Jasper's lips. "Come over to the garage and let me show you my old car. Bee said you was a car collector or collector of antiques." The two walked around the back of the house and went inside an old barn that now housed three cars. The car nearest the double doors was a, 1968 Buick four-door boat. "This is my every day car. Had her since new. My wife loved this car, she drove it until she got sick. This is my work truck." Pointing to a serviceable 1968 Ford pickup.

"And this one belonged to my granddaddy. He bought it new and cared for it like a baby." They stood looking at the 1936 Chrysler Airflow. It looked like it did the day it came off the assembly line. A look in the window told a little different story. The upholstery was worn and the old shatterproof windows were showing white streaks. On closer inspection, David could see the dark green paint was wearing through, probably from Jasper's polishing. "I don't drive it much, just in parades and such. My granddad stopped driving it during the war because of the gas shortage. It just sat in this old barn for years until I decided to get her running again. She purrs like a kitten now."

They had walked around to the rear of the Chrysler. David remembered reading about this car in a magazine a long time ago. It was an unsuccessful attempt by the Chrysler Corporation to make an aerodynamic car body during the thirties. It was not a big seller. It was ugly, but it did catch people's attention.

Jasper opened the trunk of the Chrysler, moved a blanket, and revealed two unlabeled whiskey bottles. He picked up one of the bottles, unscrewed the cap, and passed the bottle to David. "Help yourself. I likes a little nip myself now and then. All things in moderation. That's my philosophy." Jasper winked and flashed a broad toothy grin.

David was almost sorry he had brought the subject up. It was comforting to know the preacher was tolerant, but he had drunk moonshine before and the memory stayed with him for a long time. He took a little swig, and lowered the bottle while the nearly clear liquid did what it was supposed to do.

"Not bad," he took full measure, before returning the bottle to Jasper. Jasper gulped twice and sighed with relief. He returned the bottle to its place next to its mate and said, "Don't you say anything to Bee, you understand. She is a righteous women and I don't need any unpleasantness in my house." Jasper was serious. David put his finger to his lips and wondered to himself if Bee had her own stash of Wild Turkey somewhere. His stomach had a nice warm, glowing feeling that comes with drinking smooth whiskey.

Back in the house, Bee had coffee, cake, and ice cream on the kitchen table. "You showed David your car collection Jasper."

"Yes'em, sure did."

"The old Chrysler is a beauty. If you are ever in a mood to sell it, let me know," David blurted out not thinking. *What the hell would I do if Jasper offered to sell it?*

"It's already spoken for, one of my boys will get her when I'm gone. The oldest boy lives just down the road. He likes cars and I know he would take care of it." Jasper had taken a large piece of cake and was scooping out some ice cream from a gallon container. "You want some, David?"

"No thanks, coffee is fine. Bee, I want to ask you some questions about Cindy and Miss Margaret. Do you mind?"

"No, not at all. I know'd that's what you came down here for," Bee said as she sat down and poured David's coffee.

David explained his desire to write a book about Cindy and the old Chevy. He really wanted to find Cindy, if she was still alive. He told Bee how he had interviewed Cindy's old high school classmates just last week. He didn't mention Cindy's apparent loose morals.

"One thing you mentioned, Bee, was the four letters Margaret received from Cindy. Do you have any idea where they are?" David was hoping Bee would have a good answer for him on this question. The postmark on those letters would be a clue he could use in locating Cindy.

"Miss Margaret kept them under lock and key in a little strongbox. She told me about them, but I never seen 'em. The little strongbox went with all the other personal stuff to the Millards. I mean, Mr. Millard sent a truck to the house one day to pick up all of Miss Margaret's things and the old boxes of the Judge's papers in the garage. They come and gone in just a few hours. I signed a piece of paper, but I don't know where they went."

"Well, I'm going over to visit the Millards in a few days. Maybe they will have Margaret's things over there. I intend to find those letters, if possible."

They spent the rest of the evening talking about Cindy and Miss Margaret. Bee repeated most of what she had told David over drinks of Wild Turkey back in Miss Margaret's house. Bee reminded David that Cindy was gone long before she ever came to work for Miss Margaret. "Miss Margaret was an old lady when I came. A gracious old lady, but an old lady nevertheless."

"Did Miss Margaret ever mention a Mr. Carl Warren, a math teacher at the high school?"

"She said Cindy was a genius at math, all her teachers said so. She could have had a scholarship at any university she chose. I don't remember his name though."

"What happened, Bee? Cindy disappeared on graduation night. You said she was pregnant, but she still could have gone to her graduation ceremony and then disappeared. Did Margaret ever explain how or why?"

Bee screwed up her face and looked up at the ceiling as if looking for a sign or something. "She said it was the most terrible night of her life. Miss Margaret told me little bits and pieces of the story over a long period. She swore me to secrecy. I just don't feel right in telling you more than I already did." She looked at her cousin Jasper.

Jasper was in the middle of a huge bite of cake and ice cream. "You got to follow your conscience, Bee. I can't tell you what to do. You got to live with your decision."

David took the lead and explained how he would not use actual names in his book and he would change the name of the town and state. He made another stab at convincing Bee that promises like she made are invalid after death.

Bee said looking up, "Miss Margaret, if you is listening, the man said he would keep your name out of it. He would change all the names. I think everybody who could be hurt by this story is dead by now, and probably Cindy, so I guess it don't hurt now to tell."

David breathed a little easier and sat back in his chair.

"The Judge and Cindy had an awful argument in the hallway that night. Miss Margaret told me Cindy ran up to her room, crying all the way. The Judge had slapped her hard, knocking her down. The Judge was angry, he stormed into his library, slammed the door, and locked it. Miss Margaret went upstairs and tried to talk to Cindy.

"Cindy was hysterical, crying and carrying on. Finally, Miss Margaret got Cindy to calm down and talk to her. They had been on good terms when Cindy was growing up, but after she started high school, Miss Margaret said Cindy became increasingly distant. Miss Margaret said she knew Cindy was getting good grades without studying so she let her have as much freedom as she wanted.

"Miss Margaret said she held her daughter for a long time that night, and between sobs Cindy blurted out the story. She was pregnant, but Billy Sandoval was not the father. Cindy said she and Billy were in love, and she knew it was true love because Billy was the only boy who ever treated her like a lady. He really respected her for herself, not just because she had big breast. She and Billy spent hours talking and planning for the future. They were going to California and live on the beach. Billy was a really good person, she said, no one had given him a chance. He was not a delinquent or a criminal like the Judge had tried to describe him.

"Cindy told her mother she spoiled it all by getting pregnant by someone else. She was so ashamed. She knew she had disgraced her family and herself. It was the most stupid thing she had ever done. Cindy told her mother she could have any boy in school. She found out very early in life that having sex meant being popular. Miss Margaret told me she suspected what Cindy was doing, but she ignored the signs that Cindy was being what you say, promiscuous. She was popular and getting good grades and all. Miss Margaret was not proud of herself. She was crying when she was telling me this part. I think she felt partially responsible for Cindy's predicament.

"Miss Margaret said Billy had convinced Cindy sex was only one of the major ways two people in love could communicate with each other. They should wait until they were married before they had sex because it would be a hundred times better when they had no fear of being caught or her getting pregnant.

"Now she was pregnant with somebody else's child and she could not face Billy. She would rather die first. She had tried to make herself miscarry before Billy and she were to elope, but she failed. That very afternoon she had tried to commit suicide by stopping her car in front of a train at the main street crossing, but she chickened out and moved just in time.

"Miss Margaret didn't ever tell me the name of the boy who was the father of Cindy's baby. I guess it was somebody that made the situation much worse, because Miss Margaret said she went downstairs and demanded the Judge come out of his library and talk to her.

"The Judge told Miss Margaret all the things he had found out about Billy's background, his drunken father, possibly a baby in another town, his police record, a suspect in several robberies, and parole. He convinced her that Cindy would be throwing away a promising career and a rewarding life by staying with him. Miss Margaret said she told the Judge Cindy was pregnant by someone else, not Billy, but that didn't change the Judge's mind one bit.

"Together they decided Cindy had to leave town right away. I think Miss Margaret believed Cindy was really in love with Billy, but I think she also believed the Judge about Billy's future.

"It was the only time in years, that Miss Margaret and the Judge agreed on anything. The Judge would take Cindy to New York to live with his brother Thomas, and his wife, MaryAnn. They would keep her at their home until the baby came, help with the adoption, and then Cindy would be sent to a university in England.

"The Judge said he would take care of Cindy's unborn baby's father when he got back form New York. Miss Margaret never did say what happened to him. Miss Margaret said she chased Billy off the front porch the next day. I think she felt kind of sorry for him. She told him Cindy was never coming back, and she never did."

David told Bee and Jasper he had talked with Billy in prison and maybe the Judge was right. Billy did end up living the low life of crime. He told them what Billy had said about waiting all night for Cindy to show up. He said he had waited a lifetime. The three of them speculated whether or not Billy would have been successful if Cindy and he had gotten together, the jury of three could not reach a consensus.

CHAPTER 22

The transatlantic flight from Atlanta to Dublin was an all-night affair. David placed a call to the Millards from the Atlanta airport to inform them of his arrival. He spoke to "Edmond," who identified himself as Mr. Millard's personal secretary.

"Mr. and Mrs. Millard are not available at the present time Mr. Jordan. However, you are expected. If you will leave your flight number and arrival time with me, I will make sure our driver meets you at the airport. The Millards were hoping you would spend several days with them before returning to the states."

Surprised, David asked, "Does that mean they are expecting me to stay in their home?"

"Yes, Mr. Jordan. Mrs. Millard is hosting a dinner tomorrow evening in your honor and it would be quite appropriate for you to spend the night. I'll send our driver to the airport in plenty of time to meet you at the gate."

"The flight is Delta 1162, arriving at 10:20 A.M. I'll be wearing a light tan jacket." David said.

"Enjoy your flight, Mr. Jordan." Edmond hung up.

The flight had been delayed taking off from Atlanta due to poor weather conditions all up and down the East Coast. Once they reached altitude, the pilot spoke over the intercom and said he would try to make up for lost time, they should not be more than thirty minutes late landing at Dublin. David felt a surge of excitement going to a country he had never seen before.

The flight attendant served dinner and two small bottles of Jim Beam. Getting a little sleep tonight should not be problem. He would loose five hours during the night.

The Dublin airport was socked in with fog during the early morning hours and the incoming flights were circling in a holding pattern over the Atlantic. Finally, the fog cleared and the trans-Atlantic flights were landing, one after another. The delay added to a late start out of Atlanta and now it was close to twelve-thirty P.M. when David's flight touched down.

The customs officer at the Dublin airport barely looked at David's new passport and never asked to see inside his luggage. How disappointing. He was amazed by the babble of languages around him. People from all over the globe were trying to get into Dublin. Some were being searched and thoroughly questioned.

After he cleared customs, David stopped at a small booth offering coffee, tea, and baked goods. He had a great deal of difficulty understanding the girl behind the counter and she him. Her English with an Irish brogue was considerably different than the English spoken in California. After a few exchanges, he walked away with a cup of hot tea and a hard roll of some kind, it was crusty and tasted like putty.

He drank the tea, threw the hard roll in the trash and finally found his way out to the main terminal. There were half a dozen "drivers" waiting for their passengers, holding up signs with names on them. One of them held a sign with his name neatly printed. The driver was in uniform and as soon as David acknowledged he was Mr. Jordan, the driver grabbed David's bags and guided him out of the terminal into a windswept parking area. Dublin in November is a dismal place, rain, gray skies, dampness, and the constant smell of wet people.

The car had been left running in the parking lot and was warm and cozy inside. David was amazed anyone would leave a fine motorcar running without being attended. He certainly was not going to complain, the interior was very warm and comfortable. The car was an older Rolls Royce.

"What year is this car, driver?" There was no response, possibly because David could not figure out how to communicate through the closed window-partition. After a few minutes, David sat back and watched the sights of the Irish countryside go by. The back seat of the Rolls was covered in Mohair and smelled slightly old with a hint of perfume, undoubtedly left by a former passenger. The car was a standard shift and the driver shifted gears flawlessly with only the slightest sensation. They did not head into Dublin, but south into the country.

The Millard manor house looked like a picture postcard. It was a large three-story, vine, covered brick and stone structure with many chimneys, and a slate roof. The grounds surrounding the manor were immaculate. The Rolls came to a stop next to the front entrance where Edmond met David.

There was no doubt Edmond was in charge. He motioned to a young girl in a maid's uniform to take David's belongings up to the guestroom. He told the driver not to be late for the arrival of Mr. Millard at the airport at five-thirty.

Mrs. Millard appeared, dressed in a light blue, ankle-length dress, heels, and one of those annoying permanent smiles. She was attractive, despite the heavy makeup and delicate almost frail appearance. She appeared ready for any occasion.

"Welcome to Ireland and to Kingsford Manor Mr. Jordan." Mrs. Millard was very picture of graciousness. "I'm anxious to discuss my Aunt Margaret, but I do hope you will wait until tomorrow. I have so many things to do to prepare for tonight's dinner party. I'm sure you will enjoy our guest, I know they will be looking forward to meeting you." She took David's arm and guided him inside the front foyer. "Perhaps you would like to rest before dinner. Jetlag is so irritating."

David saw his baggage disappear up a wide staircase in the hands of the young servant girl.

"We dress for dinner over here David, I know in the states it's not the custom, but we try to blend in. I hope you don't mind." She did not mention Kathryn. "Dinner will be served at eight." She smiled, offered her hand, which David shook instead of kissing it and retreated down the main hallway.

Edmond indicated he should follow his suitcase. David asked the maid who took him to his room, "Is Mrs. Milliard's daughter, Kathryn, going to be at the dinner tonight?"

"No, Sir. I believe she is in London." She pointed out the bathroom facilities, linen closet, with extra blankets and the fireplace gas valve. "If you need anything, Sir, just ring."

"What is your name?" David asked.

"Martha, Sir."

"A sandwich and a glass of milk would be fine, Martha." David suddenly remembered he was hungry after not being able to eat the roll at the airport.

Martha proceeded to unpack the contents of his suitcase. She hung his suit in the closet and placed the other articles of clothing in the antique dresser. David was not used to this kind of service and was very uncomfortable with someone going through his things. However, he figured he could get used to it. The guestroom was elegant by any standard. The manor house was several hundred years old and had been "modernized" in the twenties judging by the electrical and plumbing fixtures. A gas fire was burning in the fireplace. The room felt cold and damp, despite the fire. The two large multi-paned, leaded-glass windows looked out over a rolling farm and pasture lands. The view was terrific, just like the travel brochures, green rolling hills intersected with stone fences and hedgerows. It was not hard to understand why the Irish adopted green as the national color.

A decanter of brandy was setting on the table next to the heavily draped window. He took a small drink. Not bad, not good, but okay. The sandwich and milk arrived with a knock on the door. Martha set the serving tray on the small table next to the window. He ate half the sandwich and gave thought to who might be the other guest at dinner tonight. He set his portable alarm clock to seven and lay down. Within a few minutes he was sound asleep.

The dinner party was a huge success, according to John Millard. He was standing next to his wife, seeing the last guest out the front door. They both turned and thanked David again for being so open and frank about his experiences in Dumont. The six other dinner guests, including two members of the Dublin police force, an attorney, and their wives, were extremely interested in the law enforcement aspect of David's self-defense shooting of Adam Barnet. John Millard had questioned David extensively about the confiscation of the old Chevy.

David had tried to be the listener at the beginning of the dinner, but before long he found the other guests to be engaging, and interested in him, he told the story in detail. He did not divulge the seamy side of the interviews he had had with Cindy's classmates. He thought that part of the story was hearsay, and, until he could talk to Cindy, it would remain off-the-record.

David was invited to join John and Rebecca for a nightcap of brandy. They sat around the huge, glowing, wood-burning fireplace in the sitting room. John told David how his daughter, Kathryn, had felt somewhat responsible for David's misfortune. She had persuaded him not to bid on the old convertible so the gentleman from California could satisfy an old dream. "One never knows what the future holds, eh David. Maybe you will find that old car yet."

"Tomorrow we will try to answer your questions about Margaret and Cindy. Would ten o'clock be alright?" Mrs. Millard asked.

"Fine with me." The Millards finished their brandies and trudged off to their living quarters leaving David to find his way back to his room. He made two wrong guesses before he finally opened a door and found a pair of pajamas laid out on the bed. He had not packed any pajamas, and in fact did not own any. A glass of milk and a small plate of pastry and cookies were sitting next to the armchair in front of the fireplace. What a life, he could get used to this luxury without any trouble at all.

David wrote in his journal about the Millards and the dinner party. He made a list of a dozen questions he wanted to ask the Millards. He wondered how he could ask about Kathryn without sounding forward. Staring at the fireplace put David into a semi hypnotic mood for a long time. He imagined he could see her face in the shadows. How could he ever hope to compete with the life-style Kathryn had lived since childhood?

He had known that Kathryn had come from money right from the start. Somehow, he ignored this fact because he was so infatuated with her charms. Half of him believed she was in love with him just like he was in love with her. The other half kept saying, "She is a very attractive lady who likes to flirt a little, nothing will ever come of this. You're going to make a fool of yourself if you insist on pursuing her."

David was up by eight o'clock and in the shower. He dressed and went down the stairs looking for breakfast, or at least coffee. Martha found David wandering around the vacant dinning room and asked him if he would like to join Mr. Millard for breakfast in the morning room.

Of course, the morning room. "Why didn't I think of that? Yes, I would like to join Mr. Millard for breakfast."

Martha smiled, she could tell David was not used to luxury on this scale. She led the way toward the back of the house to a glassed-in room next to the kitchen. The morning room was also a nursery for Mrs. Millard's prized flower garden. The room smelled sweet and damp. Mr. Millard was sitting at a glass-top table, reading a newspaper.

He rose as David approached, "Good morning, David. I trust you slept well. Still short a few hours of sleep, I'll wager. I hate the flight back to Dublin from the states. It takes me several days to get my internal clock adjusted."

"Yes, thank you, I did sleep well. That bed in the guest room is very comfortable." David was telling the truth. He had slept like a baby.

"After you have had a chance to eat, would you like to see part of my car collection? I keep several cars on the premises, primarily the ones I like to drive."

"Yes, I would very much like to see your collection. Tell me, how did you get started collecting antique automobiles?"

John launched into what obviously were his favorite subjects himself and his cars. The two men finished eating and exited out the back door of the nursery. John led the way a large two-story brick building with a slate roof that had once been a barn. It had probably been used to house numerous horses and cows in the days before automobiles. All the ground around the barn had been paved over with brick. There was no sign of a live animal anywhere in sight.

John explained how he had designed the heating and air-handling system within the old barn so his prized auto collection would not be exposed to the unfriendly Irish weather. Temperature and humidity of the barn were kept constant, winter and summer.

"I became interested in automobiles as a young man. I grew up in Detroit. My father was an engineer working for General Motors all his adult life. He taught me a great deal about the auto business and the engineering that goes into the design of even the smallest and least expensive models. He constantly complained about the compromises he and the other engineers had to make in order to satisfy the stylist and accountants.

"I took over a machine tool import/export business from my wife's family and was very fortunate to make some good business decisions allowing me to indulge myself with buying and selling classic automobiles." They entered a side door and were met by a gust of air, "The building is pressurized to prevent the damp air from entering the garage," John explained.

"Ah, this one was my first purchase twenty years ago. You rode in it from the airport, I believe. I found her tucked away in an old garage outside of London. I put her right myself except for the bodywork. I hired that done by a very professional shop in town. It is a 1937 Rolls-Royce Hooper Sport Saloon. Watkins, my driver, is an excellent mechanic. He lives on the premises and watches over these machines, like they were his children."

David was looking at the interior of the old barn in amazement. There were a dozen cars parked at a forty-five degree angle to the sides of the large open space. The interior of the barn had been completely sealed off from the outside world. No windows, not even a skylight. There was one personnel door with a built-in air lock and one airtight double-overhead door at the far end of the cavernous room. The floor was covered with marble slabs and polished to a high gloss. A larger than life mural, depicting a vintage car race, covered the walls. Overhead, the ceiling was painted light blue with realistic clouds, and a six-foot scale model airship floating over the assembled autos.

Next to the Rolls Royce was a very classy 1935 Hispano-Suiza, followed by a beautifully restored 1953 Mercedes Benz 300S Cabaret. There were several older Porsches and Mercedes Benzes including a gull-winged model waiting for restoration.

John directed David to an immaculate 1950 Jaguar XK 120 Roadster. "This is my favorite. I love to drive this car. The motor runs so smoothly and it's responsive as any new machine and better than many. Would you like to go for a spin?" David could see John was anxious to show off the fire engine red sports car.

Watkins had joined them and moved to open the large double-doors. The overhead door moved up silently, revealing an air lock. John opened the driver-side door and motioned to David to get in the passenger side. The Jaguar started instantly and emitted the classic exhaust note of a high-performance, inline, six-cylinder engine.

John drove the Jag into the airlock, the overhead door closed behind them as, the front double-sliding doors moved aside allowing John to exit the garage. He stepped on the accelerator and the Jag shot out of the garage as if they were on a catapult. The Jag rounded the manor house and headed down the narrow driveway to the main road about 1000 yards away.

John shifted smoothly through the gears and was approaching 120 kilometers per hour by the time he downshifted and braked at the end of the driveway. David was feeling uncomfortable. The car had no seatbelts, no airbags, no roll bar, in short, no safety equipment of any kind. The driver was obviously mad.

After a sharp, right-hand turn, which led onto the main country road to town, John drove as though he were qualifying for a major sports car race. He took up most of the road, rounding turns and topping hills. David was not used to cars driving on the left-hand side of the road, consequently he was more alarmed by the high speed than he otherwise would have been. David prayed there was no oncoming traffic. The Jag responded to John's driving input with lightning agility, one minute accelerating so as to put both men back forcibly in their seats, then turning violently as if on rails, throwing David against the thinly padded door or against John, and then suddenly braking hard.

John was a skillful driver, no doubt about it. He was a different man behind the wheel of a sports car than he was hosting a dinner party. David envied John's driving skills, but he wished this adventure to be over. He liked taking risks, but not on these narrow public roads.

The picturesque Irish landscape rushed by in a blur. John was talking all the time he was driving, but David could not make out half of what he said. The wind, passing over the low windscreen, combined with the high RPMs of the Jag's straining engine, prevented any meaningful conversion.

Finally, it was over. They cruised past the manor house and the doublewide doors in the front of the barn opened like magic. The doors closed behind them as the overhead doors opened and the Jag roared into the showroom. John left the Jag in the middle of the floor. Watkins was standing to one side. "Watkins, check the tire pressure will you. I noticed a slight pull to the left side, otherwise she ran beautifully." Watkins responded like a pet dog would when his master offers a pat on the head and a tidbit.

"Rebecca should be up and about by now, David. Lets go see her and get the information about her family for you. Did you enjoy the ride?"

"Oh yes, I enjoyed the ride very much. Do you get the Jag out very often?"

"Oh, no, seldom in fact. The local police took my driver's license away last year after I had my fourth driving citation for speeding. They are not fond of high-speed runs on local roads. Serious lot they are. No sense of competitiveness.

"I had my solicitor appeal the case, but the judge could not be persuaded. I still go out on special occasions, like today." John was smiling at David and said, half in jest, "Life is too short, minor traffic laws are for old ladies to obey." David did not reply but promised himself to avoid anymore "spins" with John at the wheel.

Rebecca was waiting for them in the library. The same young girl who had found David roaming around in an empty dinning room had just delivered a fresh pot of coffee. "Did you enjoy your car ride, David?" Mrs. Millard asked, knowing full well that Mr. Millard had given David a ride he would not soon forget.

"Yes, I did. My first ride in a Jag roadster! It was really a lot of fun." David felt the need to disguise his true feelings about the adventure he had just finished.

"I'm glad you liked it." The emphasis was on "you." "I refuse to ride with John. I have not ridden in a car he was driving for years. I expect to have to visit him in jail, one of these days or the morgue. Did he tell you the local police tried to put him jail the last time he received a speeding citation?"

She looked at John with the look wives give their husband when they have done something really stupid.

"Now Rebecca, David did not come here to listen to you lecture me about my driving. Let's just drop it, shall we." His narrowed eyes and the frown gave lie to his soft voice, but his meaning was obvious, "Stop," and that was the end of that.

Rebecca poured David a cup of custom blended Brazilian coffee. They discussed the merits of Colombian vs. Brazilian coffee and then got down to the purpose of David's visit.

"As you know, I intend to use Cindy's story as a basis for a book I plan on writing. The business with the new car, the suitcase in the trunk, and her disappearance all go together to make a terrific mystery novel. I wish I knew the ending. That's why I need to find Cindy. Do you know if she is still alive?"

Husband and wife looked at each other waiting for the other to answer. Mrs. Millard spoke just ahead of her husband, "When Cindy left New York she made it perfectly clear she did not want any contact with the family. We honored that request Mr. Jordan."

What kind of an answer was that? David thought to himself. He waited for a more specific answer but received only silence. Okay, lets try this approach, "My next question to you, Mrs. Millard, is this: Where were you living at the time of Cindy's disappearance? I know you and Mr. Millard were married by then, but did you get involved with the decision for Cindy to come live with your parents at that time? Did you know Cindy personally?" David felt like a police inspector asking a suspect questions.

"John and I were married in 1950 and we were living in London at the time. John was getting started in my father's business. We traveled a lot in those days. Western Europe was a goldmine for my father and for us as well. Much of the European industrial capability had been destroyed in the war and needed to be replaced. Of course, my father was in the machine tool business since before the war. He had made many valuable connections in the states and in Europe buying and selling industrial equipment.

"I knew Cindy, we had been together on several family occasions, but I did not know her well. My father hardly ever talked about his brother, Timothy. I really never knew the reason why they were not close. There were a few family gatherings where both brothers were together and they seemed amiable, but not close at all. It never occurred to me to ask why they were not close.

"My mother called one day and said Cindy was living with them. Her father had brought her on the train. Apparently the Judge and my father had talked on the telephone and made the arrangements without discussing it with my mother. Needless to say my mother was very unhappy about the whole situation, she was involved socially in New York City and did not want to be bothered raising another child who was going to have a baby.

"I never talked to Cindy myself. So all I can tell you is what my mother told me over the telephone. I was working for my father at the time, in our London office, and it was two months before I could take time to go to New York and see my mother. Cindy had already left by then."

"Left! Where did she go? Didn't she have the baby at your mother's house?"

"Oh, no, Cindy left for the West Coast exactly six weeks after she arrived in New York."

John interrupted. "I can add something to the West Coast move. Cindy had received a letter from her mother containing some information that she wanted. I used to talk with our New York office almost daily on the telephone about business. Sometimes Rebecca's father would tell me about the yelling matches Cindy would have on the telephone with her mother in Dumont.

"The main subject of the argument was a name and address Cindy's mother refused to give. Finally, Margaret put the information and some money in a letter. When Cindy got the letter, she packed and left the next day. My mother-in-law couldn't physically stop her. By the time Thomas got home from the office, she was gone.

"They called the police, but they treated it as a runaway and basically did nothing. Thomas called his brother in Dumont and apparently, Timothy said to let her go. We never did find out where she went. Eventually the subject just faded into the past and we all went on about our business."

"Mr. Jordan, we never suspected foul play," Mrs. Millard said. "Cindy was headstrong and she made up her mind to go, and that was it. After all, she was almost eighteen years old at the time. After Cindy left, my mother spoke with Margaret many times on the telephone, and in fact several months later she went to Dumont and stayed with Margaret for several weeks.

"When my mother came back to New York, I remember asking her what happened to Cindy and all she could tell me was Margaret had received a letter from her saying everything was fine and the baby was in a good home. We assumed that meant the baby had been given up for adoption."

"Did you know, or did Cindy tell your mother who the father was?

Mrs. Millard hesitated slightly. "The Judge and Margaret told my mother about a boy that Cindy was seeing who was always in trouble. He was a mechanic or some rather common person. They wanted to keep her away from him, without too much success I gathered. I never heard a name."

David felt the next question was extremely important, because somebody from Australia was coming to Dumont to take possession of the O'Ryan house. "Did you know anything about the Australian Margaret met in Europe before the war started?"

Mrs. Millard glanced at her husband and took a deep breath, "No, not directly. As I said, my side of the family was not very close to Cindy's parents."

"Mrs. Millard, someone from Australia is coming to Dumont to take possession of Margaret's house. You must have knowledge of that, you are the executor of your aunt's will." David was conscious of a wall that had shot up between the two of them. Her facial expression had changed from open politeness to cold and defensive. She looked again to her husband.

John spoke with measured words, practiced many times in tough sales pitches. "Mr. Jordan, my wife has openly answered your questions about Cindy's disappearance. I am afraid there are certain issues that prevent us from going further with this conversation. I'm sure you will understand Mr. Jordan. You will have to use your imagination and fill in the rest of the story. After all, isn't that what good writers do?"

David started to protest and then thought better of it. It would do no good to upset Kathryn's parents. Evidently, the new buyer did not want to be identified, maybe a restriction in the old lady's will, David was guessing. "You are right. A good author will fill in the blanks with a bit of imagination." There has to be an Australian connection, David thought. But pressing the issue will not endear them to me or make my seeing

Kathryn any easier. "You both have been very helpful and hospitable. I truly enjoyed staying here, and seeing your car collection, John. The ride in the Jag was something I'll be sure to incorporate into my book."

"Thank you for understanding, Mr. Jordan. I will be looking forward to reading your novel when you finish." Mrs. Millard had regained her permanent smile.

"There is one thing you may be able to help me with, Bee said that your aunt had received four letters from Cindy over the years. They were in some kind of small locked box she kept in her room. Do you have them or do you know were they are?"

"All of my aunt's personal belongings were sold or disposed of Mr. Jordan." The response was quick from Mrs. Millard.

John stepped up and said. "My wife's aunt kept thousands of letters she had received from people all over the country. There were boxes and boxes of correspondence dating back before the war. They were of no interest to anybody so I had them incinerated. I am sorry but that's probably what happened to the letters you're referring to." They both were standing now obviously signifying that the meeting was over.

David excused himself, saying, "I'll pack my bag and be on my way. If you could have Watkins take me to the airport, I believe I could catch an afternoon flight to London." The threesome shook hands and said farewells. David sensed a look of relief on the Millard's faces. He would try to find out exactly what was in the will when he got back to the states. Are wills recorded and made public he wondered? David did not know the answer, but he was going to find out. Maybe Sheriff Woodford could help.

Upstairs, David found Martha packing his bags. How did she know he was leaving at that moment? He started to ask, and then thought of a more important question. "Martha, do you know where Kathryn stays when she is in London?"

"No, Sir. I have never heard her mention an address, and even if I knew I couldn't tell ya." Her Irish brogue was coming through strong and clear. "The Millards would sack me for sure if I gave out her address." She picked up David's bags and left the room. David checked the closet and bathroom for anything he may have forgotten and went downstairs.

John and Martha were standing at the front door, talking. Watkins picked up David's bags and placed them in the trunk of the Rolls, and stood waiting with the rear door open.

David walked up to John and held out his hand. John reciprocated, but the handshake was not as warm and friendly as David might have expected. Together they walked toward the open car door. "David, I must say something to you. I'm afraid I must be perfectly frank." John's expression darkened, and he was very serious. David could feel the muscles in his neck begin to tighten up. He knew he had screwed up somehow.

"I sense you are looking for a way to enter into my daughter's life. Kathryn is a wonderful, intelligent, and beautiful woman. She makes friends easily and sometimes her friendliness is mistaken for something else."

"I don't understand what you are driving at, John. I have not made any inappropriate advances to your daughter. I have not seen her since she left Dumont." David was a little pissed off at being treated like an amorous teenager.

"David, I saw the look in Kathryn's eyes when she talked about you and your intentions for restoring the old car. She spent a long evening with you at dinner that night. I know her well and she was quite taken with you. I know you plan to contact her in London, and I'm asking you not to.

"Kathryn is engaged to be married to a brilliant lawyer in San Francisco next spring. The man she is marrying is a long-time family friend and they have known each other for years. He helped her when her husband was killed and took care of the messy details with the FAA, and so on. Since then, he has been at her side helping her manage her husband's financial affairs. They have a lot in common and make a perfect pair. It would be a shame if anyone or anything came between them. Do you understand my meaning, David?"

David got the meaning all right. His temper flared and he could feel his face flush. "I understand you perfectly, John. Kathryn has one quality you didn't mention. She is over the age of twenty-one and, I suspect she is perfectly capable of choosing her own acquaintances. If she accepts my invitation to dinner when I get to London, I will try my best not to molest or mistreat her in any way. Good-bye." David got in the Rolls, closed the door, and said to Watkins, "To the airport driver" and as an after thought, "step on it."

CHAPTER 23

As Kingsford Manor slid into the background, David felt more and more relaxed. He liked the experience of dining and sleeping in a "castle," but the constant attention from the servants was more than he cared for. He doubted he could get used to it, even if he had the money to support such a lifestyle. The little talk John Millard had given him as he was leaving did not set well. He was damned if he would let Kathryn's father dictate his future.

It was a foregone conclusion that John would call Kathryn as soon as he could and try to convince her not to accept any calls from David. Now that he was seated onboard his flight to London he could have kicked himself for not calling her before he left Dublin. Now he would have to wait until they landed.

The flight took a little over an hour and the plane landed as scheduled at six-twenty P.M. Gatwick airport was ten times the madhouse Dublin had been. It was eight o'clock before David could claim his baggage and find a phone booth.

Kathryn's telephone rang four times before the answering machine responded. A male voice repeated the number and asked the caller to leave a message. He hesitated, was that a canned voice supplied by the answering machine or was it a man living in Kathryn's apartment? He hung up and redialed. The same voice came only this time David was ready, "Kathryn, this is David Jordan, I'm in London and I will be staying at the Bloomsbury Park Hotel. I have no idea where it's located, except it is close to the British Museum. I'll leave it up to the cab driver to get me there. I hope to hear from you soon." He read the hotel telephone number off his reservation confirmation and hung up.

The weather in London was no better than in Dublin. He made his way out to the taxi stand and gave a driver the address and name of the hotel. The driver nodded and indicated to David to get in the back seat. He did not offer to help with the bags. *I thought the London cabbies would be more polite and helpful than the ones in the states, but I was wrong.*

The traffic was incomprehensible. David was still not comfortable with driving on the left side of the road. The shear number of cars and trucks speeding along the boulevards produced a maze of light and color. The streets were wet with a light rain. Traffic signals were confusing. People crossing the street dared cars to hit them, their faces hidden under black umbrellas. David had considered renting a car in London and driving out into the countryside, but he quickly abandoned any notion of driving in heavy traffic. .

The travel agent that booked David's trip said the Bloomsbury Park Hotel was half the price of the Mayflower Hotel and just as good. From the outside, it was difficult to determine the age of the building the hotel was in, but it looked to have been built during the reign of Queen Victoria. The doorman opened the cab door and held an umbrella as David stepped out of the taxi. He fumbled with the strange currency before finally settling with the cabdriver. A bellhop was summoned to pick up David's bags and lead him inside.

The Hotel was definitely left over from the Victorian era, but the lobby appeared to be in excellent condition. David hoped the rooms were in similar condition and all the plumbing worked.

"Welcome, Mr. Jordan. We have been expecting you." The desk clerk could easily have passed for Sir John Gilgood, the Shakespearean actor. Your room is number 408." David filled out the card the desk clerk handed him and gave him his credit card and passport in return. "We hope you enjoy your stay with us, Sir. If there is anything we can do to make you more comfortable, please let us know right away. There was a telephone call before you arrived, Mr. Jordan, I'll transfer it to the voice mail on the phone in your room." He handed David's key to the bellhop and they headed for the elevator.

David's heart was racing. Kathryn must have called. No one else knew where he was staying. Kelly had a copy of his itinerary, but she would not be calling unless it was an emergency. It must have been Kathryn. What message did she leave? Why didn't she wait until he got here so he could talk to her? Maybe she didn't want to talk to him. Maybe her father convinced her not to see him and she just called to tell him not to bother. Maybe …. "Stop it," he told himself. "Your imagination is working overtime."

The bellhop unlocked the door to 408 and led David inside. The room was spacious with a king-size bed in the center, and a huge TV mounted in a cabinet with a small refrigerator. Paintings on the wall depicted the English countryside. Quite adequate, David decided. The bellhop began to open David's bags. David stopped him and handed him two one-pound notes. The bellhop accepted the offering and left without giving any indication if it was too much or not enough. David could not remember exactly what conversion factor to use when going from American dollars to English pounds. Worse yet, he didn't remember if he was supposed to tip people in England. He knew there were some countries where restaurant and hotel employees were paid enough so they did not have to grovel for tips like they do in America.

He went to the telephone and read the instructions on its face: "How to retrieve messages." He pushed several buttons without being able to retrieve Kathryn's message. Finally giving up, he called the operator. The operator said she would put the message through for him.

"Hello David. I'm so glad to hear from you. My father called and said you might contact me when you arrived in London. I'm so glad you did. I can't wait to hear all about your experiences in Dumont. Did you find the car? I'm sorry, I'm carrying on so. I live not far from your hotel, if I leave now, I should be there in twenty or thirty minutes. I'll call you from the lobby. We can have a drink together or maybe a late dinner. I know several great restaurants near there. See you soon." Her low hushed voice was music to David's ear. He called the operator and asked her to replay the message again.

Her voice was soft and warm as a summer night. The way she said "See you soon," made David's heart stop. He stood motionless, holding the telephone receiver in his hand. He called the operator and asked her to replay the message for a third time. He had to be sure he wasn't imagining his good fortune.

"Kathryn is coming to the hotel to meet me. What the hell did her father say to me about contacting her? What difference does it make now?" Looking in the large gilded mirror on the wall, David answered himself, "None, absolutely none." He had to get cleaned up before she got here. David ripped off his shirt and tossed it in a corner. Should he shower? Not enough time. He rushed into the bathroom and ran his electric razor over his face in record time. A quick "Navy" wash followed by underarm deodorant. Toothbrush, where is the damn toothbrush? Hotel mouthwash will have to do.

Finally, hair combed, face shaved, mouth cleansed, clean shirt and now what? Wait for Kathryn's telephone call or go down to the lobby and meet her? Decisions, decisions. "It's better to wait here, don't be too anxious, don't let her see you're dying to see her." David stood by the window and looked down at the street below. He was turned around, he didn't know if his room was on the same street as the front lobby or not. It didn't make any difference, he couldn't make out people's faces from this vantage point anyway.

He thought back to the time when he was giving advice to his son, Chance. It was Chance's first date in the family car. He was sixteen and the girl was from across the street. He told Chance most boys make the mistake of chasing the girl. "The best way to get the girl you want is not to appear to be to interested, just polite and a little mysterious. The girl will be doing the same of course, so you have to be patient. In the meantime, date other girls. If she is interested in you, she will make some kind of small move toward you. You'll know when it happens, then do what your heart dictates." Well Kathryn had made a small move toward him, hadn't she?

The telephone rang. He deliberately waited until the second ring, "Hello."

"Hello, David, it's Kathryn."

"Hello, Kathryn, I'll be down in just a minute." David quickly put on his jacket, picked up his room key and wallet, and was out the door. The elevator was vintage and slow. God, it was slow. David wished he had taken the stairs when the elevator doors finally opened and he stepped out into the lobby. There she was, standing near the concierge's desk.

"David, over here." They met in the center of the lobby, carefully embraced each other. "You look wonderful, none the worse for wear," she said, standing back and looking him over.

"You look fantastic, Kathryn. Let me look at you." He held her at arm's length. Her dark hair fell on her shoulders. The lights from the lobby chandelier reflected like hundreds of diamonds in her deep brown eyes. Kathryn was wearing a stylish sweater and a skirt revealing what David had known all along, her curves were correctly proportioned.

"Lets find the hotel bar, I could use a drink about now." They both looked around for some indication of where the bar was. Together they walked down a wide hallway toward the sound of a piano playing. Outside the hotel pub entrance, a billboard displayed a poster advertising Donald Schofield at the piano. "Perfect," David said to himself. Polished oak, brass, and leather was the predominant decorative motif. The pub was nearly empty, two couples sat around the piano and a few more solitary patrons sat at the bar. David and Kathryn chose a booth off to one side, across the room from the piano.

The piano player actually had a five-piece orchestra at his command, via the miracle of electronics. The music was designed to facilitate conversation and relaxation without being overwhelming. The resulting atmosphere was conducive to a romantic meeting. Schofield played mostly soft jazz. He would take musical requests according to a small sign on top of the piano.

Kathryn ordered a glass of wine and David ordered a scotch on the rocks. A little class, David thought. Scotch tasted like something burnt, to him, but he thought it gave a good impression. Kathryn wanted to know how his visit had gone with her parents. He explained briefly and asked, "Did your father tell you I was coming to London with the intention of seeing you, or did he simply mention I was stopping in London for a little sight seeing?"

Kathryn looked straight at David and said, "My father thinks you have ulterior motives, Mr. Jordan." She cocked her head slightly raising one eyebrow, looked up at David with an impish grin, "He told me what he said to you before you left Dublin. I am afraid my father still thinks of me as a young girl. I apologize if he offended you."

"He offended me all right, but that's between him and me. Why did you come here tonight, if he didn't want you to see me?"

"I told my father I was perfectly capable of making my own decisions regarding the people I associate with. I consider you a friend and a gentleman, and if I wanted to see you, I would. Besides, I still feel somewhat responsible for your injury. I'm afraid he is a little upset with me, but it's not the first time." Kathryn looked the part of a triumphal teenager who had just outfoxed her parents.

"I knew you would make your own decisions. That's exactly what I told your father when I closed the door on the Rolls, as I was leaving, and I was right." David too, felt triumphant.

"Now tell me about your upcoming wedding." An impulsive question, but David decided to find out where he stood and get that bit of unpleasantness out of the way.

Kathryn looked as if she had suddenly remembered something disagreeable, but quickly recovered, "The wedding is set for April 22nd. I'll send you an invitation, if you think you could make it." The last part of that statement sounded too polite to be believable.

"No, don't bother. I wish you all the happiness in the world. Your fiancé is a very lucky man."

Kathryn hesitated for a moment before speaking, "Look, David, I didn't come here to talk about me. I wanted to find out about you, the events in Dumont, and your car, where is the car?" She brightened up with the change of subject.

David also felt relieved to be talking about something else. He was determined to enjoy this evening and pretend he didn't hear anything about her wedding. He began by telling her about the events leading up to the shooting of Adam Barnet and his own near-death experience. He went into detail about the Chevy being confiscated and lost in the bureaucracy of the Los Angles police department.

The hotel pub offered food service and seemed to be a great place to carry on a conversation, David suggested they take advantage of it. They ordered a bottle of Merlot and a large Cesar Salad with French bread. David could not help but notice Kathryn never took her eyes away from him. She took in every word he uttered. He was feeling the same closeness he had felt the last time they were together. There was no doubt in David's mind that this was much more than a simple infatuation, a powerful attraction existed between the two of them

"Now, it's your turn Kathryn. What is it you do here in London?"

"Oh, I have been quite busy developing a language based software for the company Richard and I started a couple of years ago. Richard is my fiancé. After Brian was killed, Richard became a large part of my life. He helped me through some very difficult times.

"He and my late husband worked together in my father-in-law's law office, and they were good friends. Well, they invested in several business opportunities, and one of them now looks like it will develop into something very profitable. It is a computerized language training company. The software is designed to be used by people from the European continent who want to learn English.

"I'm fluent in French, German, and some Italian. I work with a group of language experts here in London who are putting the course material together. It will be one of those dot com companies I'm sure you have heard about. I don't think it will make as big a splash on the stock market as some companies have, but it should turn a profit, and who knows, maybe it will grow into something quite large." Kathryn's eyes were glowing with enthusiasm as she talked about her business prospects.

"It sounds quite challenging. What part do you play, besides being part owner? Are you actually designing the course material?"

"I work in the editing office as one of the language editors. We have to be very precise when we interpret from one language to another, and that is my responsibility. I review the French and German language course subject matter for correctness. Other people do the same. It takes more than one pair of eyes and ears to catch the more subtle nuances in the English language."

"Here, I'll give you my card. Maybe you will want to watch for our web site when it becomes available on the Internet. If we are successful, we plan to go public, and you could buy stock," Kathryn pulled a business card from her small handbag and gave it to David: "Philips Language International", Kathryn Philips, Editor." The card contained all the usual information, address, and telephone numbers. Useful information, David thought, as he tucked the card away in his wallet.

David was beginning to feel the effects of the Scotch whisky and Merlot. He kept trying to find a way to determine how Kathryn felt about him. How can I bring up this subject without sounding immature, and crass? He thought he could sense her desire to talk about "them" as well. Then the idea came.

He excused himself, and walked over to the piano man. The two couples that had been sitting at the piano bar had left, the only other patrons besides Kathryn and David were the two men sitting at the bar. He explained what he wanted and the piano man nodded, knowingly. David pushed a ten-pound note onto the keyboard and thanked him. On the way back, he stopped at the bar and told the bartender to put the piano man's drinks on his tab.

As David approached the booth, Kathryn was returning from the ladies room. The piano player began playing a romantic composition reminiscent of Moonglow from the movie, Picnic. "Would you care to dance m'lady?" David mimicked a British accent bowing slightly.

"Of course, m'lord, I would be honored." Kathryn curtsied. David's imagination clothed her in an elegant gown and sparkling jewelry.

They came together, looked into each other's eyes, and began to dance. No one else was on the small dance floor. The music tempo was just as David had requested. Kathryn was light as a feather in his arms. If the world ended right now, David knew he had already entered heaven. She put her head on his shoulder, her hair was silky smooth, and there was a hint of a fine perfume. David was afraid to say anything for fear of destroying the mood. Her hand caressed the back of his neck, softly.

He held her ever so gently, but close, their thighs touched, the two dancers moved as one. The music and Kathryn's embrace were intoxicating. He could not possibly do or say anything that would improve this fantastic moment. They danced for a long time. David had no idea how long, and couldn't have cared less about stopping. The piano man ended the piece. "We close in five minutes ladies and gentleman. Thank you, for being with us this evening. Please join us again." He launched into his theme song.

The two dancers stood on the dance floor, in each other's arms, unwilling to admit the mood was gone. Suddenly, the house lights came on. David signed the bar bill with his room number and left a tip. Kathryn took David's arm and they left the pub, walking toward the lobby. "How far do you live from here?" David asked.

"It's on Bedford Place, it's an apartment building about 10 minutes by taxi, I don't know how many blocks. London is not like American cities with nicely laid out streets and avenues," she replied.

"I would love to walk you home."

"David that's a lovely thought, but it may start raining again," she protested.

"No problem. Stay right here."

David approached the front desk and spoke to the desk clerk. The clerk disappeared into the doorway behind the counter and returned with an umbrella and two raincoats.

"Now I can walk you home and the weather be damned." He helped Kathryn put on her raincoat and they walked out into a light mist. The doorman started to signal a waiting cab and David said, "No thanks, we're walking." The doorman looked at them and then up at the rain and shrugged.

With arms locked tightly they walked at a leisurely pace, stopping at some of the store windows to comment on the displays and prices. Kathryn was well versed in the quality of different brands of clothing and jewelry. She explained, in detail, how to determine the quality of various types of clothing, and how to keep them stylishly by adding accessories like scarf's, belts, and costume jewelry. They stopped for a long time in front of a bookstore and discussed the various novels each had read. David expressed a preference for historical novels and Kathryn was a mystery fan.

They bought two cups of hot tea from an all night newsstand, next to the subway station entrance. There were two teenage girls laughing and making a lot of noise in one of those instant photo booths. Without thinking about it, David said, "Let's have our picture taken."

"In these rain coats? We will look like a couple of school children."

"You mean a couple of wet school children," David added.

They waited until the two girls left and then entered the booth. Sitting close together, Kathryn helped David assemble the right amount of coins to place in the coin slot. They smiled and looked at each other and the camera. After few minutes, four pictures on a stripped of film dropped out of the machine. They laughed at themselves as David placed the filmstrip in Kathryn's handbag.

They walked hand in hand down a nearly deserted street. The rain was falling softly and steadily. The drenched figures huddled close under the borrowed umbrella. Neither noticed the rain or paid any attention to the occasional passersby. David would have been content to walk to Scotland. The reflections from the street and sidewalks of the multitude of colored lights glowing from the shop windows offset the dreariness of the English weather. The feeling of closeness David felt with Kathryn pressing against his body thoroughly warmed him.

The last few blocks to Kathryn's apartment was a long, narrow, dark, cobblestone side street. The houses on either side were two and three story brick buildings sharing a common wall. With a little imagination, David could see horse drawn carriages clopping along the wet street.

"This is it, David, pointing up to a narrow three story, brick town house. I could call you a cab so you won't have to walk back to your hotel in the rain." Kathryn looked at David, her face was wet with raindrops, or was it tears? They stepped up and under the front door entryway.

"I prefer to walk." David took Kathryn by the arms and looked directly into her eyes. "Kathryn... I, I know you are engaged, and I respect that, but I have to tell you how I feel. There is an old saying and it goes something like this: 'Never fail to tell somebody you love them when you have the opportunity, because you may never have that opportunity again.'" David's voice faltered for just a moment. "Kathryn, I love you, I have from the very first day we met." he paused. Kathryn's face and eyes were irresistible, they kissed a long passionate kiss. For a few moments David was completely oblivious of the world around him. His knees were shaking from the cold and dampness. Or was it the intensity of the moment?

They clung to each other, catching their breaths. The rain had started again. "David, our lives are so different, I wish it weren't so." Kathryn's voice was quivering, tears were forming as she took David's hands in hers. "I'm leaving tomorrow for Berlin to meet Richard and some business people." She swallowed hard. She reached into her handbag, pulled out the photo strip, and tore it in half. She gave David one half, her voice full of emotion, "Keep this someplace where you can look at it once in awhile, and I will do the same. Maybe, if we do it at the same time, our hearts will know we are thinking of each other." She turned, opened the door, and left David standing alone in the dark.

CHAPTER 24

The walk back to the hotel was long and wet. David felt like he was on automatic pilot, he did not recognize any street names or landmarks, and yet the hotel marquee appeared through the rain in the distance.

He could not get Kathryn out of his mind. The evening had been the most bittersweet experience of his life, holding Kathryn in his arms one minute and losing her the next. He was positive Kathryn harbored the same burning emotions for him as he did for her, but she was committed to another man and it was clear she would not betray him.

It was impossible to be angry with her. David felt as if his life had suddenly fallen into a dark hole. He had too much respect for Kathryn to blame her for his misery. He was positive she felt miserable as well.

Back in his hotel room he peeled off his wet clothes and left them in a heap on the floor. In the shower he let the hot stream of water beat on his back and shoulders. He wanted to cry, but the tears would not come.

Lying in bed, David stared at the ceiling, wondering what other men would have done in the same circumstance. Would they go charging after her? Challenge Richard to a duel? He recalled the movie The Graduate in which the young suitor barged into a church wedding, and physically dragged the bride, the love of his life, off into the sunset. If David did break into Kathryn's life, would she accept or reject him? The answer was not clear.

He knew he was beating himself up for not acting, but what action could he take? Kathryn was an adult. If she wanted to break off her engagement, she could have. She could have at least given him a signal she might consider such action in the future, but she had not. In fact, in David's mind giving him half the photo strip was an act of final farewell. "Don't call me, I'll call you," was a quote that came to mind.

Sleep finally came as the sky turned a light gray in the east. David slept until the maid knocked on the door and actually came into the room before she realized there was someone in bed. "Oh, dear. I didn't know you were still in bed sir. I'm going." She closed the door behind her. David got up and made up his mind to put plan B into operation. Plan A was to spend the next six days with Kathryn. Plan B was to spend the next six days alone in London.

David's original intention, to see Buckingham Palace, the Tower of London, and the other famous sites in London, evaporated. He could not get interested in his surroundings. He was sure he would regret this decision, he may never have the opportunity to come back to London. He called the hotel concierge and asked him to make flight reservations for Chicago as soon as possible.

After his shower, he called Sheriff Woodford in Dumont, hoping the sheriff would still be in his office. "Sheriff! How the hell are you? Caught any bad guys lately?"

"David, where are you? I called your daughter and she said you were in Ireland or England, but her twin boys had lost the letter you sent with the hotel telephone numbers on it. I've got some news for you and you are not going to believe." The sheriff paused, waiting for a reaction.

"Don't tell me they let Billy Sandoval out of prison." David felt a sudden cold twist in his stomach as he said Billy's name.

"No, this is good news. At least I think it is good news. Cindy O'Ryan is back in town. For some reason, I cannot fathom, she bought the house back from the estate, and paid the asking price. Cindy arrived two days ago from Australia and this town has not stopped talking about her." Woodford stopped and took a deep breath. "You still there, David?"

David could hardly believe his ears. Cindy was back in Dumont? What an incredible turn of events. "Yes, tell me about her Sheriff. Have you met her? What kind of woman is she? Is she a lady?" David was instantly ashamed of himself for making that last remark. He had no business judging her.

"Yes. I met her last night. I drove over to the house after I heard she was in town. She is a very imposing woman. Strong willed, I mean, not physically. Speaks her mind like she is used to being in charge and giving orders. She has a slight Australian accent, but not like those advertisements on TV.

"I asked her if she planned on living here and she said, 'What business is it of yours if I do or not? I'm a US citizen, and unless they've changed the law recently, I can live anywhere I damn well please.'

"I told her about the murder and the car and you getting shot, she stopped me and said she knew all about it and she knew you were looking for her, and if I saw you, I'm to tell you she has nothing to say. That was pretty much the end of the conversation.

"When are you coming back, David?"

David was scribbling notes on hotel stationary trying to record the Sheriff's words as accurately as possible. "I'll be back in the states by the day after tomorrow. I'll be staying with my daughter for a couple of days and then I'll drive over to Dumont. I'll call you when I get into town. Find out all you can about Cindy O'Ryan for me. I intend to meet her and talk to her whether she agrees to or not. She is the last piece of the puzzle and I am not going to give up without doing my best to have a conversation with her.

"Oh, one more thing that just occurred to me. Could you speak to your friend at the escrow desk in the bank and get an address in Australia for Cindy? The reason I ask is, I would like you to contact the local law enforcement agency down there and get a printout of any police activity she might have had. It would be interesting to see if we could find out what she has been up to all these years."

"David, I need to remind you Cindy is not under investigation. She has not broken any laws I know of. I cannot start asking a bunch of questions, especially in a foreign country, just because of your curiosity. We have laws forbidding that kind of police activity. You get my point David?"

"Yes sir. I get the point, but consider this. She left the country under suspicious circumstances. I am sure you could just ask a few questions to satisfy yourself she is who she claims to be. What if she's an impostor?" David was impressed he thought of the impostor angle spontaneously. Of course, if she were an impostor the sheriff could launch a full-scale investigation.

"What about it, Sheriff? It sounds and looks like she is hiding something, maybe the real Cindy is buried in Australia and this gal is out to fleece the estate."

"Shit, I suppose you've got a point, a weak one, but I could do a little investigation on the QT. I'll contact somebody I know at the state capital and get the ball rolling. I've never contacted any police agency in Australia so I'll need some guidance. Call me as soon as you get to town."

David hung up. Now things were starting to get exciting. He wished he could knock on Cindy's door right now, but he knew he had better have his ducks lined up before he tried to talk to her. She sounded like her guard was up, based on what the sheriff had said. He could hear the bar-talk in Murphy's Bar and Grill, in Dumont. "Cindy O'Ryan is back in town".

The British Airline flight to Chicago was a dream. The sky was clear and David had made a point to be at Gatwick airport in plenty of time to find his way around. He had a cup of coffee, a sweet roll, and people-watched until it was time to board the plane.

The coach seat next to a window was forward of the wing, so David had an unobstructed view of the blue Atlantic below. Fortunately, the seat next to him was empty, so he could stretch out and enjoy a little extra comfort. To his surprise, Chicago was clear and sunny also. The good weather improved David's disposition considerably. Kathryn was still in the forefront of his mind, but he had rationalized his emotions into a neat memory storage box.

Whenever he felt like it, he would pull out the box and remember Kathryn's face looking up at him in the rain. *Those eyes, God, what secrets they held.* The feeling of her body next to his when they were dancing was fresh in his mind, sensual and electrifying. She moved when he moved, she followed so exquisitely David felt he was dancing with a shadow.

He spent several hours writing in his journal and reviewing his notes regarding Cindy's classmate's recollection. He made a list of questions he wanted to ask her, assuming she would see him. Why was she so against seeing him, he wondered? Was she still embarrassed about having someone's child besides Billy's? Did she know Billy was in prison? She must, if she knew all about the killings and the car. Maybe she was in contact with somebody in town besides her ex-classmates. He still needed to locate the math teacher that Cindy was seeing after hours.

Kelly and the twins met David at O'Hare. The boys had made a big banner and decorated it with all kinds of things they wanted to do with their Grandpa. Basketball and hockey were high on the list, followed by a visit to the children's museum. The Christmas season was approaching, and the boys were busy generating a list of wants and needs. They talked about going skiing during the Christmas vacation period. David had never skied in his life and decided if Kelly, Fred, and the boys wanted him to go he would tag a long. If nothing else, he could keep the fire going in the fireplace and work on his book.

Later in the evening, at Kelly's apartment, after the twins had been put to bed, Kelly and Fred sat listening to David describe his visit to the Milliard's Kingsford manor house. He went into detail about the exciting ride in the Jag and all the fancy cars in John Milliard's stable. The dinner party got Kelly's attention and she wanted to know how the women were dressed and what kind of food was served. "Did they have a butler and maids serving dinner?"

David added the part where John lectured him not to see his daughter, Kathryn. He felt sure Kelly sensed he was after more than just a story for his book, so he decided to let her in on his feelings. The photo strip of Kathryn and him brought a "Gee Dad, that was really romantic." He tried not to let on how much Kathryn had meant to him, but he could see in Kelly's eyes she knew.

David stayed with Kelly and her family through the Thanksgiving Day celebration. After dinner, Kelly asked her dad if he wanted to go for a walk with her. The day was cool and sunless. A stiff breeze was blowing off Lake Michigan. They bundled up in windbreakers and gloves.

"Dad, I need to talk to you about Mom." They had just exited her apartment building and headed into the wind. "She and Gerald have separated. I've been on the phone with her every day for the last two weeks. She is not taking this well at all. I think she feels like a failure with you, and now Gerald." Kelly was holding on to her father's arm and trying to keep out of the wind.

"Am I supposed to feel sorry for her, or what?" David could not help but feel a twinge of joy at Ellen's expense.

"I love you both, Dad. It still hurts me not to have you both at least able to talk to one another. I miss our family. I remember how it used to be when Chance was home, we had such a good family. I didn't think it would ever change." Kelly's voice quivered ever so slightly and the tears came.

David was not thinking on sentimental terms, "She didn't bother trying to talk to me in person when she decided to go after my pension money. Instead she sicked that scumbag lawyer on me, threatening to take me to court." David had not thought about the pension money lately but now the thought of having to share it started a flame in his stomach.

"Look, Kelly, I busted my ass for years at HIC in order to have a little something when we retired. When she bailed on me, she gave up any rights to that money as far as I'm concerned. I'm sorry she didn't make a good choice with Gerald what's his name, last name, Folk, Poke, or whatever the hell it is."

"Pope. Daddy, you know things were not right with you and mom for a long time before she started seeing Gerald. She told me your marriage was never the same after you left her and went on the second tour of duty in Vietnam when you didn't have to. She had a baby and another one on the way, with very little money to live on and no one to help her.

"Legally, I think you are fighting an uphill battle, the law is pretty clear about community property. You may want to reconsider before you end up paying the scumbag most of the pension money." Kelly was giving David good advice and he knew it.

Why was it he let himself get boxed in like this? He remembered at the time of the divorce there was talk about the pension and having to share it. He had ignored the issue and now his daughter was telling him the facts of life.

"I don't want to get in between you and Mom, but I wish you could bury the hatchet. Actually, what I'm getting at is this, I want you and Mom here for Christmas." Kelly hurried on: "The boys would really enjoy having you both here at the same time. They love their grandma, too." Kelly looked up at her father, the way daughters do. That look turns most fathers to mush including David.

How could he resist Kelly's logic? Of course the kids loved their grandma. He guessed he could swallow some pride for the sake of the twins and Kelly. He hated to admit it, but he had always felt guilty about serving the second tour of duty. He had tried to hide behind his patriotic duty and loyalty to the Corps, but in his gut, he knew better. It had been a spur of the moment decision on his part, he could not bring himself to back out and lose face with his buddies. That decision damn near cost him his life, and eventually did cost him his marriage.

"You're right, Kelly. Thanks for making me see the light. I'll call your mother and tell her to call off the dogs. I give up."

Kelly wiped her face. "Thanks, Dad, I knew you would do the right thing." They cut across Lakeside Park and stopped in a small coffee shop for some hot cappuccino.

"Now, tell me all the dirt between your mother and Gerald Pope."

"You know I can't do that. I didn't tell mom about you and Kathryn." Kelly gave her dad a long sideways look. David hugged and kissed her on the forehead. She was Ok, he thought. At least something good came out of his marriage to Ellen.

David left Chicago Sunday evening and checked into the North Star Motel, in Dumont. The town was deserted at 8:00 PM. He drove his rental car down Main Street, turned right at the Methodist church, and onto the street where the O'Ryan house was. The house stood stark, illuminated by a lone street light at the corner. A dozen naked, giant Elm trees guarded the property. There was a single light on in one of the upstairs windows, but no activity he could see. No cars were parked in the driveway and the garage doors were closed.

Back at the motel, David zoned out on the Sunday night movie.

"Good morning, Sheriff. How are you? Can I buy you some coffee?" It was 9:00 AM Monday morning, and David had been waiting for Sheriff Woodford to walk into his office. Woodford's secretary told David on the telephone the "man" was on his way to Dumont and should be here any minute.

"Hell, yes! I'm about two cups low right now." The two men shook hands and walked over to Sherry's. The waitress brought coffee and doughnuts without asking. Sheriff Woodford got right to the point. "I received a reply from Australia. Cindy lived in Perth for the last few years. The only thing that showed up on the police record was a couple of traffic violations. I found out she owned quite a lot of property down there. I have a listing if you need to see it, I would estimate she's worth quite a bit of money. There was no marriage license or any law enforcement record.

"She is an officer in a corporation, Samson Mining and Milling Inc., so her photo is on the corporate records and also on her driver's license. She is for real. She is Cynthia O'Ryan, as far as I am concerned. I know you were talking to her classmates before you left for Ireland, did you turn up anything interesting?"

"Nothing I would consider out of the ordinary. She was a popular girl in high school. She dated a lot of guys. Some said she was more than just friendly, but you know how guys exaggerate. No one I talked to could tell me exactly why she left. The rumor mill speculated that she was pregnant. But she left everything including her boyfriend. It was a mystery to them. Has she talked to anyone in town yet?" David asked.

"Not that I know of. A moving truck unloading a lot of furniture last Friday. Her neighbor said it looked like the same stuff Bee shipped out when she closed the house. So, what's your plan David? Are you just going to knock on the door and invite yourself in?"

"That is my plan, Sheriff, the direct approach. I'll put on my best shirt and tie and try to make a favorable impression. Maybe bring some flowers." David smiled as he spoke, but that was exactly what he planned to do. Why not? She had already told the sheriff she didn't want to talk to him, so he had nothing to lose. The sheriff got a call on his radio and had to leave in a hurry. "I'll call you after I visit Cindy O'Ryan," David said, as the sheriff climbed into his patrol car.

David waited until one o'clock before he parked under the carport of the O'Ryan house and walked up to the side entrance and pulled the door chain. He was holding a large bouquet of mixed flowers. He had to go all the way to Rockford to find a flower shop, but it was worth it. The flowers looked better than usual in contrast to the gray and dismal overcast December sky.

David pulled the door chain twice before it was unlocked and opened. "Yes, who are you? What do you want?" said the woman standing in the doorway, a cigarette in her left hand.

It was Cindy O'Ryan. David recognized her face from the faxed copies of the driver's license and corporate papers Woodford had shown him. Stern face, faded blond hair pulled back, bags under her eyes, showing her age, a long way from the prom queen he saw in the photo Bee had shown him. She looked every bit of sixty years old, thin frame maybe a hundred and ten pounds, five foot five or so, makeup expertly applied, dressed in slacks and wool sweater.

"I'm David Jordan, I would very much like to talk to you. I bought your car. The one the Judge gave you for your graduation. These flowers are for you, a peace offering." He smiled his best smile and tried not to look offensive in any way.

Cindy looked at David for what seemed like a long time. Finally, she reached out for the bouquet and held it close. Smelling the fragrance she gave a curt, "Thank you." She cradled the flowers in her left arm, "I have nothing to say to you except, enjoy the car!" She stepped back inside, closed the door and slid the dead bolt in place.

CHAPTER 25

David stood on the porch, stunned. He did not expect to be dismissed this abruptly. Maybe he should have been more prepared, Sheriff Woodford had warned him. He said Cindy was strong-minded, he did not use the word rude, but that term fit the situation. Feeling like a door-to-door salesman who had just had the door slammed in his face, David retreated to the safety of his car.

Cindy had made her wishes clear, changing her mind would take some doing. He started driving out of town, down a backcountry road. He needed to think this situation through. There had to be a way to convince Cindy he was not going to hurt her or anyone she knew. All he was trying to do was put together the pieces so he would have a plot for a novel and satisfy his own curiosity. He realized the only way to get her to cooperate would be to find something she wanted and exchange it for the information he needed.

Only one other loose end came to David's mind: the missing math teacher, Carl Warren. He never did find out what happened to him. The letter he had sent to the high school administration office had not been answered. Okay, he decided, he could afford the time to do some investigative work.

The next stop was a phone booth and a call to the information operator. There were six Carl Warrens or C. Warrens listed in area code 815. David wrote down the numbers and called each one, asking for the Carl Warren that used to teach math in Dumont. No luck. David was not surprised, that would have been too easy.

The Internet was another possibility. He thought of going to the library and using their computer to get on the Internet and search for Carl Warren. The problem was, he did not know Carl's middle initial, or social security number, nor did he have any clue which city or state to search. Carl Warren was not an uncommon name, there were hundreds, probably thousands, of people with the same name in the Midwest.

Even if he did find the math teacher, assuming he was still alive, what did he expect to find out from him? He probably would not admit to anything. The Judge told Margaret he would take care of the Warren person when he got back from New York. What did he mean exactly? How did he make the math teacher disappear?

One place to search would be the dead file in the local newspaper office. It was a long shot but that's what they did in the movies. Dumont had a small semi-weekly newspaper called the Dumont Advertiser. The paper specialized in store ads, garage sales, farm commodity prices, marriages, and the local athletic team scores. There was a copy of the paper on the counter where David had eaten breakfast this morning. The first two pages carried stories about local events that masqueraded as news.

David found the Advertiser's office on a side street next to a secondhand furniture shop. The office manager dressed in Levi's, a tee shirt and ink stained apron, recognized David and wanted to know if he could be of service. "I'm trying to find out what happened to a Dumont high school teacher who dropped out of sight years ago. I thought I might be able to browse through your dead files for some information about this individual."

"How far back do you want to go?"

"1956"

"That's not possible." The response was quick, without thought and the abruptness immediately irritated David. The young man stepped back, took a breath, and explained, "This office and all the files down in the basement and in the backroom went up in smoke three years ago. I know who you are. You are Mr. David Jordan. I wrote news articles about you, Mr. Jordan. I tried to get a personal interview with you, but the sheriff wouldn't let me, so I interviewed everybody else I could corner. Some of the wire services picked up my stories. It was the most exciting news story I've ever covered. Did you read any of them?"

"Ah, no, I can't say that I did. To tell you the truth, it didn't occur to me this town had a newspaper until this morning. I'm sorry, it just didn't dawn on me."

"That's all right, we're pretty small, but we're growing. As soon as I finish college, I've got some ideas that will make people take notice."

"Would you be looking for Carl Warren?" the young man said, in the same manner as someone asking, "Would you like sugar in your coffee?"

David's mouth must have dropped open a foot at the mention of the math teacher's name. "How did you know I was looking for Warren?"

The office manager was a young man, barely out of his teens, and obviously pleased he had surprised David. "Someone else was trying to find information about the missing teacher last week."

David immediately tried to think of who else would be interested in someone who had left town over forty years ago. "Who was it?" asked David, leaning over the front counter.

"I can't tell you her name that would be unethical."

"Bullshit. What's printed in the newspaper is public information." David was trying to think of a convincing argument he could use. One he could convince the young reporter to reveal the name of the person who was looking for the same man he was. It was a female, he suspected Cindy O'Ryan, but he had to know the name for sure.

"Nah, that information is confidential. I can't tell you who it was."

"Now listen to me, son. It is very important I find Mr. Warren. Can you at least tell me what information you have on Warren?"

"That's just it, he left town many years ago, before I was born. There may not have been anything printed about him. This is not the Chicago Tribune, you know."

"Look, here's the deal, son. I'm working on a really important story. If I can find Mr. Warren, he may have the key to missing information I'm looking for. Now, I don't know a lot about computers, but I'll bet you have computer access to news agencies and sources of information that are not available to the average citizen. Am I right?"

"Sure, were linked to the Rockford Free Press news network. I have access to all kinds of news sources," replied the young man, not knowing just what David was getting at.

"Here's fifty dollars." David opened his billfold and laid out two twenties and a ten-dollar bill on the counter. "You search all the old files you can find for the name Carl Warren. He used to teach math here at Dumont, in 1956. He was in his twenties at the time, married and had a child. He organized science and math contest. See if you can find mention of his name during the period, say between 1956 and 1966.

"If you find some information that allows me to find him, you'll earn another fifty dollars. Can you do it?"

The young man, Eric Jenkins, could use a hundred
dollars. His father owned the paper and Eric was working for
starvation wages. "I'll do my best. I'll have to wait until we
close the office tonight, so I can stay on-line without
interrupting incoming business. Tell me where you're staying
so I can get in touch with you if I find something?"

"The North Star Motel, room nine. If I don't hear from
you this evening, I'll stop by tomorrow morning. Do you want
to tell me who else is looking for Warren?" David thought
maybe the money had loosened the kid up.

"I can't tell you that Mr. Jordan, she's a long time mail
order customer. It wouldn't be right. I'll get on the computer as
soon as we close, promise."

"Do you suppose you could find back copies of the
paper with the articles you wrote about me? Maybe all of the
June, July and August issues? I never thought to keep any of the
news accounts. I would like to read what you wrote."

"Sure, I can do that, Mr. Jordan. I keep copies of
everything I write."

David walked over to Sherry's Coffee shop and ordered
the Monday special: chicken fried steak, baked potato,
vegetables, and desert. He sat in a booth in the back of the
restaurant, away from the busy cash register and noisy entrance.
He asked the waitress if she had any back copies of the local
paper, the Dumont Advertiser, lying around. "Sure, I got a
whole stack of them in the back, I save them for my boy. He
collects papers for the Boy Scouts paper drive."

"I'm just interested in the last couple of weeks, if it's not
too much trouble."

The waitress brought David a hand full of papers and his dinner at the same time. "I want them back when you're finished," she said.

The papers were only a few pages thick, it must take a year supply to help with the paper drive, David thought. He didn't expect to find anything useful, he just wanted to get an idea of the type of articles appearing in the news section.

The local news was just that. Births, marriages, police activity, city council meeting, news of record, and a column entitled "Dumont Gossip." The gossip column contained just what the title implied. It listed people visiting from out-of-town, local residents in the hospital, dinner parties, who was seen with whom at the last VFW meeting, and so on.

David was positive the other person inquiring about Carl Warren was none other than Cindy O'Ryan. She must have had the paper sent to her in Australia so she could keep up on the local news in Dumont, but why would she be trying to locate Carl Warren after all these years? David let his imagination run wild with all kinds of scenarios that would put Cindy on a collision course with Carl Warren, the man who fathered her child forty-three years ago. Where was the child now? Could it be that Carl ended up with Cindy's baby?

Snow was falling as David drove back to the motel. It came down in fluffy flakes and stuck to everything. Living in southern California most of his life, David seldom had the opportunity to watch a snowfall in person. It was quite nice, he thought. The leafless elm trees in the town square took on a softer, more pleasing look with the snow covering the bare branches. It occurred to him that at the rate the snow was falling he would be stuck here for a while. It was a week before Christmas and he wanted to get back to Chicago so he could do a little shopping for the twins.

As soon as he entered the motel room, he turned up the thermostat, located the extra blanket in the closet, and flung it on the bed. After his shower, he climbed under the covers and flicked on the TV. Finally, locating an interesting movie, he propped himself up with both pillows. He let his mind relax with the help of a little Jim Beam he had packed in his suitcase.

The eleven o'clock news had just started when a loud knock on the door woke David. He jumped up and pulled on his trousers. "Who is it?"

"It's Eric, Mr. Jordan. I have the information you wanted."

David opened the door and Eric came in, covered with snow. Quick looks past the figure covered in layers of clothing told David the first winter snow had covered the town. "Come on in, Eric. Let's see what you have for me."

"I had almost given up, when I remembered something the other party that was looking for Carl Warren had told me. Anyway, here it is." He handed David a brief description of a newspaper article that appeared in the Rockford Free Press in October of 1962. The article was entitled: "Former Lt. Governor Killed in Car Crash."

The article was about the death of Timothy O'Ryan, former Illinois State Lt. Governor. Eric had highlighted the third line, "A passing motorist, Carl Warren, discovered former Lt. Governor Timothy O'Ryan's partially submerged car at around 3:00 AM." The entire article was on microfilm at the Rockford Free Press. Eric had called someone at the news desk in Rockford and had them fax a copy of the article to him.

"That's great, Eric. I really appreciate what you did. That was a good job." David flipped open his billfold and gave Eric three twenties. "A little extra for doing this in quick time." Eric took the money and stuffed it in his Levi's.

"Thanks, Mr. Jordan. Anytime you need some research done let me know. I'll have the back issues of the paper for you in the morning if you want to stop by." He turned and started to walk out the door, flipping his jacket hood up against the snow.

"Eric, have you told this other person about what you found?

The door closed with a thud and Eric was gone. If he answered, David could not hear.

David read and reread the copy Eric had provided. Evidently, the Judge had been driving late at night on a highway, north of Springfield. According to the deputy sheriff interviewed by the reporter, Judge O'Ryan was apparently traveling at a high rate of speed on State Highway 29, when he lost control of his car on a curve and went off the road into the Sangamon River. The rain slick road and lack of skid marks indicated the Judge might have fallen asleep at the wheel. Mr. Carl Warren, traveling in the same direction, at approximately three AM, saw the taillights of the partially submerged car and called the sheriff's office from a nearby farmhouse. The farmer, Mr. Eggleston, and his son were able to attach a tow chain to a tractor and pulled the car out of the river.

Judge O'Ryan was found inside the car, he was pronounced dead at the scene. An autopsy had been ordered to determine the exact cause of death. No other vehicles were involved in the accident. There was no mention of the reason for the Judge to be on the highway at night.

Most interesting to David, was the absence of any mention of where Carl was going or why he was traveling on the same highway at the same time as the Judge. The article did not mention Carl Warren's address, or hometown. Sloppy reporting, David thought.

He lay awake half the night thinking about the connection between the Judge and Carl Warren. There had to have been some kind of meeting or contact before the accident. They could not have been at the same place, at the same time purely by coincidence, especially at three in the morning. Did Cindy know about this connection? All the sudden it seemed there were more questions than answers.

Tomorrow, he would call Sheriff Woodford and see if he could dig up a copy of the autopsy. That would be vital information. He decided he would go to the public library in Dumont and talk to the librarian who had helped him in the past. He wanted to find out what kind of information they had on the former Lt. Governor.

At 8:30 AM, Eric barged through the front door of Sherry's coffee shop, looked around and spotted David sitting at his favorite booth in the back of the restaurant. "Mr. Jordan, I thought I might find you here. I got some more news about Carl Warren. You're going to like this."

Several customers turned and looked at Eric and David. "Keep your voice down, Eric. I don't want everybody in town listening in on my conversation," He was a little annoyed at the kid for causing a scene that would surely be all over town by mid-morning.

"Sorry, I guess I'm a little excited because I think I found something that you wanted in the first place, an address. This came in during the night from the Illinois State News Agency. I had posted an inquiry last night, but they were busy, and didn't respond till this morning." He handed David another computer printout of an article that appeared in the Peoria News Dispatch, 3 April 1966.

The small back page column was entitled: "Eastside High School Announces Math Contest Winners." As before,

Eric had highlighted the line drawing David's attention. "Carl Warren, Eastside High School math instructor, announces two of his students have placed first and second in the Illinois State Science and Math Contest." Towards the end of the article was Mr. Warren's phone number. He wanted parents to call him so he could give them the contest scores of all the students who had participated.

"Here are your back copies of the Dumont Advertiser. Dad always prints more than we need. Is that the information you need?" Eric was beaming with self-importance.

"This is great Eric. I'll take it from here and see if Mr. Warren is taking any calls this morning. I have another job for you. Do you want to make another hundred?"

"Sure. My car is broke down, and it needs new brakes. Who or what do you want me to track down now?"

"Judge Timothy O'Ryan. There should be a lot of material out there about him, but limit your search for the years between 1962 and 1966." David knew the Judge died in 1962, but if there were any fallout from his accident, it would be after the date of the crash.

Back at the motel, David sat at the small table and entered notes in his journal and phrased questions he would ask Carl Warren, assuming he still had the same phone number and was alive. Considering the time lapse, Carl could easily be dead or long gone from the state of Illinois.

David dialed the Warren's number. Four rings, then finally a female voice: "Hello."

"I would like to speak with Carl Warren please, this is David Jordan calling."

"What is it you want to talk to him about? What are you selling?"

"I'm not selling anything. Is this Mrs. Warren?"

"Yes. Who did you say this is?"

"David Jordan. I want to talk to Carl and get some information about one of his former students.

The silence on the other end of the telephone lasted nearly a full minute. "If you want to talk to Carl, you're too late, about ten years too late. He passed away in 1989. He died from prostrate cancer. Which student do you want to know about and why?" Mrs. Warren sounded a little testy.

"Mrs. Warren, I'm driving down to Peoria this afternoon. Could I please meet with you? I'm trying to gather information for a book, I'm writing, and I think you may be able to help me fill in some blanks. The student I'm interested in is Cindy O'Ryan."

Another long silence. "I wondered how long it would take her to find us. Are you a private detective or something?"

"No, absolutely not." David's brain was racing ahead: why did she think Cindy would be looking for her? He had to see Mrs. Warren now. "Cindy O'Ryan does not know I'm talking with you. I am a private citizen, and I am not on anybody's payroll. Please, Mrs. Warren, give me your address. I could get it from the telephone company."

"I don't suppose there's any stopping you now. All right, but no funny business. My son will be here, I'm not buying anything."

David picked up his journal and the small tape recorder he borrowed from Kelly. The drive to Peoria would take about three hours. He figured he could be at Mrs. Warren's house at 1:00 PM easily.

The excitement was building in David's head. He sensed he was on to something important to Cindy O'Ryan. If he could uncover some hidden secret about her past or the Judge's, he could use it as a lever to encourage her to talk to him.

The drive to Peoria was boring. Interstate 39 and then US 24 to Peoria. The scenery could only be interesting to people who thought corn fields, rusty farm machinery, and cows standing knee deep in manure was pleasing to the eye. Fortunately, snow shielded the most unappealing junk from the passing motorist. The highway department had dumped tons of salt on the roads, so they were passable and traffic was flowing near normal. The further south David drove the less snow remained on the ground.

Peoria appeared in the distance and David started looking for lunch. Without trying, he found himself in the center of town next to the Illinois River. He found a small dinner advertising, "Home Cooking." The waitress who took his order was able to give him directions to the street address he had gotten from Mrs. Warren.

She lived on the outskirts of Peoria in an aging subdivision. The street address was easy enough to find. The house appeared to be a well-kept-split level brick and aluminum sided home with a fireplace chimney on one end of the composition shingle roof. Two late model cars were parked in the driveway.

The weather had turned cold after the snow and the wind blew the cold up David's pant leg, and down his neck. The walk from the warm car to the front porch of the Warren house brought lounging memories of southern California.

One ring of the doorbell and the door opened. A tall, fair-haired, slender, man greeted David. He was about forty years of age. "Hello, I'm David Jordan. Mrs. Warren is expecting me."

"Come in. Wipe your feet off in the entry hall. I'm Chuck Warren, Mrs. Warren's son." David cleaned his feet as directed and took off his windbreaker. The house was decorated for Christmas. Presents surrounded a large Christmas tree opposite the fireplace. A heavyset woman, well into her sixties, with gray streaked hair was sitting in a wheelchair parked next to the fireplace. A plaid car-blanket was draped around her legs. Another woman, wimpish and forty-something, was sitting on the couch.

Chuck introduced his mother, Mrs. Warren, and his wife, Ethel. "Mr. Jordan, would you please get to the point of your visit. My mother is not well, and I don't want her to be upset or inconvenienced in any way." Chuck did not play the role of protector well, it was not natural to him and he was uncomfortable playing the part.

"Then I'll get to it," David said as he sat on the edge of the recliner he had been offered.

"Are you folks aware of the events that took place in Dumont this past summer?"

Mrs. Warren answered in a firm but small voice, "We have not lived in Dumont for many years, Mr. Jordan. I do not keep in contact with anyone who lives there." Mrs. Warren had turned her wheelchair toward David. She wore the textbook picture of a poker face. He could not read her at all.

David felt very uncomfortable. He knew he had stumbled into the heart of the Cindy O'Ryan story, but he did not have a road map on how to get to the bottom line.

"I'll start by telling you how I got involved this summer, in Dumont." David spent several minutes explaining the bare highlights of the estate auction. He told them about the killing of Jim Ballantyne, his involvement in the killing of Adam

Barnet, the attempt on his own life, and finally his desire to write a book using Cindy's life story as the plot.

"I know Cindy was a student of your husband's, Mrs. Warren, she took four years of math classes from him in high school and won academic honors in the process. I assume you knew her."

"Yes, I did know Cindy O'Ryan. What is your question, Mr. Jordan?"

She's not going to cut me any slack. He had no way of knowing if Mrs. Warren knew about Cindy and her husband's affair. He was afraid to mention Cindy's pregnancy for fear of revealing a family secret the son may not have been aware of. He wished he could talk to Mrs. Warren in private.

"I can see you're uncomfortable, Mr. Jordan, but if you think I'm going to make it easier for you, you are mistaken."

David looked around the room hoping to find a quick exit if he needed it. He was in deep water and he was fumbling for the correct words to phrase the next question. "Mrs. Warren, Cindy O'Ryan and your husband were very close. He spent a lot of time after school tutoring her and helping her with her math skills. Cindy was good. She won the state math competition in 1956.

"Some of her classmates I talked to recently implied there was more to the relationship than student, teacher. Did you know Cindy's father took her to New York on graduation night, to live with his brother and sister-in-law? Cindy was pregnant."

"Mr. Jordan, you haven't told me anything I didn't already know. Now what is your question?"

Chuck came off the couch. "Mom, I told you I thought this was a bad idea. The doctor said no excitement. You're getting yourself worked up. Mr. Jordan, my mother has a bad heart. They gave her a pacemaker four months ago, but it has not provided the relief we had hoped for." Chuck was standing next to his mother and held out his hand. "We should ask Mr. Jordan to leave, Mom. I don't see the point in this conversation anyway."

Mrs. Warren took Chuck's hand in hers. "I've known all along this day would come. Your father and I discussed it many times. If Mr. Jordan found us, it won't be long before Cindy finds us." Mrs. Warren looked straight at her son and said, "Chuck, sit down. Ethel, why don't you make us a nice pot of tea? I have to get this off my chest, I may not have long before the Lord calls me. It's time."

David was holding his breath. Apparently whatever her secret was, her son was unaware of it. He had switched on the tape recorder in the car and placed it in his shirt pocket under his jacket. He hoped it would at least pick up enough of the conversation so he could transcribe it later to his journal.

"Mr. Jordan, Cindy O'Ryan got pregnant by my husband. I'm sure you knew that and were afraid or too polite to blurt it out." Chuck stood up and started to say something, but the words were not there.

"Chuck, sit down and be quiet. You need to hear this. Your sister, Gloria, will want you to tell her all about it when she gets here for Christmas. And poor Steward, I hope he understands. Ethel, where is my tea?"

Mrs. Warren began telling a story that had been bottled up for years and a look of relief gradually came over her. "Cindy O'Ryan was a beautiful girl and she knew it. She could have any boy in high school, and did, if you believe the rumors. She was also very intelligent: her mind was like a calculator.

She could do complex math problems in her head. Her talent constantly amazed my husband.

"She squandered her gift. I don't believe she ever appreciated the fact God had given her the ability to become a great mathematician or scientist. She was too busy doing what girls like her do, teasing and flirting to get what she wanted.

"I knew something was going on between my husband and her, the last year we were in Dumont. I had my first baby, and I was happy being a mother and wife. I didn't want to see what was before my eyes. One week after graduation my husband came into the house like a wild man. 'We're moving' he said. 'I'm tired of this place, they don't pay enough. We are going to Rockford, I'll get a job teaching paying twice as much as they do in this dump.' I knew something had happened to set him off like that, but he wouldn't tell me.

"The next day he rented one of those U-Haul trailers, and we packed everything in it and left town. That night we stayed in a motel in Rockford, and I begged him to tell me what had happened. Finally, he broke down and cried. It must have been twenty minutes before he could talk, finally he got it out: 'Cindy O'Ryan is pregnant and I'm the father,' he said.

"I wasn't shocked, I had seen her constantly flirting with Carl. The shame of it was, she had a boyfriend, he used to come by our place and pick her up. Carl tried to act like he wasn't jealous, but I knew he was. That night, he told me she had made up her mind at the beginning of her senior year, to seduce him. He tried to talk sense to her, but she was too much of a temptation for him. Carl told me that during spring break he finally gave in. After the first time, she was too bold to ignore. He had sex with her several times during the next six weeks.

"He said he did not know she was pregnant until graduation night. He knew something was wrong, because

Cindy was to receive an award for winning the state math championship. Everyone was asking what happened to her and no one knew. She just disappeared.

"The next week, Judge O'Ryan confronted my husband and told him he was the father of Cindy's baby. The Judge was furious, he accused Carl of ruining his daughter's life, jeopardizing his political career, and causing a major disgrace in the school system. He told Carl, Cindy was in New York with relatives. After she had the baby, she would put it up for adoption. He wanted Carl, our child and me out of town immediately. We were never to come back and never tell anyone about Carl's relationship with Cindy.

"Carl was not a big man Mr. Jordan, he was a gentleman. The Judge intimidated him by saying if we refused to go, he would have Carl arrested for statutory rape and thrown in prison for at least eight years. We both knew the Judge had the power to carry out his threat.

"That night in the motel room, we both got down on our hands and knees and prayed to God for help. We prayed for guidance. Carl prayed for forgiveness. Chuck, I forgave your father and I believe God did too. Your father was a good man. He was a good father to you, Gloria, and Steward."

Mrs. Warren stroked her son's hand. Chuck looked tenderly at his mother and said, "Mom, I really think you should rest now. Mr. Jordan got what he came for." He looked at David, "Enough is enough."

"No son, there's more and I've got to get it out now." She finished her tea and indicated to Ethel, she wanted more.

"I knew that night in the motel God had spoken to us. We had to find Cindy before she gave the baby up for adoption. It was Carl's child just as much as it was hers. We both knew we had to take the baby as our own." Chuck's eyes were popping out of his head. Obviously, he couldn't believe what he was hearing.

"I know the question in your head, Mr. Jordan. How did we know it was Carl's and not some foolish boy in high school? Cindy was seeing a young man who was working in town, but I didn't know his name. Carl told me Cindy said her boyfriend would not have sex with her out of respect.

"She told Carl she had fantasized about making love to him since the first of the year and not to believe those exaggerated locker room stories about her. He knew Cindy had a reputation for sleeping around, but Carl was convinced it was a charade. He knew he was not Cindy's first lover but he felt she lacked the experience of a woman who had been sexually active.

"Cindy was the biggest flirt and tease in town, but according to Carl, she was unresponsive in bed. Don't ask me to explain it, I can't. In my heart, I knew that baby was Carl's, and he did too.

"Carl called everyone of Cindy's girlfriends and finally talked to someone, I didn't know who it was, who said Cindy was on the West Coast. She gave Carl the address, and we decided to go to Los Angeles to try to talk Cindy into letting us have the baby. It was in late November before we got enough money to take the trip out west. We found her in a Catholic home for girls in West Los Angeles. By the time we got there she was due to deliver any day.

"At first Cindy wouldn't see us. I asked one of the nuns at the home if she would talk to Cindy for us and convince her we meant no harm. Finally, we were allowed to see Cindy the second evening we were in town.

"Carl and I both talked to her and convinced her we could give the child a better home than any stranger. I asked

Cindy point blank one day, when Carl was out of the room, if the baby was his. She looked me straight in the eye and said it was.

"She accepted our offer after she realized Carl had legal rights, as the baby's father, and we would not be raising the baby in Dumont. Actually, I think she was relieved to know God-fearing people would be the baby's parents. So, we stayed ten days, until the baby was born. It was a boy, and we left for home two days later. We named him Steward, we call him Stu. He lives in Boston with his wife and two beautiful children.

"We raised him as our own, and I loved him just like he was my own. We told Steward he was adopted, right from the start. Carl never wanted to admit he had sex with one of his students, so I agreed with him that we would not tell anyone Carl was Steward's real father. We new Cindy was going to Australia because she already had her airline ticket when we saw her in Los Angeles. She swore she would never come back, but I guess she did. I know she will want to see Steward, I would if I was she.

"Mom, I can't believe you kept this secret all these years." Chuck was in major disbelief.

Poor Ethel was holding a tissue to her nose and sniffling quietly. "Are you going to tell Stu?" Ethel asked.

"I have to now, don't I, Mr. Jordan? He'll find out from Cindy, or from you and your book."

"Mrs. Warren, I can assure you, I had no idea you had taken Cindy's baby as your own. I have no intention of confronting your son, so whatever course you take, it's between you and him." David was having a problem digesting the revelations Mrs. Warren was pouring out.

"I guess in a way I want to thank you, Mr. Jordan. I have been carrying this burden around a long time. Carl wanted to tell Stu who his real mother was because he was always afraid Cindy would come back at least want to see her child. He was afraid Stu would find out the truth from someone else and then not forgive him. Carl did not have the courage and I didn't either till now. I think when Stu and his family come home for Christmas, I will be able give him a present he won't forget." She seemed pleased with herself for unburdening her soul.

David was sitting on the edge of his chair the whole time Mrs. Warren was telling her story. Now he relaxed enough to sit back. "Mrs. Warren, I want to thank you for letting me in on your family secret. I can assure you when I write my book, I will change names and places so as not to cause you or your family any embarrassment."

"Thank you, Mr. Jordan, you sound like an honorable man, I believe you. Now are there any other questions on your mind?"

"Just one." David hesitated to mention the Judge's accident and Carl's presence at the scene, but it was now or never. "I found an old newspaper article telling how Judge O'Ryan was killed in a car accident not far from here. Apparently, he went to sleep at the wheel and drove off the road into a river south of here. Your husband discovered the wreck at three in the morning and called the sheriff." Mrs. Warren sat motionless with a blank look on her face.

"You do your homework, Mr. Jordan, I'll give you credit. That was a long time ago."

"Mom, what are you saying? You think Dad had something to do with that man's death?" Chuck was getting an education about his parents and was not taking it too well. "What was Dad doing out at three in the morning?"

"To tell you the truth, I don't know. All I do know is Judge O'Ryan would send letters to school administrators where Carl was teaching and imply Carl had to be watched and could not be trusted to be alone with the female students. Your dad had to change teaching jobs several times in the early sixties because of those letters.

"Carl was gone the night of the accident. The next day, when he came up the driveway, I was frantic to see him, I was getting ready to call the police. I had already talked to the hospital and asked if they had Carl in the emergency room. I asked him, 'Where have you been?' He walked right past me and started taking off his clothes in the bedroom. He looked at me with a funny look and said, 'I can't tell you, and please never ask me again. It's none of your business. I will not discuss it.'

"He meant it. He did not discuss it, ever. I knew better than to press the issue. Your dad was strong willed that way. Once he had made up his mind that was it. Of course, I heard about the accident, I read the papers. Some people even called your dad and asked him about it. He acted like it was a fluke, and he just happened to be passing by.

After your father died, I was going through his things and I found a letter in the back of his desk. It was another one of those awful letters from Judge O'Ryan, it was addressed to the chairman of the school board here in Peoria. There was no postmark on the envelope. I have no idea how Carl got hold of it. The Judge was asking the school board to investigate Carl for improprieties involving his female students.

"I burned the letter." Mrs. Warren let out a sigh of relief and settled back in her wheel chair. "That is the end of the story, Mr. Jordan. I have no idea how or why the judge went off the road that night and I don't want to know. I'm tired now." She looked directly at David and her expression said, "Don't bother trying to ask anymore questions."

"Ethel, help me to my room please. Chuck, see Mr. Jordan out."

CHAPTER 26

The drive back to Dumont was a blur. Not from the weather, but in David's mind. Mrs. Warren had filled in the missing link. He did not have to see Cindy now. It did not make any difference, as far as his book was concerned. He could make up the rest and throw a little imagination in on top of the real life events. Isn't that what a legitimate writer would do? That's what Kathryn's father told him he would have to do. Good authors write based on people's real life experiences, maybe their own, and add a lot of dialogue to make the book interesting to the reader. He could do that.

It was Tuesday, December 21st. Christmas was on Saturday, and he had to get his shopping done. David planed to head back to Chicago first thing in the morning. He wondered if Ellen would be at Kelly's. He and Ellen hadn't said a civil word to each other since the divorce. This Christmas most likely would be a very interesting holiday season. It would be the first time in years, in which the two of them would be in the same room without lawyers present.

Sherry's was closed when David drove into Dumont. Damn, he should have thought of that. There was an all night gas station, south of town that had a mini mart attached. He was hungry and almost anything sounded good.

Back in the motel, two leathery hot dogs, and a couple of beers later, David was ready for a good night's sleep. Then he noticed the message light was blinking on his telephone.

The recorded voice belonged to the motel office manager. She said in a smoker's rasping voice, "Mr. Jordan, I have a letter for you in the office. Please stop by and pick it up." The motel office was closed and locked. He would have to wait until morning to find out what the message was. Who could it be from? Sheriff Woodford, maybe, with the autopsy report.

David felt good about the conversation with Mrs. Warren. She needed to get it off her chest and he needed the information. They were both happy. Her children were in shock. What about poor Steward? David was thinking about what it would be like to find out your adopted father is your real father. He hoped Stu would be understanding and not flip out and cause his mother a heart attack or something.

By 8:30 AM, David was in his usual booth in Sherry's when the sheriff walked in and sat down opposite him. Woodford had been outside in the twenty-degree cold, investigating a break-in somewhere. He was chilled to the bone from the wind and snow. The cold traveled over to David's side of the table, causing him to silently long for the sunny skies.

"David, I received your message about wanting a copy of the Judge's death certificate. It's a matter of public record. I don't know what you were expecting but the medical examiner listed the cause of death as a blunt- force trauma to the forehead. Most likely received as a result of the Judge's car smashing though a guardrail and crashing down the embankment into the river. His car did not have seat-belts, or, if it had them, he wasn't wearing any, it was a '60 Buick."

David thought to himself, "Carl Warren probably had something to do with that blunt-force trauma. In fact, I would bet on it. How did Carl make it look like an accident? How exactly did he take revenge on the Judge? If he hit the Judge with an object, he would have had to put the body back into the car and some how drive it off the road into the river. Well, there is no point in thinking about it now. It will be a mystery forever, because both parties are dead and buried."

"Thanks, Sheriff. That pretty well wraps it up for me. I'm heading back to Chicago this morning and I don't know when I'll be back. You will have to let me know when Billy's trial is scheduled. I plan on spending the holidays with my daughter, her family, and my ex."

"Your ex-wife? That should be cozy. Take some pictures so I can see how well you get along." The sheriff laughed then he got a call on his radio and had to leave.

David finished his breakfast and was about to walk out when Eric made another grand entrance. "Mr. Jordan, I'm glad I found you. Look at what I have for you." He handed David a manila envelope stuffed full of newspaper clippings about Judge O'Ryan. Some dated back to the 1930's.

"How did you get these Eric? They didn't come over the fax machine. These are the original clippings." David was very impressed, but surprised by Eric's resourcefulness. "Tell me how you got them."

Shuffling from one foot to the other Eric blurted out, "The other person I told you about came by yesterday afternoon. She wanted to know if I could go to Rockford and look in the archives in the Rockford Free Press office. I told her I didn't need to go anywhere because I had the information about Mr. Warren on my computer. That is when she asked me if you had been in to see me. I know I should have kept quiet about it, but she knew who you were. She said you two were working together, so I figured what the hell. It's public information, just like you said."

David tried not to let on he was pissed that Eric had told Cindy about Carl Warren. On second thought, Cindy would find her way to Peoria eventually. He was more interested in knowing what Cindy was up to.

"She asked what other information you were looking for and I guess I kind of let it slip about the Judge. That's when she offered to help by supplying all of this information. Isn't it great? She had it at her house and brought it over about an hour later. She said to tell you she would exchange this file for information about Mr. Carl Warren."

Eric said he didn't have time to sit and have breakfast. The fact that David had not invited him didn't seem to make an impression. He had to get to work on Thursday's Food Mart sale sheet. David laughed as Eric left. This kid has a lot of personality, he hoped Eric got a chance to be a reporter for a real paper someday.

David glanced through the hundreds of clippings, he could see that it would take some real analysis to put all the information in any kind of order. Maybe there wouldn't be anything here that would contribute to the book. But who knew? Some evening, he would pull out the folder and read through it.

As he drove back to the motel, David began to wonder if Cindy was ready to talk, or did she intend to trade information and that was all? He was debating on what his next step should be. Should he knock on Cindy's door, call first, or send a note? He made up his mind after he picked up his message from the motel office.

Dear Mr. Jordan,

It seems we are looking for the same people. I would like to meet with you and exchange information. I will be free to meet with you tomorrow morning at 10:00 AM. Please be prompt.

Cindy O'Ryan

Did she think he would come running at her request? "Please be prompt," my ass. "Fat chance sweetie", he said to himself, as he drove out of town headed for the interstate and Chicago.

CHAPTER 27

Ellen was the picture of a devoted grandmother. She doted on the twins and they in return were constantly pulling on her and begging for favors. The warm atmosphere pleasantly surprised David. Kelly had decorated the house with old-fashioned, home, made decorations. He had no idea how she found time to take care of the house, the kids, Fred, and work for a demanding boss like Jeff Carver.

Fred was constantly feeding the CD player with Christmas music and keeping the adults in the proper mood with heavily spiked eggnog. After two drinks, David had to resort to coffee to avoid exhibiting his usual slurred speech. He didn't want to give Ellen any excuse to criticize him in front of the kids or Kelly.

On Christmas Eve day, Ellen and David found themselves alone in Fred's office. David had been sleeping on the couch and Ellen had offered to take care of David's laundry. A peace offering of sorts.

"I was sorry to hear about you and Gerald, Ellen. What happened? I thought you two had a lot in common."

"Oh, we did have a lot in common, but this past year we just seemed to grow apart and talked less and less until we finally both realized it just wasn't working. He was devoted to his medical practice and political activities. I had my own job at the hospital taking up a great deal of time, as well, we just drifted apart." She looked like she was going to cry, but then changed the subject and said, "Did Kelly tell you I was promoted at the hospital? I'm the Director of Personnel now."

"That's great, congratulations," David said, meaning every word. He was glad to see she had made a good career move. Maybe she would have a good pension plan now and would leave his alone. Actually, he had noticed that Ellen was taking good care of herself physically. She was trim and fit for a woman in her middle years. She should not have trouble finding another partner.

"How is your book coming? Kelly filled me in on your meeting with the woman from Australia. Tell me, how did you get the idea for a book anyway?"

David and Ellen sat alone in Fred's office for most of the morning. They exchanged news about each other and discussed Kelly and Fred's success with raising two young boys in midtown Chicago. They both recalled the day they received the news about Chance's death. It was then that they held each other for a long time. There were tears on both sides.

Christmas morning was hectic. Like the scene in most American homes, the boys were tearing open presents at a frantic rate. Being twins, they both received the same type of gifts. No one wanted to be responsible for making one appear more deserving than the other. David's gift made a big impression on the boys. For Danny, David gave a basketball autographed by Michel Jordan, and to Steven, a Sammy Sousa autographed baseball.

The day after New Year's, Ellen was preparing to return to California, and David was contemplating returning to Dumont and meeting with Cindy. A letter had been delivered to David via Federal Express on New Year's Eve day.

The letter was from Cindy O'Ryan. In it, she explained how she had gotten Kelly's address from Eric. She indicated David must have overlooked the message she sent to him at the motel. She would be home the week after the holidays, and she would like to meet with him to discuss mutual interest, at his convenience, of course. It was signed simply, "Cindy" in the beautiful script as was the body of the letter.

"Your damn right, at my convenience," David said aloud after he had read the short letter.

"What are you going to do, Dad?" Kelly quickly expressed her own opinion, "You should go at once, and find out what kind of women Cindy O'Ryan was...or is"

"I'll go, but on my terms, not hers." David was adamant.

David dropped Ellen off at the O'Hare airport, on his way to Dumont. The weather was crappy, a light snow was falling on top of the six inches accumulated two days ago. The roads were icy and dangerous. David drove with both hands griping the wheel trying his best to avoid driving next to eighteen-wheelers and the blinding clouds of slush and water being thrown up by their wheels.

He had made reservations to fly back to California the day after tomorrow. He hoped he could finish with Cindy so he could get back to warm weather. He missed the early morning walks on the beach just a few bocks from his place in San Pedro.

Dumont looked sad and dreary. Snow was piled high along the curbs of Main Street. Some cars were buried and had not moved in several days. The motel manager greeted him and handed him the key to room number nine without asking for a credit card or signature on the guest ticket. He planned to stay one night only. He turned up the thermostat in his room and took stock of himself in the mirror. Not bad. He was wearing a very expensive and stylish new variegated sweater Kelly had given him. A light lunch at Sherry's would be nice and then he would drop in on Miss O'Ryan.

The old Victorian house seemed somehow deteriorated in the cold light of this January day. The snow had not been shoveled off the driveway. Previous tire tracks leading into the garage had frozen in place. They would be there until a spring thaw. Ice and snow covered the porch. A footpath had been shoveled through the snow, up the porch steps, and to the house.

David gave three pulls on the cranky door chime before the door was unlocked and opened. "Mr. Jordan, how nice. Did I miss your call?" Cindy's greeting was cold as the January morning. "Do come in so I can close the door."

"Thank you, Miss O'Ryan. I was passing through town, on my way to California, so I thought I would stop by to see if we could exchange information." David could be cold also. He had the upper hand, he knew where her son was.

"Let's stop with the games, Mr. Jordan. Come in and sit by the fireplace. The furnace in this old house is not functioning properly, and I can't get any decent help to come and look at it, so I'm forced to live next to the fireplace. Fortunately, there is plenty of wood in the basement.

"Make yourself comfortable, I was about to pour some tea, would you care for some?"

"Yes, please." David took a quick look around while Cindy was in the kitchen. The living room had been converted into a one-room apartment. A bed was positioned in a corner, a desk and chair in another. An overstuffed couch and easy chairs were positioned in front to the fireplace for maximum comfort. A glowing fire in the fireplace was burning vigorously, producing a good amount of heat. David moved the easy chair back away from the fire screen, the left arm was very hot.

Cindy returned with a serving tray and set it down on a small coffee table in front of the couch.

"I moved this chair back because it was getting pretty hot. I'm sure you don't want a fire in here."

"No, that would be disastrous. Thank you. This house would go up in minutes. It's over a hundred years old, built in

1898, I believe. My grandfather built this house for his wife. How do you like your tea, Mr. Jordan?"

"Straight up, thank you. Please, call me David. I feel as though I know you. I have been investigating your past. I'm sure you know that. My goal is to write a book based on your life. Not a biography, but a novel using your life as a basis for the story line or plot. I was hoping you wouldn't mind." David was embarrassed that he had blurted out those last two sentences without more introductory conversation.

"I'm well aware of your intentions, Mr. Jordan. I'm not pleased. How would you like someone snooping around in your past, exposing you to all kinds of ridicule? I have consulted a lawyer about getting a restraining order against you. He assured me he could, if I tell him to go ahead with it."

"Why haven't you done that?" David asked, taking a sip of hot tea. It was very good tea. Strong, not bitter.

"I was waiting to talk to you in person, to see if that was really what you are about, and also to determine if you are any good, as a writer I mean. Are you a good writer, David? What have you written?"

"This will be my first book, Miss O'Ryan I'm a retired manufacturing engineer. I know that's not a qualification in itself, but I have written numerous technical papers so I'm familiar with the English language. The book would be a novel, using fictitious names, and places. I don't think anyone outside of you and your relatives, or the Warrens, would be able to recognize it." David sat, drinking his tea and taking stock of the woman across from him.

She was still beautiful, older, gray hair mixed with blond and pulled back in a bun, lightly lined face, clear blue eyes, erect posture, and although she was thin she still had domineering presence. She wore a full-length dress with a high collar and a wool sweater. She reminded David of an old-fashioned schoolteacher. He wondered if she resembled her mother.

"I can't say that your background causes me to jump at the chance of immortality, but let's skip that subject for now. What did you find out when you visited Carl Warren's wife?" Her directness came easily, with confidence. David could picture her at a conference table with men and being in charge.

"I thought you would make your own journey to Peoria, Miss O'Ryan. You had the same information that I had."

"Please, call me Cindy. Yes, I did. In fact, I did make the journey, as you put it. I found the address in the reverse telephone directory. When I got there, it was the day after Christmas. I had called from here before I left, but no one answered. So I drove to Peoria and went by the house. There were lights on, but no one answered the door. So I went next-door and inquired.

"The neighbor lady explained they were all at the hospital. Mrs. Warren had suffered another heart attack Christmas day, and her children were standing by, expecting the worse. She told me Carl had passed away years before."

"I find it difficult to believe you would just walk up to the front door and announce yourself as Steward's mother. You have no idea of how your actions would be taken." David was truly astonished at Cindy's lack of respect for the women who took an unwanted child off her hands.

"David, I simply have no time for formalities." Her voice was commanding and final. "I went to the hospital and found the room where Mrs. Warren was being treated. No, I did not announce myself. I stayed back and observed. I'm sure you know why I was there in the first place, don't you?"

"You wanted to see your son. Did you know which one he was? The Warren's had two sons."

"Yes, of course. I recognized the birthmark immediately."

"Birthmark?" David was stunned. Mrs. Warren had made no mention of a birthmark. "I never met Steward in person, he was not at the Warren's when I was there." David was surprised. A birthmark that was visible on a fully dressed person added a new dimension to the story. "I didn't know about the birthmark."

"He has a port-wine birthmark, about the size of a silver dollar, on the left side of his neck, just below the ear. I knew I would always be able to recognize him because of it. Don't worry, David, I did not make my presence known. I do have some sensibilities. I had to satisfy my maternal instinct to see my child. I had no others. I don't expect you to understand. Do you have children, besides a daughter in Chicago?"

"No." There was no reason to mention there was another child. "What is Mrs. Warren's condition now?" David knew the answer would not be good.

"She was in intensive care the day I was there. I called the hospital two days later and inquired. She had passed away later the same day I was there. So now, you understand why I wrote the letter and asked to meet with you, David. I know you must have had some kind of conversation with Carl's wife." Cindy was looking at David, with her head lightly tilted. He sensed a pleading tone in her voice.

"I am wondering why you are so interested in my conversation with Mrs. Warren. After all it was Steward you came to see. I never met him so I really don't have any information on him other than he was adopted by the Warrens."

"I have my reasons, they may not seem logical to you, but they are sincere."

Pulling out a small cassette tape out of his jacket pocket David said, "I have my conversation with Mrs. Warren on tape. "I'll let you listen to it, if you will answer some questions for me first."

"Go ahead, ask away. According to a couple of my old girlfriends I've talked to recently, you have interviewed half the graduating class of 1956. I spoke with my mother's housekeeper, Bee Canady. She said you two were good friends and had some long talks. You've been to Ireland to visit my cousin Rebecca and her husband John. You probably know more than I can remember."

"I doubt that." David was surprised Cindy had uncovered his trail. How much more did she know about him? Did she know about Kathryn? "You were a top student, a math wizard, you won the state science contest in the math division that year. It appears that your mental powers are still in tact." Cindy looked directly at David and nodded slightly to acknowledge his left handed complement.

"Tell me, why did you go to Australia, and when?"

"You should know that. Bee told you about my mother having an affair with the man from Australia. He was killed in the war, he was a pilot for the RAF. When I left my uncle's house in New York, I was headed for someplace as far away from here as I could possibly get. I had a schoolgirl's romantic notion about joining my father's family in Australia." Cindy was nervously fidgeting with her fingers. David sensed something was on her mind and he was about to find out what it was. He was glad he had a new tape cassette and the tape recorder was on.

"Maybe you could start at the beginning. You and Billy Sandoval were very close during your senior year. Why don't you start with him?"

"First of all, Mr. David Jordan, I want you to know, that if a book is written about me, I want the right to edit it before publication. Will you agree?"

"No. There is no point in writing anything if I have to spend the rest of my life rewriting to suit you. I told you I would use fictitious names, this is not a biography"

"Stop Mr. Jordan. I know what you said. If you don't agree to my editing, will you agree not to publish your novel until after my death? That is your only other option." It was plain to see that Cindy had plenty of experience issuing orders and expecting them to be carried out.

"No. I can't do that either. Christ, you could live to be a hundred, your mother almost did."

A long silence came over the room. Only the crackling of the fireplace broke the silence. Cindy stood, walked around the couch, and stood behind it. "David, having a book published about my life is not important to me personally, my ego does not demand it or prevent it. What is important, if it is published, it must be factual. I'm at a stage in life that I need to put certain past events in their places. You don't understand that now, but perhaps you will when I finish. When I decided to come back to Dumont, I didn't know about you or your book. I think, after I finish answering your questions, you will agree we are mutually beneficial to one another.

Cindy circled the couch, sat down, and took a deep breath, "I have cancer. Cancer of the cervix, adenocarcinoma, to be specific. Twenty years ago, I had radical surgery to remove the cancer. All my female plumbing was removed, to be perfectly blunt. I'm sure you will find a message in my misfortune, Mr. new book author. At any rate, the cancer returned, chemotherapy and radiation, followed by a short period of remission, and now it's back again.

"My doctor says I have less than six months. That's why I decided to come to Dumont. Not because of this house, it does not hold happy memories for me. When I found out my mother had died and she left the house to the local women's club, if I couldn't be found, I decided to buy it from the estate so the money could be applied to the girl's foundation in Rockford. I may setup a similar foundation, here in Dumont, I haven't gotten that far in my thinking yet.

"I wanted to see my son before I died, maybe talk to him, if he wants to talk to me, but first, I had to know what Carl and his wife have told him about his past. That's my sole reason for returning to Dumont.

"I'll agree not to interfere with your project if you will agree not to publish for one year after my death. Can we agree on that?" She held out her right hand. David hesitated and then shook Cindy O'Ryan's hand. He knew he would not be ready to publish before a year was up anyway. So, no big deal.

"I don't see any need for a legal contract, David. I spoke with your former employer, Stanley Becker, he gave you a glowing recommendation. 'Jordan is a man of his word,' he said, 'a fine fellow, we were sorry to see him retire, we wish him well.'"

David was shocked by the revelation Cindy had contacted his old employer. Stanley gave him a good recommendation! David's head was spinning and this was just the beginning of a long afternoon.

"Now, let's get started with Billy." Cindy seemed at ease now, she made another cup of tea, and took several pills from a small bottle.

"Billy wasted his life. He had so much to offer, but nobody would let him get out of the gutter. He came from a truly dysfunctional family, yet somehow survived with a decent set of morals and a good head on his shoulders, until the Judge got hold of him." Her face turned cold and dark just mentioning the Judge.

Cindy sipped her tea and sat staring into the fireplace, as if transfixed by the flames. She talked non-stop for an hour and a half about her childhood, her relationship with her mother, the Judge, Billy, and Carl.

"If Billy and I had made it to Hollywood like we planned, the whole world would be different. At least it would have been different for Billy and me.

"Did you know that Billy knows all about cameras? That was his passion, he wanted to be a cinematographer. We used to go out into the country and make mini movies, I would pose and act out silly skits, Billy would take home movies. We had so much fun. Can you picture us? Billy behind the camera, and me in front of it?" Cindy almost smiled for the first time since David had met her.

The fire in the fireplace was dying when the conversation ended. David sat motionless for a few moments. "Cindy, I don't know how to thank you. You have given me more than I expected. I know it was difficult for you. I promise I will do my level best to present your character in my book honestly, and Billy too, even if he did try to kill me."

"That was not the Billy I knew, that was a stranger to me," Cindy said, with indignation. "The Billy I knew was sweet and kind, a real gentleman. I was sorry to find out he had lived up to the Judge's expectations." A tiny bit of emotion had crept into Cindy's voice.

"I sincerely hope you will be here to read the book when it's finished." David said.

"You had better get busy, David. I don't have a lot of time left. There is one thing you can do for me. I know it will be difficult for you, but it would be payment for me giving you the material for your book. I would be grateful if you could see that Billy has whatever comforts he is allowed in prison. I know he will never get out with his record. Care packages would be nice, cigarettes, toiletries, chocolate, and perhaps a book about photography. He doesn't have anyone on the outside, you know. Could you do that for me, please?" Cindy was visibly tired.

"Yes, I will do that for you. Do you plan to visit Billy?" David asked.

"Good heavens, no! I choose to remember him as he was. A bright and charming young man, full of promise. I suspect he would choose to remember me as the young girl who promised to start a new life with him."

David agonized in his head whether or not he should tell Cindy about his visit with Billy, especially the part where Billy said, "Tell her, I waited all my life for her." He decided not to, but to describe it clearly in his book.

David placed the few remaining pieces of wood on the fire and went to the basement for more. He filled the woodbin and left several large pieces standing next to the fireplace. "I could see if I can find a repairman to come over tomorrow, if you like. The sheriff and I are on good terms. Maybe he knows someone who could fix the furnace for you."

"Thank you David, that would be nice. Will you be leaving tomorrow?"

"Yes, my plane leaves tomorrow evening. I'll leave you my phone number, in case you think of something I should know." David wrote his address and phone number on a note pad next to the phone. "I'll leave the cassette tape of my conversation with Mrs. Warren, if you're interested. I have my notes, so take your time."

Cindy walked to the door and shook David's hand. "If you ever find that old convertible David, be careful with the movie film in the trunk, after you publish your book, the film will be classic memorabilia. Billy was very proud of his photographic work. He was going to use it for demonstration purposes to try to get a job."

David left the house and started his ice-cold car. As he pulled out of the driveway, the tires crunched on the frozen snow and ice. He was thankful he had not repeated Billy's last statement. Cindy was carrying enough baggage without adding to it. Some people believe everyone has a soul mate. If that were true, Cindy and Billy would be good candidates for a life together in the hereafter. David hoped it would be so.

A young boy who looked way to young to be driving delivered the pizza to David's motel room. He took out his tape recorder and replayed the entire conversation with Cindy O'Ryan. All the while he was listening to the recording, he was writing in his journal and looking at the photograph of Judge O'Ryan. Cindy had given him the photo just before he left the old house. The photo was a rare picture of the Judge with his left side turned toward the camera. The picture was black and white, but the port-wine birthmark on the left side of his neck was clearly visible.

CHAPTER 28

The evening flight to California was a good choice. This flight was not crowded, and David could sit back and replay in his mind the conversations with Carl Warren's wife and Cindy O'Ryan. He was thankful for his detailed notes. His brain was overloaded with emotions and images that sometimes distorted the facts. He knew he had a good story line, but he was having trouble putting everything into perspective. He actually had several stories to deal with. Any of the main characters could be portrayed as the hero or the villain.

After dinner and coffee, David pulled out his journal and went over his notes about the Cindy O'Ryan conversation. It was incredible the way she related the whole story as if she were talking about somebody else. She never shed a tear, her voice never cracked, and she was almost emotionless, almost, but not quite.

David had asked Cindy to start at the beginning, assuming Billy Sandoval would be the beginning. He was wrong. The Judge was the beginning.

The Judge and Margaret had separate bedrooms for as long as Cindy could remember. Whether or not that had anything to do with what happened at night, in Cindy's bedroom, was something she could not answer. According to Cindy, her parents were seldom in the same room together at the same time.

It began when Cindy was about eight or nine years old. At least that is when the memories started. The Judge would come into her room at night and hold her hands and tell her how beautiful she was and how proud of her he was to have a daughter like her. At first, Cindy felt special. Her father telling her how much he loved her and how they had to take care of each other. "We must keep these visits to ourselves. It will be our secret. You can keep a secret can't you, Cindy?" Of course, Cindy wanted to please her father by keeping a secret, even if it was from her mother.

David supposed what happened next was typical of child molestation cases. He could not visualize how a grown man could molest a child, especially his own daughter, but these things did happen and they happened to Cindy. It took place gradually over several years. The Judge's visits, although infrequent, were increasingly intimate, especially after Cindy began to develop into a young woman.

When Cindy was twelve, they actually had intercourse. Cindy knew it was wrong, but she could not tell anyone. The Judge made her promise not to tell her mother or he would have to punish her. Cindy was obviously intimidated by the commanding presence of the Judge. He was not a large man, but he definitely was large in her mind. She was ashamed and confused, there was no one she could turn to. The visits, although spasmodic, continued. Cindy was in high school when she discovered she could manipulate the Judge by resisting his attempts to get under the covers with her. She would threaten to tell her mother and he would offer her just about anything she wanted.

"Anything" usually meant a new dress, or piece of jewelry, perhaps a new phonograph, even a car to drive around town in, it was a lesson well learned. Her mother was so busy with her teaching job and counseling other girls, she did not have time for her own daughter. David asked if she thought her mother knew about the nighttime visits. Cindy stared into space without answering. After a moment she said, "I really can't say one way or the other. We became increasingly distant when I began high school. We seldom had a meaningful conversation. By the time I was old enough to realize what was happening to me was wrong, I felt so guilty, I actually felt guilty about feeling guilty. He never physically hurt me or forced himself on me, I let him. I know it does not make sense but that's the way I felt. I could not tell my mother. There were times when I felt she had to know, but we never discussed it."

During high school, Cindy learned to flirt and tease the boys to her advantage. The prospect of having sex with her was enough to manipulate boys and men alike. "Men are such easy prey, they think with their peckers instead of their heads," Cindy had said, with an air of satisfaction. "A girl could use boys and get what she wanted if she dressed right and used a little common sense."

Cindy found she could have any boy in school, if she put her mind to it. She felt no remorse about it. It became a game with her. Then she met Billy at a New Year's Eve party, and her life changed. He worked on her car, the one her father bought for her after she threatened to stop the late night visits.

Billy was different. He was mature and he treated her with respect. In fact, he refused to have sex with her, saying it would be better if they waited until they were married. Sex was an act of love, according to Billy. It was not something to be experienced in the back seat of a car at the drive-in movie.

David was sure Cindy had actually fallen in love with Billy, and he, with her. They planned to elope right after high school graduation and to go to Hollywood and make movies. She would get acting jobs, and Billy would get a job working from behind the camera.

It was a silly teenage dream, David thought, but now that he knew each dreamer, it could have worked. Except for the nightmare. The Judge was seldom home because of his political campaigning, he was trying to ensure his nomination for Lt. Governor during the spring of Cindy's senior year.

Then one night, he came home late, and stepped silently into Cindy's room. She resisted his touching at first, but after awhile it seemed useless. It had happened so often in the past, one more time didn't seem to make any difference. She closed her eyes and laid motionless, not encouraging the Judge but not stopping him either. She closed her eyes and forced her body to not respond in any way. That was the last time he came to her room.

A few days later, the Judge bought Cindy a new convertible, the Chevy, it was an early graduation present. In reality, it was an attempt to keep her away from Billy. At least she would not have the excuse of taking the old Ford in for repair all the time.

His verbal outburst about that worthless grease monkey was not having any effect on Cindy. She continued to see him. When Cindy missed her second menstrual period, she knew she was pregnant. In near panic she went to an old woman in Rockford who had helped other girls avoid unwanted pregnancies. The woman sold Cindy a bottle of medicine that she said would cause a miscarriage, but all it did was make Cindy violently ill to the point she thought she would die. Her mother made her go to the doctor and that is when all hell broke loose. The doctor told the Judge, and the Judge shamelessly blamed Billy.

Cindy described the role Carl played in this nightmare, as though she was reading it from a newspaper account. It was almost like she had a split personality. On the one hand, Cindy and Billy had an innocent romance, a young love affair, on the other, Cindy had set a goal to seduce a teacher before the year was out. Coincidentally, Carl was preparing Cindy for the state science contest, taking place the first week in May.

They spent several afternoons together, going over possible math problems, in the nearly deserted schoolhouse. She finally succeeded in bedding her favorite teacher in the teacher's lounge. They made love several times after that. Finally, Carl said he could not continue with their love affair, his conscience would not allow it.

When Cindy discovered she was pregnant, she did not know who the baby's father was. Admitting it could be her own father was out of the question, she could not accept that as a possibility. Bearing her father's child, then facing Billy and confessing her affair with a teacher was simply more than a seventeen-year-old girl could handle. The father of her child would have to be Carl.

Cindy was near committing suicide those last few days in Dumont. In fact, she did try once, by driving on to the train track at a crossing, but at the last moment she stomped on the gas and accelerated across the tracks just as the train approached whistle screeching.

Billy was beautiful she said. He had planned every detail of their elopement. He was ready with maps and the names of people to contact when they got to Hollywood. He had even lined up a furnished apartment in Santa Monica. Cindy looked off into the fire when she described how excited Billy had been at the thought of making his dream come true. He was escaping the misery of a small town with the girl he loved and who loved him in return. Late that afternoon, as she walked into her front door, Cindy was met with a storm of accusations.

The Judge had talked with Dr. Whitworth and found out Cindy was pregnant. He immediately accused Billy of being the father and never once acknowledged any other possibility. Cindy's mother begged her to go with the Judge to New York City. "It will be better for everyone concerned," she had told Cindy.

Cindy was devastated. She did not know which way to turn. She was pregnant, but she could not be sure who the baby's father was, the Judge or her teacher. The boy she loved had never been intimate with her, he respected her too much. She could never force herself to confess to Billy her stupidity, her infidelity, or her guilt. There was no one she could turn to, no one to help her. How could she possibly resolve this mess? There was no way out. The burden of guilt was overpowering. Cindy described it as a "...heavy, black, wet, cloud engulfing me, I was paralyzed with quilt. I wanted to die." New York seemed like the only answer at the time. At least she would be far away from Billy. She would be able to avoid the face-to-face confrontation she knew would shatter his life. She prayed he would never find out the truth. "Billy was so sincere and trusting that I just could not tell him what a stupid and selfish girl I had been. I know it would have broken his heart. So I took the coward's way out. I let the Judge take me to New York and I promised myself that I would never contact Billy again. In time, I believed he would come to understand that I had decided against marrying a poor mechanic and instead decided on a life without him. That in itself was deceitful, but better than the truth."

Cindy's last night in Dumont was full of revelations. Her mother had told the Judge he was not Cindy's father. In Cindy's room, her mother broke down and told Cindy her real father was from Australia and had been killed in the war. "I didn't comprehend the full meaning of what she was telling me at the time. All this business of her having an affair in Europe and then losing her lover in the war on top of everything else was just too much. Mentally I just collapsed. My whole world disintegrated." Cindy said she didn't understand the implication of her mother's confession until several days later.

"And then it hit me. The judge was my step father. All those years I never even dreamed that he was not my real father." David thought he could see glimmer of softness in Cindy's eyes even though her face remained hard and sharp. "The person coming into my room late at night, all those years, was not my father. My father was a good man."

She said she felt sympathetic toward her mother for the first time in years. The emotional upheavals that had taken place that evening provided some kind of avenue for the rekindling of the mother daughter relationship that had been missing for several years. She felt that this was the time to confess her own sins. "I told her I had been having sex with Carl Warren. I thought she would faint, but she held on. I could not bring myself to tell her about the Judge, that part of my quilt was just too great. The possibility of him being the father of my baby never registered with me until the baby was born. Even if the Judge was not my real father, the shame and guilt was too much of an obstacle to overcome. I had given in too many times for my own selfish reasons."

They both packed Cindy's clothes for the trip to New York. At least she would be away from Dumont and have a little time to think of a plan, some way out of this situation. Then a glimmer of hope sparked in her mind. If she could make contact with her father's people maybe she could make some kind of life for herself.

Cindy forgot all about the car parked in the garage, ready for the trip to California. She could not bring herself to contact Billy and say Good-bye, her stomach turned at the very thought of facing him. She said, "Even after all these years, I still get this terrible feeling in my stomach just talking about facing Billy. I know I hurt him badly. I never allowed myself to become emotionally attached to anyone ever again." Those last words were said with the finality of a closed grave. The trip to New York on the train was made in silence. She spent the time in utter despair. The Judge was right about one thing, her life was in ruins.

Cindy's aunt and uncle were not happy to be put in the position of guardian, but, because she was family, they promised to take care of Cindy and help her find adoptive parents for her baby.

In the days following, Cindy began to see clearly, what she had to do. After many tearful, sometimes screaming, sometimes pleading telephone calls, her mother finally gave her the address in Australia of her father's sister. She sent it in an envelope containing two thousand dollars cash. Cindy packed and left New York the following day.

The St. Mary's Church in Los Angles was the next stop. She was sure the priest would arrange for her to stay at a home for unwed mothers. The church would help with the adoption. Then she would be free to leave all her past sins behind, start a new life in a country as far away from Dumont as was possible, and still be on this planet.

Cindy stayed in contact with her mother from time to time, writing a few letters. "I wrote mother several times over the years. She sent letters routinely telling me about my school friends and various happenings around town. She even had the local paper sent over. She acted as though I would someday come back, but I never considered it until after she passed away and my own health was in jeopardy." Soon after arriving in Perth, she found a job in an accounting office of a large mining corporation. She was good at her job and began earning a good salary. She eventually advanced to the position of Chief Financial Officer and was responsible for a staff of twenty. "I was promoted to chief financial officer in a male dominated mining company. I did it on my feet and not on my back. Make sure your book gets that part of my story correct."

Although Cindy returned to the states on several occasions, to handle business matters for her company, she never came back to Dumont or saw her mother in person again. She traveled extensively in the Orient and Europe, usually alone or with business associates. She never married or indicated that she was even remotely romantically involved with anyone.

The remaining hours of the flight were spent trying to put the events of the last six months in some kind of order. In the beginning David had found the car of his dreams, only to loose it to the police. Second, he was unwittingly associated with a murder and a drug deal. Third, he killed a person in self-defense, and someone tried to kill him. On top of those events, he had uncovered a long smoldering scandal seriously affecting several people's lives. And how could he forget the possibility of a murder on a deserted rain swept highway late at night, and a successful cover-up? The icing on the cake was his relationship with Kathryn. Put it all together properly and he was sure he had the making for a best selling novel.

CHAPTER 29

The first morning David was back in his duplex apartment, the sun rose on a beautiful Southern California day. Winters were the best time of year in southern California, as far as he was concerned. The air was cleaner, the days warm, and the nights cool. He rose early and walked down the hill to Cabrillo Beach. Several anglers were dodging waves breaking over the huge boulders forming the breakwater between Los Angles Harbor and the Pacific. The air was fresh with the scent of salt and kelp. Two large, heavily laden tankers were anchored off shore, discharging their cargo via a under sea pipe line. The day promised to be bright and sunny with the air temperature in the seventies. A perfect day, for a ride on his Harley Davidson. Anticipating a great ride, David hurried back to his duplex apartment, rolled out a chrome and deep maroon, two-wheeled beauty.

Two hours of ridding were enough to convince David he had not totally recovered from the two gunshot wounds. His gut hurt and his back was complaining. With the Harley safely back in the garage, David walked around to the front of the duplex to collect his mail. The old lady in the front unit came out her door and handed David a large bag of mail she had been collecting for him during his absence. The bag was nearly full. He thanked her and took the mostly junk mail back to his place.

Inside his apartment, he set the bag down next to his desk and proceeded to take off his riding boots and then to undress. He took a long hot shower, concentrating the spray on his lower back. The Harley was fun to ride but not good for his wounds which were still healing.

Dinner consisted of a frozen chicken potpie with the evening news, followed by a cup of good coffee. He picked up the bag of mail, went outside, and sat down on a deckchair facing the harbor lights. The mail was junk except for a few bills, one birth announcement, and a marriage invitation from friends at HIC.

David had programmed himself to dedicate the next two weeks to getting organized and arrange the material for his book. Several trips to the stationary store provided all the supplies he needed to start writing. He had a computer with plenty of memory, large enough to store any book he was likely to write. He set up two large-flip charts on either side of his desk. Over the desk, on a wall-mounted bookshelf, he lined up various reference books: dictionary, thesaurus, Farmers Almanac, and a half dozen other source books he bought at a garage sale. After he had everything at his fingertips, he sat in the new ergonomically designed desk chair and surveyed his writer's nook. Perfect, he thought, "Now, where do I start?"

On one flip-chart he wrote with a felt tip pen the names and description of all the main characters, including birth dates, relationships to each other, etc. On the second flip-chart David plotted a timeline with dates of major events.

The first thing to do, he assumed, was to establish the main characters. His book would have six, the father, mother, daughter, boyfriend, housekeeper, and mother's lover. Of course, the young girl would be the heroine. There would be an assortment of minor characters: police officer, doctor, teacher, and various suitors. One chore that became time consuming was giving each character a fictions name. Several hours browsing through the phone book provided names to get started with.

Locations were also listed on his timeline. David invented places and landmarks, but not before checking the map of the state where most of the action would take place. He did not think it was a good idea to use actual place names.

David hammered away at his computer for the next three months. He tried to be as professional as possible by spending at least two hours in the morning and two hours in the afternoon working on the book, often times he worked late into the evening. He had a vague idea of how the pieces of his story would fit together, but it was while sitting at the computer and letting his imagination run wild, he actually put on paper something resembling a book. He had no idea of how a professional writer would go about writing a book, but this routine seemed to work for him.

The story unfolded as a murder mystery with a valuable clue locked away in an old car. Murder, sex, money, and greed were the essential elements that were required to make an enjoyable read. David kept at his writing every day, rain or shine, the pages added up quickly.

Near the end of April, he had completed nearly four hundred pages and was nearing what he hoped would be an exciting ending. The last chapter was giving him trouble. He could not visualize an ending that made him feel good. The real life ending to Cindy's story certainly was not a happy one, nor would it provide the reader with closure David felt he needed. He was stumped. For three days he had not written a word. Several long motorcycle rides, a couple of new release movies, and dinner with Ellen had not provided the spark of inspiration he needed.

During this period of writer's block, David invited the old lady in the front apartment back to his place for dinner one evening. They had been neighbors for several years, but had not really gotten to know one another. Mrs. Neely was seventy-two years old and in full possession of her faculties. Physically, she had some major problems limiting her to the confines of her apartment. She had moved to San Pedro from North Hollywood after her husband died. She wanted to be closer to her son, who owned a small auto repair business downtown San Pedro. The part of her life's story that got David's attention was the thirty-three years she had spent as an English teacher for a well know-military academy in the San Fernando Valley.

David told her about his writing project and his need for an editor. He needed someone who could correct all of his grammatical mistakes and spelling errors. Spell check was great but not good enough. She agreed to undertake the project, for a price, so long as it did not interfere with her twice-a-week bridge club meetings.

Mrs. Neely was a whiz at correcting David's manuscript and she became totally involved in the story itself. She began making comments and asking questions regarding the characterization of the various players. At first, David was a little reluctant to accept her critiques, but it was evident she had read thousands of books and knew what elements a good story needed in order for the reader to stay interested. Consequently, many of her suggestions were useful, adding color to David's character descriptions.

The two collaborators, writer and editor, could not come up with an ending that suited them both. They had several discussions, but no idea either one suggested seemed right. Finally David said, "Let's give it a rest, stop thinking about it for several days, a week, and see if our subconscious imaginations can come up something that fits."

After dinner one evening, David was sitting on the patio watching the setting sun turn the western sky to brilliant red. The outline of Catalina Island was silhouetted against the horizon. He was about to fix his second drink when Mrs. Neely came onto his patio holding a large brown envelope. "This came several days ago, special delivery. " You were gone, so I signed for it and forgot all about it. Just now I found it lying under yesterday's newspaper. Isn't that sun-set beautiful?" David could not agree more. He offered her a drink, knowing she would refuse anything with alcohol in it.

The envelope was postmarked "San Francisco." The return address was simply a post office box. David's mind raced and his heart stopped. Could this be from Kathryn? She was the only person he knew who lived in San Francisco. He opened the envelope, and pulled out two sheets of paper. One was a hand drawn map and the other, a neatly typed message, signed by Kathryn.

Dear David,

You will no doubt be surprised to hear form me. It seems like each time we were together, I said Good-bye in a most conflicting manner. I promise I can be open and honest with you now. I have broken my engagement to Richard.

I have a good friend who owns a cabin on the Big Sur Peninsula. She offered it to me as a means of recovering from a near disastrous wedding. It would be wonderful if you could join me. If you decide not to, I will understand.

The cabin is located high up the side of the mountains overlooking the Pacific Ocean. The view is one of the most beautiful in the entire world. I hope you can find the time and are inclined to give me another chance.

I will be arriving Saturday the 29th. You may come any time, the combination to the gate is on the map. My friend promised the refrigerator would be full and the wine cabinet stocked.

I hope to see you soon

Kathryn

P.S. I have a surprise for you.

David read and reread the letter a dozen times. She broke off the engagement. Unbelievable! Her father must be beside himself. There was absolutely no question he would meet her in Big Sur. Sleep was not possible.

She had a surprise for David. What in the hell could it possibly be, he wondered? David spent what seemed like hours staring at the photo strip he and Kathryn had taken in London. He could not believe Kathryn had broken her engagement and invited him to a cabin in Big Sur. The gods were definitely smiling on him. He pasted Kathryn's note on the back of the door to the tiny kitchen. Every time he passed by, he would read it.

He had two days to get his butt up to Big Sur. Decision time, drive the pickup or the Harley. The highway to Big Sur from Los Angeles is along the coast, California's State Highway 1. From Malibu he would go north to San Louis Obispo, where Highway 1 actually starts. It snakes along the most beautiful coastline found anywhere in the world. The coast highway, built by convict labor during the twenties and thirties, is a premier biker road, especially the section between San Simeon and Carmel. The road is a two-lane blacktop with numerous switchbacks, narrow bridges, and non-existent safety rails. The shoulder less roadbed, sometimes low next to the ocean and sometimes a thousand feet or higher above it, is dangerous in and of itself. When motorists and bikers are gawking at the blue Pacific below, the road takes on a real sinister aspect. Add fog or a pacific storm and it can be one of the most dangerous roads in the country. Perfect for a bike trip.

David packed the saddlebags on the Harley with a minimum of wardrobe, toilette kit, candy bars, and rain gear. He was on the road by ten, Friday morning. Plenty of time to sightsee along the way. Riding a motorcycle for any length of time requires frequent stops to stretch the legs, and get the circulation going in areas that are cut off while sitting in one position for a long period of time.

The town of San Simeon marks the beginning of the most scenic portion of the highway, this would be a good place to spend the night. The whole place exists to provide tourist accommodations for people visiting Hearst Castle. The motel David selected was within a few yards of the beach and the pounding Pacific. A nice steak dinner and a glass of wine while watching the sunset from King Neptune's restaurant put David in the mood for a good rest after the long ride from Long Beach.

The coast was covered in fog early the next morning. It could be hours or it could be minutes before the fog lifted. This time of year a marine layer hangs on the California coast and the sun may or may not break through before noontime. He packed his saddlebags, checked out, and decided to head up the coast despite the low visibility.

Driving a motorcycle in the fog is not a pleasant experience. The cold moist air creeps under the motorcyclist's jacket and any other openings that it can find. The face shield is blurred with moisture. The road is slick and the visibility poor.

Several close calls with oncoming vehicles and nearly stopped cars in front of him caused David to seriously question his decision to start riding in weather like this. After an hour, the highway started to climb and the fog began to lift, the road opened up. Muscles in David's neck and forearms were beginning to tighten and cramp. A small wide spot in the road called Gorda, about a thousand feet above the ocean came into view. Perfect timing, the gas station, restaurant, and store offered a welcome place to rest.

Two cups of hot coffee and David was back in the saddle, heading north. An hour later he passed Big Sur Lodge and slowed down to look for the gravel road leading up the side of the mountain. The road was not numbered, nor was it identified with any kind of sign. According to the map, two-tenths of a mile north of the Lodge, he was to turn right and proceed up a steep gravel road to a locked gate. A four-digit lock combination was penciled in on the margin of the map. The cabin was two miles further up the road. The key to the cabin was under a rock next to the front step to the cabin.

The steep gravel road leading to the unlocked the steel gate provided David with a challenge. Closing the gate behind him, he proceeded carefully up the winding trail. Looking up the side of the mountain, he could not see a structure of any kind. The green grass covering the hills was starting to turn golden brown. Tall pine trees stood in the ravines between the steep hills, live oaks dotted the hillsides. The cabin came into view on the last turn. The view from this altitude, at least three thousand feet, was magnificent. The fog was still clinging to the valleys and lower reaches of the coastline. The sky was brilliant blue and the sun was as bright as it was possible for it to be.

The cabin, built on a steep hillside, was exposed on all sides to the surrounding seascapes and landscapes. No sign of life in or outside the cabin was visible. Parking the Harley was a relief. David shed his leather jacket and pants exposing a denim shirt wet around the neck and in front where the fog had crept in.. He hoped he could change his clothes before Kathryn showed up.

Finding the key, where it was supposed to be under a rock next to the steps, he unlocked the huge wood framed double glass doors and went inside.

The cabin was mostly glass, huge redwood beams supported the roof and ceiling. The view from inside the cabin was like a wraparound movie screen. Once inside, every turn a person took afforded a magnificent view of the ocean, cliffs, mountainside, forest, meadow, or huge chunks of the sky. The first floor of the cabin was open, except for the bathroom. The kitchen and dining areas were separated from the living room by a centrally located circular fireplace. Bookshelves containing a mini-library and stacks of CDs lined one side of the wall separating the bathroom from the rest of the cabin. A loft provided space for two double beds and a bunk bed pushed next to the far wall. Room dividers separated the sleeping areas.

A multi-level redwood deck surrounded the cabin, neatly accommodating a rock out-cropping. On the south side, built into the deck, was a ten-foot diameter redwood hot tub. David lifted the cover, tested the water, and found it hot and ready for use. He must be dreaming. The road leading to the cabin dead-ended at the cabin's front door. No other structures or signs of civilization were visible from any angle, not even utility poles or fence posts.

A sheet of instructions covered in plastic was hanging from a hook next to the kitchen counter. The note read in part, "... cabin has no telephone, limited electricity is supplied by solar panels on the roof and a battery pack under the deck. A propane tank supplies gas to the kitchen range, refrigerator, and hot tub. Use electric lights, CD player and TV sparingly. Water is from the spring up the hill, so do not walk in or play in the water."

David unfastened his saddlebags from the Harley and took them inside. He changed into dry Levi's and a clean shirt. The refrigerator contained a wide assortment of foodstuff including imported beer. He helped himself to a bottle of Becks, a slice of cheese and a couple of slices of weird-shaped bread. Situating himself on the deck, under a sunscreen, he could see the road leading to the cabin. His watch indicated it was half-past one in the afternoon.

The view from this vantage point was spectacular. Kathryn was right, this had to be one of the most magnificent vistas in the world. He was planning what to say to Kathryn when a bright flash caught his eye. It was like somebody flashing a mirror. Then he saw it. A car driving carefully up the narrow trail that barely passed for a road, leading to the cabin. It was a convertible with a lone driver.

The car disappeared behind a stand of trees and re-emerged around a switchback, before turning onto the last hundred yards of driveway. It was a black convertible with a woman driving. She had a yellow scarf tied around her head and she wore sunglasses. The car was a 1956 Chevrolet convertible, black and chrome.

Unbelievable! David was stunned, shocked, and unable to move. Kathryn pulled the car up next to the Harley in front of the cabin. She gave a little hand wave to David who was rooted to the deck. He could not believe his eyes. Could it be the '56 Chevy he bought at auction? No, not possible, that car was lost in the bureaucratic maze of the Los Angeles Police Department.

Kathryn opened the door of the Chevy and stepped out, holding it open. "Well, come on, let's go for a ride."

David nearly tripped over the steps leading down to the driveway. He approached Kathryn and she stepped back and motioned with her left hand for David to get in the driver's seat. He did.

The car was immaculate. The black lacquer paint was so deep reflections seemed to be in 3D. The chrome was brilliant and the stainless trim had been polished to perfection. The deep red leather upholstery felt smooth and rich. The pile carpeting matched the seats perfectly. David looked at Kathryn and said, "Is it? Is it Cindy's convertible?"

"Yes, I hope you like it. It was so much fun driving down from San Francisco this morning. The car runs beautifully. I attracted all kinds of attention in Monterey when I stopped for coffee. There were three of the cutest guys gathered around the car when I got out of the restaurant. They wanted to know all about it. They followed me until I got to Carmel."

David thought to himself, "Those kids were no fools". The car and its driver fascinated them just like he was fascinated year's ago.

"Lots of people looked and waved. Please tell me you like it." Kathryn's eyes were brimming with light.

"Like it? I love it. How did you find it and who did all the work?

"My father found it. He has connections all over the country when it comes to cars. I was so afraid you would be unhappy if someone else restored it. These past two months have been absolute hell for me. I want to sit down and tell you everything that has happened since the last time we saw each other." Kathryn was running out of breath, she was talking so fast. "I'm so relieved you came. I was worried you had given up on me."

David stepped out of the Chevy, looked at Kathryn, and said, "I love it. And no I'm not the least bit angry someone else restored it. They obviously did a fantastic job. The car is perfect shape from what I can see." He pulled Kathryn to him and they kissed.

"David, please, I have to sit down. I have been running on adrenaline all morning. I could use a drink and I need to talk with you." She took David's hand and they went out on to the deck facing the sunlit Pacific.

"Just a minute, I'll be right back." In the kitchen, David found the ingredients and made two Bloodymarys.

They sat for a few moments, taking in the surroundings. "This is one of the most beautiful places in the world, don't you think, David?" Before he could answer, Kathryn continued, "I'm so glad you decided to come. I was afraid you were tired of my saying Good-bye each time we met. All the time I was driving down from San Francisco, I kept praying you would be here. When I saw the motorcycle, I knew it was you."

Kathryn looked like she just stepped out of an advertisement for a fashion magazine. She wore tailored slacks, a silk print blouse, a yellow scarf around her neck and a smile that would light up any occasion. Kathryn's dark eyes drew David into her with a mystical, irresistible attraction.

"Yes, it is a fantastic view from here. I would not have missed this opportunity to be with you. Now, tell me about your decision to break-off your engagement." David thought that this would be a good place to get started. He felt like he had won the fair maiden, but common sense told him not to rush. He needed to know the entire story before he committed himself to some stupid statement he might later regret.

"All right" Cindy adjusted herself so she could face David. Then she looked down and took a moment to get her thoughts in order, "David when I last saw you in London I was a wreck for days afterwards. The business trip to Berlin was successful despite my lack of participation. Richard and I sold our language conversation software company to a German company that will continue with the development and do the marketing. It was a very good deal for Richard and me. We got," she hesitated, "a lot of money and still retained a minority stock position.

"Richard was after me all week, wanting to know why I was not participating fully in the negotiations. He said it was like my mind was somewhere else. I couldn't tell him that it was. I faked an illness.

"After the Berlin meetings, we both traveled to Dublin and stayed with my parents for a week before returning to the West Coast." Kathryn fell silent for a few moments and looked out to sea before continuing. "One day, while I was walking down the hallway, I accidentally overheard my father and Richard discussing the purchase of large blocks of stock of a Liberian shipping company. They were pooling their resources in an attempt to take control of the company." Her voice was beginning to falter and her eyes were brimming with tears.

David shrugged his shoulders and said, "It sounds like a great business deal, if they could pull it off. Why did that bother you? And apparently it did, I can see it in your eyes."

"Richard was patting himself on the back because he knew he could use my share of the money from the software project, add that to his own and my father's and make a bid for the shipping company. He as much as told my father outright that he wanted to marry me so he could control the project and use me as a pawn in the negations. He was talking as if I were a commodity or a chess piece he could push around at will." She broke down and began to cry softly.

David comforted her and silently thanked Richard for being an asshole. "Did you confront Richard about your suspicions?"

"They weren't suspicions. I heard him say 'After Kathryn and I are married I will have total control of x amount of dollars and we can proceed with the tender.' My father said, 'Don't you think you should consult Kathryn first? She may have something to say, after all, half of the money is hers.'

Richard laughed and said, 'Don't worry, I've been cultivating this relationship ever since the accident. After we're married she will agree to whatever business deal I present to her. I know she's your daughter, but she really doesn't understand money matters very well. I have researched the California community property law extensively and I know I'm on solid ground. The deal is in the bag.' He laughed that awful laugh of his. I never minded it till now."

"Your father went along with Richard's plan?"

"I didn't stay and listen to any more of the conversation. I was so mad and upset at being used like that. Richard had been a true friend when Brian was killed. He took care of everything. The language conversation company was his idea, but my language training and contacts in Europe were essential to its success, so we became business partners. We gradually became close and after a while it seemed like a logical next step, agreeing to marry him. I felt it would be the right thing to do.

"Two years ago, when our software project started to take off and it looked like it would be a very profitable business, Richard began to change. Looking back, I think he saw an opportunity to be a Bill Gates or like one of those other dot-com billionaires. I really don't know what happened, but I do know after I overheard that conversation our relationship was over. I could not believe one thing he said.

"My father came up to my room the next morning and said he had something important to discuss with me. He said he had asked Richard to pack his bags and leave the house. I could not believe my ears. He proceeded to tell me about the conversation of the previous night. I had not eavesdropped long enough the night before to hear all of my father's comments.

"Apparently he stuck up for me and told Richard he was an unscrupulous bastard. He had used me for his personal gains, he was after my money pure and simple. They had a very heated argument and my father told him to leave.

"I was dumbfounded. On the one hand, I was proud of my father for taking my side, but on the other hand, I was ashamed because I actually had thought he approved of Richard's plan.

"When I got back to San Francisco, I officially broke off our engagement and notified our friends and relatives. I wanted to call you, but it was too soon. It didn't feel right. Shortly afterwards, my father came to San Francisco to visit with me and to look at some cars he was interested in. Actually, the car auction was down at Pebble Beach. I went with him to dinner one night and he mentioned one of the cars he was going to make an offer on, had been confiscated by the police and later, auctioned to its current owner.

"Impulsively, I asked him if he could find your car. He asked why I was interested and I told him because I was interested in you." Kathryn took a sideways glance at David through half closed eyes, she brushed a lock of hair out of her face and David felt his cheeks turning red.

"My father wanted to say something, but he held his tongue and he promised he would ask around and see what he could find out. To make a long story short, two weeks later a man I had never heard off called and asked what I wanted done with this old Chevy convertible.

"He was a mechanic in San Jose who specializes in restoring mid-nineteen fifty Chevrolets. Somehow, a friend of my father's found Cindy's car at a collector's warehouse in Pasadena. He made an offer and the man sold it to my father. He had it transported to San Jose, and now the mechanic wanted to know what I wanted to do with it. I told him I wanted it like new and I wanted it by May first. He had six weeks to finish. I think he did a terrific job. The car looks and runs great."

"I can't believe you did this for me," David exclaimed. He was truly in a state of shock. Not only had the woman of his dreams set up this terrific romantic rendezvous, but she also went to the trouble to locate, buy, and restore, the car of his dreams. "This is a dream come true."

David stood and pulled Kathryn to him. She put her arms around his neck willingly and they kissed. Every nerve in David's body seemed to be on fire. He was aroused with anticipation of what was surely to come. They parted, breathless staring into each other's eyes, "I want to make love to you, I've wanted to for a very long time," he said.

"I expect nothing less," Kathryn said, in a low seductive voice causing David's knees to weaken. She took David's hand and led him into the interior of the cabin. They turned toward each other and kissed again, two people completely oblivious to the outside world. Somehow they negotiated the stairway to the loft and the king sized-bed.

David had fantasized making love to Kathryn many times over the past few months, nothing he imagined in his mind came close to the ecstasy of the real thing. They tore each other's clothes off, fell on the bed, explored each other's bodies shamelessly, and made love twice before finally resting from sheer exhaustion.

Never in his entire relationship with Ellen, or any other woman, had David experienced sex with the intense passion he felt with Kathryn. They became one, their bodies and souls were united. David never dreamed that love for a woman could become the center of his universe, but that is exactly the emotion he felt.

CHAPTER 30

Last night had lasted until two in the morning. Kathryn had raided the refrigerator and found cold cuts, cheese, breads, and fruit, while David uncovered the hot tub and discovered the wine racks hidden under the stairwell. They feasted while they soaked and watched shooting stars over the Pacific. It was a moonless, clear night, and the heavens were bright with starlight.

The two lovers talked for hours, confiding in each other intimate secrets about themselves. David confessed his reasons for taking the second tour in Vietnam and leaving behind a pregnant wife and small child, deep emotions he had never allowed to surface, even in his own mind. He admitted his fear of accepting responsibility for Ellen and the children. It was a longtime after the war before he finally realized his absence had caused a gulf between Ellen and himself that could never be fully bridged.

Kathryn admitted allowing Richard to take over her life after her husband was killed. She was vulnerable and failed to take hold of her life, she let Richard make all of her major decisions regarding her future and he included himself in her life and she allowed it.

Their two bodies became one. David had never felt so close to, or so much in love with, any other person in his life. He had not realized it was possible for two people to be attracted to one another to the point where nothing else in the world mattered. He would do anything for this woman and he felt she would do the same for him.

The following morning David was first to rise and make coffee. The sun was well up into the blue sky and the coastal fog was lifting from the low headlands. "How do you like your eggs?" he called up to the sleeping mound he had left under the covers.

A muffled reply came back, "You can cook too? A great lover and a cook what luck. Scrambled would be great," Kathryn replied. "Toast crisp and fresh squeezed orange juice, while you're at it."

Ignoring the orders from upstairs, David proceeded to make a Spanish omelet that would satisfy the most discriminating egg connoisseur. It was one of the few meals he took pride in cooking. David set the table on the front deck overlooking the sea cliffs. Kathryn came down the stairs yawning and wearing a long tee shirt, she looked as fresh as the morning.

They ate their breakfast while watching the fog disappear. The vista, from the over hanging deck, brought remarks on how beautiful this place was and how lucky they were to be here together.

Kathryn asked about the book. How far had he gotten? Could she read it? Had he talked to a publisher? Did he have someone in mind to edit it for him?

"The first draft is almost complete. And no, I have not talked to a publisher or book agent yet. Yes, I have an editor who lives next door to me, she is a retired English teacher. She has really been a great help, not only with the grammar, but with the story line as well. I am at the point now where I need a professional editor."

He told her, he would rather she did not read his book until it was complete. He did discuss the basic story line, describing in detail the main characters. Kathryn asked pointed questions and made several suggestions that actually helped define the story. David immediately made a mental note of them. Maybe he ought to let her read it, she has a good imagination and a second opinion would be better than his alone or his neighbor's.

Kathryn was curious about the real-life Cindy and Billy. That's when she suddenly remembered. "Oh my God. I nearly forgot." Kathryn began talking excitedly, "The garage, where the restoration took place, called a couple of days after they got the car and asked me what I wanted done with the stuff they found in the trunk.

"I couldn't believe the suitcase was still there after all that had happened to the car since you last opened it. So I told him to keep it under lock and key and I would be there the next day to pick it up." Kathryn could see David was looking at her in disbelief.

"I can't believe those suitcases were still there. What about the fur stole?" David asked.

"It was all there. I couldn't believe it either. Alex Johnson, the man who owns the restoration shop, said the trunk was locked, but he had some old master keys and one of them worked. He had opened the suitcase, but he claimed he didn't take anything. I brought all of it with me. Come on lets go get it, it's in the trunk."

They walked hurriedly out to where the Chevy was parked and Cindy opened the trunk. David was slightly disappointed to see the dried flowers were missing. Inside the trunk was spotless. The rubber mat and trunk lining had been replaced. They carried the suitcases into the cabin.

The newer suitcase contained Cindy's clothing. Typical girl stuff, including cosmetics, under clothes, nice dresses, casual slacks, sweaters, swimsuit, and two books detailing how to break into the movies. There was an envelope, sealed, containing five hundred dollars in hundred-dollar bills. The fur stole was a mystery. David had meant to ask Cindy why she had taken it. Of course in those days some movie stars wore fur pieces even in warm climates just to create a special look. David wondered if that is what Cindy had in mind. Was the stole hers? Or did she "borrow" it from her mother?

Inside the leather suitcase were Billy's movie film and camera. It was an old Keystone model with three rotating lenses. There were several books describing the art of making home movies and a book about the making of Hollywood westerns. There were twelve rolls of 8mm movie film still in their yellow Kodak boxes. Each box was dated and inscribed with a location, "March 15-the fishpond," "March 25-sunset," "February 12-backyard," etc.

Keystone cameras were considered top-of-the-line home movie equipment for the time. There were two boxes of unopened film and the camera was loaded with film and ready for action.

"I think we should try to find an old move projector and see what kind of movies the kids were making," David said.

"Do you think we should? What if they were into some kind of personal activities? You know what I mean, they were kids in love." Kathryn raised her eyebrows.

"The impression I got from Billy was that he was a serious photographer and he intended to use this film as an example of his work. As far as Cindy is concerned, she wanted to be an actress, so I think she may be trying to impress someone with her screen presence, which probably included her sex appeal, but I don't think it would be anything explicit. I think we should look at the film. I may use the making of the film in my book. If we could find a movie projector that is."

Kathryn rose from the table, walked around behind David, threw her arms around his neck, and began to kiss his ears. "Last night was wonderful. I never dreamed two people could be so compatible physically, and emotionally, in such a short period. Oh, I know we've known each other for months, but the actual time we've spent together has been very short. Do you think we are rushing into something?"

David responded immediately, "No, hell no. As far as I'm concerned if anything feels this good it must be right." David turned and pulled Kathryn down onto his lap. They kissed for a long time. Kathryn wore nothing on under the tee shirt and David's hands were all over Kathryn's body and there was no resistance. He could fill his blood rising, he seriously thought of taking Kathryn back to bed, but then thought better of it. He had risen to the occasion more times last night than he had ever been able to do in his past life and he wanted time to replenish his manhood in anticipation of the evening to come.

"Let's get dressed and go for a ride in the Chevy and see if we can find an 8mm movie projector somewhere," David said, kissing Kathryn's neck and breast.

"We had better get going or else we'll never get out of here," Kathryn said, pushing herself up and fondling David's crotch at the same time. "You can save that for later," she laughed, and hurried upstairs to get dressed.

The sky had turned brilliant blue, the clouds had dissipated, and the coastline was visible from horizon to horizon. David, already dressed, went outside and raised the hood of the Chevy and stood marveling at the engine for some time. His eyes scanned the Rochester four barrel carburetor sitting on top of a fresh Chevy 265 cu.in. motor, painted traditional Chevrolet orange. The engine compartment was expertly furnished with new hardware, neatly bundled wiring, new rubber molding, and bushings. The car looked newer than when it came from the factory. He noticed a small imprinted bronze plaque neatly riveted to the top of the firewall.

"1956 Chevrolet Convertible

Fully restored to factory specifications for David Jordan, May 1, 2000 by Alex Johnson, San Jose, California."

David could not wait to get started driving his dream machine. A thin film of dust had settled over the deep black paint. David found a soft towel and gave the car a quick dusting.

"The car looks great, don't you think, David?" Kathryn had emerged from the cabin dressed in white shorts and a flower print blouse with a matching scarf tied around her neck. Sunglasses perched on top of her pulled back hair. "Beautiful" was the only word could possibly describe what David was seeing. He helped her into the passenger side of the car, neither wanted to let go of the others hand.

"Yes, the car is great. Alex did a fantastic job. The car is definitely show quality. It must have cost a pretty penny to put it right. I will pay you back in the....," he couldn't finish the sentence before Kathryn put her finger to his lips, "No, you won't pay me back. This is my gift to you. The title is in your name, I even had the car appraised and insured. I wanted to do this for you David, please accept it." She had moved across the seat and gave David a warm kiss.

David could only say, "Thank you, thank you, thank you. I don't know what else to say."

"That's all you have to say, now let's get moving. I want you to feel how nice this car drives."

David drove cautiously down the driveway, through the gate and onto the coast highway, heading north toward Carmel. The car responded with amazing quickness. The dual exhaust gave off that exclusive Chevy deep rumble. With the top down,

David was realizing his dream, the car, the girl, the road, this was as close to heaven as he was likely to get.

Traffic was moderate and David drove the winding, cliff hugging, forty-plus miles to Carmel at a conservative speed, covering the distance in just under an hour. They stopped at a phone booth and called several rental businesses, but no one had an old movie projector for rent. David found a camera shop and talked to the owner about finding an 8mm projector. The owner had a Bell and Howell projector in the back room, he loaned it to David with a screen after hearing about the old film found in the trunk. He offered to convert Billy's film to VHS format for a modest fee. David promised he would take the owner up on his offer after he had seen the film himself.

Kathryn wanted to stop at the market and pick up a few things for dinner, including the wine she favored. She bought a large bouquet of flowers for their table setting. The drive back to the cabin was interrupted by several stops along the way to admire the view and to have a drink at the Ventana Inn.

By the time they arrived at the cabin, it was after six and Kathryn started preparing dinner. She told David she had taken a cooking class in France and wanted to show him she could be domestic by fixing him her favorite French dinner.

David set up the movie projector and placed it in position so the screen was outside on the deck and the projector was in the center of the cabin. He built a fire in the circular fireplace. The temperature was mild, but the evenings tended to be cool and a fire provided a soft glow that artificial light can not duplicate.

The dinner was a success. David was impressed with Kathryn's ability to prepare a very nice dinner without doing a lot of work. They ate by candlelight, toasting each other with a fine wine.

David put the film in order of the date written on the box. They viewed three rolls of film before deciding they could watch the rest later. It was hot tub time. A thin sliver of a new moon was just rising over the Santa Lucia Mountains to the east.

Kathryn had found six candleholders with fancy glass chimneys and placed them around the hot tub. The setting was a photographer's dream.

"I would like to find a camera and try to capture this setting." He was holding his hands up in front of his face framing the scene.

"We can recreate this scene at a later time, now is the time for us alone." Kathryn moved closer to David, they touched wineglasses.

David took that statement to mean Kathryn was including him in her future, but there were more immediate needs to satisfy now.

It was long after the sun had set before the two lovers discussed Billy's movies. Both agreed Cindy could definitely establish an emotional connection with the camera. Of course, the film was soundless, but David knew from talking to Cindy's school friends her voice could be very seductive. She instinctively knew how to move and gesture to the camera, her use of the fur stole was reminiscent of Betty Davis, but much more believable. There was childish clowning on parts of the film and in other parts, a serious attempt to copy the moves and actions of screen actors of the day.

Billy's camera technique was amateurish in the beginning, but toward the end of the third roll of film, there was marked improvement. The camera work was steady. There was very little of the jerkiness exhibited in the first roll as demonstrated in the third. Billy had a good sense of light and shadow, always keeping his subject in focus and in the best light. Each roll of film seemed to be better in terms of the camera to subject position. David felt sure the last roll of film would be the best. They agreed to watch the remainder of Billy's film the next evening.

The second night of lovemaking was a prolonged exercise in self-indulgence. The rush and intensity of the night before was gone, replaced by a leisurely exploration of each other's bodies. The evening was punctuated by moments of giddiness, intensity, animal lust, and tenderness. Sleep came to both simultaneously as they lay wrapped in each other's arms.

The marine layer from the Pacific Ocean covered the entire mountainside on the second morning. The air was chilled and damp. Kathryn and David sat on the deck wrapped in blankets, drinking hot coffee and staring off into space, each lost in their own thoughts. "David," Kathryn finally broke the long silence, "have you thought about our future?"

David looked at Kathryn as if she had asked the most obvious question in the world. He had thought of nothing else but their future and now was the time to put it on the table. "Yes, and I have a plan that includes you and me together." He hesitated on purpose building anticipation of the moment, "I was debating with myself, actually hoping, you would be willing to take a cross-country trip with me."

"Cross country trip?" The expression on her face said that was not exactly what she was thinking. "What did you have in mind?"

"I have my book nearly completed in draft form. Now I need to get it professionally edited and then see if I can find an agent and publisher. But I can take care of that in the next few weeks and we could take all summer to drive back to Chicago.

"I would like you to meet my family. Kelly has two of the brightest twin boys you could ever want to meet and her husband, Fred, is a nice person too. I'm sure you would like them. I know they would be delighted to meet you. We would stop at Dumont and see Cindy, assuming she is still alive. I want to return her belongings, and the film. I'll get a couple of copies of the film on a VCR tape, keep one for myself, and try to get a copy to Billy. I need to put together a care package for him anyway. I'll talk to Sheriff Woodford and find out what items I can send into the prison."

"It sounds wonderful, David. I would love to meet your family. Spending the summer with you on a driving holiday, that is really a great idea. I have never done that. My parents always flew when we went on holiday, this will be a real treat for me."

David was elated to think Kathryn would be sitting beside him all the way to Chicago. Then he switched gears for a moment and got serious. "I think I've got an ending for my book. Watching Billy's home movies gave me an idea. The Hollywood angle is something every teenage girl dreams about, well, maybe dreams come true in my book. What do you think?"

"That could work. You would have to come up with a new angle on 'small town girl makes it big in Hollywood.' That has been done a million times, but I am sure we can put our heads together and find an unusual twist to this scenario. We can watch the rest of Cindy and Billy's film and maybe they will provide us with a story line from real life. Maybe the Billy character could break into movies with his camera skills and pull Cindy along with him or something like that."

David could see the wheels turning in Kathryn's head. She was excited at the possibility of inventing a new ending to an old Hollywood love tale. He decided to use her as a sounding board for any future book ideas.

"My idea for the next book is the adventures of a couple making this same trip, only make the date in the fifties. Traveling route 66, what do you think?"

"David, you have to know I would go anywhere with you. The route 66 idea has been done before, but I'll bet we could act out the role of the couple you intend to write about," Kathryn smiled, putting on a Bette Davis over-the-shoulder look. "I think we could find a new twist for that story also." The look Kathryn gave David told him the experiences she had in mind included more than just a travel commentary.

The End

Printed in the United States
85222LV00002B/80/A